Move Over

To Grace

Margaret Marie O'Carroll Support

Move Over

Martha Marie

To [scribbled out]

From
Martha Marie O'Carroll Lynch

PATJAC

Copyright © Martha Lynch 2012
First published in 2012 by Patjac Publications
24 Farmilo Road, Walthamstow, London E17 8JJ

Distributed by Gardners Books, 1 Whittle Drive, East-
bourne, East Sussex, BN23 6QH
Tel: +44(0)1323 521555 | Fax: +44(0)1323 521666

British Library Cataloguing in Publication Data
A catalogue record for this book is available from the British Library.

ISBN 978-0-9570454-0-8

Typeset by Amolibros, Milverton, Somerset
www.amolibros.com
This book production has been managed by Amolibros
Printed and bound by Lightning Source

About the Author

The second eldest of ten children (one of whom is now a very well known Irish comedian) Martha Marie was born and went to primary school in Dublin. She immigrated to London in the late 1950s after the clothing factory where she had worked since she was fourteen closed. She is now seventy three, a widow of nearly two years, three grown sons, two teenage sons, eight living siblings and a few dozen nieces and nephews; studied with The Open University and gained a BA in 1984.

As a form teacher in a multicultural state school she was responsible for teaching the personal social and health course to her pupils. Many of the discussions she had with them involved talking about different cultures and families. During lessons she was constantly pressed to talk about growing up in Ireland, and what it was like to be one of twelve living in one house. It was through telling these stories about her own life and the life of her friends also from large families that she decided to write a book.

Move Over is the first of several!

Chapter One

Sheila Malone lay in her bed and ignored the knocking on the hall door. When she heard footsteps walking down the garden path she got out of bed and looked out the window through the net curtains and saw the postman walking up the path of her neighbours' house. She waited until she saw him crossing the road then went downstairs.

Her heart was as cold as the house when she bent her small body and picked up the letters on the floor beneath the letterbox of the hall.

There was no mistaking her eldest daughter Josie's large scrawl on the white envelope, but she sighed with relief that the letter had come. The neat writing on the blue envelope with the Canadian stamp told her the second letter was from her daughter Pauline. She put both letters into the pocket of her housecoat and went into the small front room off the hall in her Corporation house.

Heat from the gas under the kettle, and the grill over the bread brought some warmth into the small kitchen while Sheila made her tea and toasted some bread.

She placed the letters on the table in front of the plate of toast like she was going to eat them for dessert. By the time she had eaten her toast the heat from the cooker had dissipated so she brought her cup of tea and the two letters into the living room across the hall from the kitchen.

Agreed by most people who were living in, or waiting to

move into a Corporation house this room was large, or a fair size. A standard-sized room would be large enough for a small suite of soft furniture and a coffee table, or a dining table with four chairs and a small cabinet.

This morning the living room in Plunkett Road was cold but it had a warm turfey smell from the fire that had been burning most of the day and evening before. There was a pull-out table against the wall where the stairs ran up from the hall. Three chairs sat comfortable at the sides, another one was against the wall.

What the family called a bunk was under the window at the back of the room. This was the inside seat from a bus that served as seats when the lid was closed and was used to hold roller skates, balls and other small toys when the children were small. It now contained everything from gloves, scarves, and anything that needed to be put away.

Two easy chairs by the sides of the fireplace and a low armless chair under the window at the front were the only soft furniture in the room. A television stood in the far corner from the door beside the press that housed the boiler that heated water from the fire. The water was piped to the kitchen, and the bathroom that was at the back of the house on the ground floor behind the kitchen. White painted wooden shelves ran along the walls on both sides of the chimney-breasts. The wall-to-wall patterned carpet was speckled with burns around the hearth.

Sheila placed her cup of tea on the tiled mantelpiece, opened the door of the cupboard that housed the boiler to allow some heat into the room. She then removed the page that had the cinema advertisements from yesterday's evening paper, and rolled the remainder of it into branches and placed them on the dead embers in the fireplace and lit them.

She pulled her easy chair nearer to the fireplace, sat down, and tore the top off Josie's letter as if she were opening a sachet of shampoo. She pulled out a small sheet of white paper wrapped round an English five-pound note. She put the money into the pocket of her dressing gown and tore the letter up without reading it and tossed it into the burning newspapers.

After Sheila had read Pauline's letter twice she looked up at the window into the back garden, and as if her words would fly to Canada on the clouds she whispered, 'Stupid girl.' She tore the letter up, then inserted her fingers into the envelope to check there was nothing else in it and tossed the shreds of the two letters onto the burning paper in the grate.

As she watched the flames curling around the shredded paper she thought about what cinema she would go to in the afternoon. She opened out the page from the newspaper she had kept and read the films that were showing like she was studying the horses that were running in the Grand National. There were two films she wanted to see, and one she would like to see again. She didn't want to bring the paper with her so to avoid walking back and forth across town she wrote the names of the cinemas and the films they were showing on the back of the blue envelope and put it in her pocket.

As she watched the flames die, and the burnt paper turn grey at the edges Sheila decided that April was a month away and she would probably have a letter from Pauline's husband Harry by then. Then to make sure every scrap of the letters had burnt away she spread the ashes among the other embers with the poker.

The only sound in the house came from the purring, and soft movements of the minute hand moving on the clock on the wall beside the boiler. As if the clock had spoken to her, Sheila raised her head from the paper ashes to the wall. She wasn't concerned about the time so she rested her eyes on the haphazard frames of photographs under the clock.

She never looked at any of the pictures, but she knew

there were old and new photograph of her ten children, six grandchildren, and other members of the family. Her second eldest daughter Una had collected them and framed them a couple of years ago when she had come home from England for a holiday.

Sheila seldom thought about her children but right now she wondered if Pauline had also written to Una. She wasn't worried if Pauline had written to Josie because she knew Josie would believe her when she said that she hadn't received any letter from Pauline.

Still Sheila worried about what she would do to make Pauline change her mind. The smartest thing the stupid girl ever did was to marry Harry Harper. She threw the end of her cigarette into the grate, then went upstairs to get ready to go into town.

An hour later, with her short grey hair tucked under a crochet hat, and wearing her favourite navy crimplene dress, black low-heeled shoes and check coat Sheila slid her arm into the straps of her large plastic handbag and left her Corporation house in the Ballyglass estate on the North side of Dublin. She had reached the gate when the door of her neighbour opened.

'Mrs Malone,' her neighbour called, waving a blue envelope, 'this came for you this morning. As I signed for it the postman asked me to give it you personally.'

Sheila took the offered letter, looked at the stamp, and recognised the handwriting. She felt the contents before she said, 'Thank you.' She went back into her house and phoned for a mini cab before she opened the letter and counted the Canadian dollars.

Later that same evening and after enjoying two of the films on her own and the late evening one with her friend Ena Dwyer Sheila sat beside the fire in her friend's small house in Arbour Hill.

There had been many times during their friendship of over forty years when Ena had been annoyed, and sometimes angry with Sheila. Now after hearing what Sheila had told her about Pauline and her children she was disgusted and ashamed of her friend. She took the bottle of whiskey off the small table that was beside her chair. 'I little top up?' she said holding the bottle towards Sheila.

Sheila finished the whiskey in her glass, then held it out to Ena.

Ena filled Sheila's glass then put the bottle back on the table. They talked about the film they had seen together until midnight by which time Sheila was so drunk that she went to bed without her handbag. Ena searched through her friend's handbag but was unable to find what she was looking for. She was locking the front door when she noticed Sheila's coat hanging on a hook beside her own. She almost cried with relief when she found the blue envelope that had contained Pauline's letter. She choked back tears when she saw the neat childish handwriting. She couldn't rid her thoughts of her own shame for the years she had watched Sheila manipulate her husband and her children.

In her small kitchen while she washed the whiskey glasses Ena could hear Sheila snoring while she made a plan about what she would do with Pauline's envelope.

Chapter Two

At half past seven on a Monday morning in late April, walking behind Josie down the platform in Euston Station, Mike Cullen told himself not to worry about his lovely wife and his sixteen-month old daughter Eileen. His lean frame just about kept pace with Josie's long strides as she walked purposefully behind the pushchair.

When she reached the first class carriage, Josie unstrapped Eileen and lifted her out of the pushchair. She then took her holdall from her husband. The nylon fabric of her dark green anorak squeaked when she pressed her arms to her body, so she could hold her baby and the bag. Her dark brown hair swayed like shaken silk tassels when she tossed her head back, fixed her oval face in a smile but kept her thin lips closed and said, 'I'll wait here.'

Mike promptly folded up the pushchair then carried it, with the suitcase, to the baggage carriage. He was pleased for Josie that she was going home. God knows; she worked hard and deserved the holiday. And the salon could manage without her for a couple of weeks. He knew the coming weekend was a big affair for her family. It would be the first time they would all be home together since before their daddy died nearly two years earlier: at least, most of the family would be home; Josie hadn't said anything yet about her sister Una.

The porter in the baggage carriage; a red haired round-faced short tubby man with yellow stained fingers appeared to Mike to be in his late sixties, and he wheezed so much that Mike doubted he would be able to carry Josie's holdall let alone her suitcase. He lifted Josie's case into the carriage then shrugged his shoulders back into his tailored overcoat and swept his hand over his neatly cut black hair.

As the porter dragged the suitcase into the carriage Mike's worry over Josie travelling on her own increased. He knew now that he should have continued to ask Josie until she had given him answers about Una. He was used to the sisters falling in and out of favour with each other, but it was months since Una had been down to have her hair done. 'She's going all the way to Holyhead,' he said to the porter when the man jutted his head out of the carriage.

The porter smiled at the paper money in Mike's hand then pointed down to the tall woman and said, 'That her in the green anorak?'

Mike waved up to his wife and nodded to the porter to show her he was the man he paid to look after her.

'Don't worry, guv. I'll see she gets on the boat all right. Just the one child, and the one case?' he said keeping his eyes on Mike's hand. 'Thanks, guv,' he said, after he had taken the two pound notes.

Walking up the platform, Mike vowed he would talk to his wife when she came back about her attitude towards her sister. Sisters should help each other and not be fighting all the time. He envied his wife for her large family and he was very proud of her because she cared so much about them.

Although he hadn't spent much time with any of Josie's brothers and sisters, Mike felt that he knew them because Una was always talking about them. Recalling now the time Josie had told him that the tall girl with the dark red hair was her sister he now wondered if he knew her at all.

Una had been bridesmaid at his wedding to Josie, and godmother to Eileen. She was married to a tall blond man called Jack. They had a son older than Eileen and they lived in Dagenham, where Jack worked in a factory. Una and Jack came to tea once a month, and he and Josie went to tea in Dagenham once a month.

Still he had to admit that Una aggravated Josie whenever she talked about when they were children. He often suspected that Una exaggerated most of the stories she told, just to annoy Josie. A slight curl grew on Mike's thin lips as he recalled that Una's stories were always funny; better than listening to Jack go on about the unions and the Labour party. This was the Una that Josie often told her friends and some of her customers about. This Una was the cleverest girl ever born in Dublin. There was nothing that Una couldn't do with her hands, given a piece of cloth, a bit of thread or a ball of wool.

Before he left the train, Mike gave Josie a handful of half-crowns in case she wasn't able to find the porter he had paid to look after her. He suspected the man would have a heart attack when he lit his next cigarette.

When the train was moving too fast for Mike to walk beside it, he waved. Josie gasped when she saw the man Mike had given the money to for to carry her case standing on the platform. She picked up the pile of half-crowns that Mike had left on the table and put them in the pocket of her trousers.

The carriage jolted when the train moved out of the station, and Josie swallowed whatever doubts she had had about travelling on her own, it was too late to change her mind. She was on her way.

It was unusual for Josie to have doubts about anything because she tended to ignore everything she didn't understand. But there were many things about this visit to her family home that bothered her and the least of them was this fourteen-hour journey, travelling on her own with her young daughter.

Josie's thoughts were torn between trying not to dwell on

why her mammy had decided not to go out to Canada for her sister Maura's wedding and why the family were now having a party for her and her new husband. She would never admit she was jealous of her pretty twenty-one-year-old sister, but it had always annoyed her that Maura was always given a birthday party.

Two hours into her journey the train was moving smoothly towards Birmingham. Josie had eaten her sandwiches and shared a pint of milk with Eileen who was now lying down asleep. She closed her thoughts to the worry about the lost porter and sifted through her memory for recipes to cook for her family when she was home. Whenever Josie was worried she cooked.

Chapter Three

While Josie was thinking cooking, her youngest brother Liam was being careful not to let the clothes fall into the long grass as he un-pegged them from a clothes line in the back garden.

He dumped the bundle of clothes on the table in the living room, swept his thin curly hair back from his forehead and called out, 'They're as dry as the ragin wind out there.' He knew his mammy wouldn't answer him but he continued, 'If yeh do another lot, yeh'll get them dry in a couple ev hours.' He also knew that she wouldn't even open the washing basket to see if there was more laundry to be done. For as long as he could remember Monday as washday had never been part of his mammy's life. His sisters had always taken care of the washing. Today he was bringing in the washing for his younger sister Joan.

Depending on what he was asked to recall, Liam could remember thirteen years of his life, but he could never recall his mammy using the washing machine. In all this time the frequent showers that were credited to the month of April never bothered him. Whatever the month, it rained in Dublin every time the clouds felt like crying. And sometimes they cried every day. But today he knew his sister Josie was coming home on the boat crossing the Irish Sea and he wanted her to have a good voyage so he was pleased it wasn't raining.

'Yeh'll be delighted te know that these are bone dry as

well,' Liam called into the kitchen. He didn't expect his mammy to answer him this time either, and he didn't care if she hadn't heard him over the sound of water gushing into the kettle. He dropped the bundle of towels on the easy chair beside the fireplace in the living room and left to get the sheets.

The white clouds were flying in the bright blue sky as if they were competing with the wind that was waving the two sheets. Liam stood in the doorway to the back garden that was big enough to build another house on and still leave enough ground for grass and flowers.

'One of yeh is too big, and one of yeh is too small,' he said into the wind that carried his voice away but he felt some of his temper easing so he continued, 'but the both ev yeh have always demanded too much work and too much attention.' He was thinking about his mammy and the garden.

Liam's daddy had tried to tame the grass and keep the weeds in check. Una had planted some rose bushes under the window and around the coal shed, but they were neglected when she went to England.

Five feet four inches was short for a man, but Liam wasn't worried about being short now because two of his brothers continued to grow until they were eighteen. Already he was more than two inches taller than his mammy. After his daddy had died Liam had stopped believing that his mammy never did housework because she was small. He still hadn't worked out why his daddy had done so much but he was sure that it had nothing to do with his mammy being small, because his two younger sisters Joan and Cathy were smaller and they were expected to do everything.

'That's teh lot,' Liam said, dropping the sheets on top of the towels. He wiggled his toes while he watched his mammy pull a sock over her left hand. He hated holes in his socks. He didn't care how often she mended the holes in his brother's socks. He bought his own socks now, because the darns she used to do were always so lumpy they were more uncomfortable than the holes. Una told him that their mammy fumbled with wool and a needle just to let them all believe that she was working.

Liam was Sheila Malone's youngest son, and the eighth of her ten children. He was also the younger of the only two that weren't afraid of her even though she had never beaten any of her children. Her small stature limited her physical ability, so she added that chore to all the others she expected her husband to do.

Yeh can puff, pant and wheeze as loud as yeh like; the beam from Liam's eyes would have told his mammy if she had lifted her face from the sock she was slipping over her left hand. He was surprised she was at home. She always went into town on a Monday afternoon and the shabbiness of the clothes she wore now told him she wasn't going out. She hadn't even combed her hair.

Liam didn't read the newspapers, or books. He had been so confused in school with learning English and his native Irish language that he stopped even trying. But he had learned to read people.

Liam didn't know why, but he could tell by his mammy's behaviour that she was furious over the party that was organized for the following weekend. He smiled in his heart because he wondered what she would do if she found out how the party came about in the first place. Still he was looking forward to having all his family home together for a while, before he went away. 'I'll be off now,' he said moving towards the door.

He had more than enough time to walk down to the village, but he intended to call in for his friend Brian on the way. His future depended on getting his friend to have his photograph taken, and he wanted them to keep the appointment he had made.

Chapter Four

Sitting on a low wall in front of the Church in the Ballyglass village Liam said, 'I wonder if it means anythin with yerself bein teh eldest and me bein teh youngest in er families?' He didn't believe that it did, but it was something to say as he worried if the beating his friend had suffered recently would prevent him from coming away with him.

Brian continued to gaze at the ground.

'Did yeh hear me?' Liam stretched out his hand and pulled on the sleeve of his friend's jumper. He wanted to talk about going away.

'Yeah, I heard yeh,' Brian replied into his lap. He shifted his heavy body on the hard wall and kept his chin pressed into his neck while he watched, through his eyebrows, a heavy noisy lorry growling its way up the short hill.

Brian always watched the lorries on the roads. He often dreamed of stealing a lift on one of them down into the country. He was sure he could get a job in one of the quarries where the lorry drivers loaded up the stones.

Because he was big and tall, and had been shaving since he was fourteen, Brian believed he would pass for eighteen. He hadn't had to shave very often at first, and he only did so because his dark hair made his face look dirty and the girls laughed at him. Now, two years later, he was shaving properly at least three times a week, and the girls smiled at him. When the lorry he was staring at passed by he started to swing his legs and bash the heels of his shoes against the wall.

'Yer jaw still hurtin yeh?' Liam asked bending his shoulders towards his knees and recalled a couple of hidings his daddy had given him but he had never suffered more than a sting on his bum. 'At least yeh saved yer ma from gettin teh worst of it,' he said knowing his remark wouldn't take the pain away from Brian's face, but he also knew that Brian gladly suffered the pain when it meant his da hadn't hurt his ma again.

Brian continued to swing his legs and bash the heels of his shoes on the wall. Every thud he made with his hard shoe vibrated up his body and into his face. He stared at the road but all he saw was an image of his ma. She was smaller then his sister Margaret, and Margaret was only fourteen. He thought that his ma must have been very pretty because Margaret was the image of her, except that his ma had creases on her forehead and around her mouth. Also his ma's eyes were darker around the outsides.

The two boys were silent for a few minutes. Liam swung his feet until they were moving in unison with Brian's. The heel of his right foot bashed the wall with the heel of Brian's right one so that they made one whishing sound with the two feet.

After they had completed four bashes Liam held one foot out and broke the motion. This time Liam's left foot kept time with Brian's right one. After another four bashes it was Brian's turn to change his feet, but instead he held both of his feet out to indicate that the game was over. He felt a sharp pain in his face when he jumped down off the wall onto the pavement. He knew that the pain would go away if he didn't jump any more. It always did, so he shoved his elbows back and rested them on the wall tilted his head back and gazed up at the sky. 'De yeh think there really is a heaven up there over all them flyin balls of steam?' He asked moving his head around as if searching for a sign that would tell him that there really was something up there.

Liam slapped the palms of his hands down on the wall to take the weight of his light body and swung himself out on to the pavement. He turned his back to the wind that was coming over from the building site and blowing his thin curly hair around his small face and worked his hands down into the tight pockets at the waist of his jeans and said, 'I still have nightmares over them clouds.'

'Why's that then?' Brian asked holding a hand over his eyes to shade them from the sun so he could see his short skinny friend. He was sorry now he was in a bad mood.

Liam lowered his head to his feet.

Not for the first time Brian noticed how Liam always looked at the ground when he didn't have a quick answer, and he was often amazed at how his friend could find some of his best solutions in the concrete that he was standing on.

Liam looked up quickly, then pulled his eyes away from his friend's bruised and swollen face. He turned his head up into the sky and said, 'I dream that I am riding around on me bike lookin fer me teeth.'

'Yer teeth?' Brian said smiling even although it hurt his face.

Liam returned his friends smile and continued, 'I was eight at the time and I was ridin up the road on me friend's bike waving both me hands in the air when me sister Una turned the corner. She ran out on the road, pulled me off the bike, pointed up to the sky and told me if I didn't keep me hand on the handlebars when I was ridin teh bike then I would spend the rest of me days lookin fer me teeth in heaven.'

'And yeh believed her,' Brian said smiling again.

'I did when I was eight,' Liam said, 'and I didn't ride a bike fer six weeks. What about yerself?' he asked. 'Do you think there is a heaven up there?'

Brian took a couple of steps backwards from the church. 'None ev us will ever know,' he said, 'but the main thing is that we believe there is.'

Liam moved towards the village. 'Come on,' he said, 'let's get yer pictcher took.' He raised the heels of his feet off the ground and clicked them together then nodded his head after a bus that was making its way into the city.

Chapter Five

Another lorry struggled to get up the short steep hill on the main Ballyglass road as Brian moved away from the wall. He closed his eyes against the dry dust and called out, 'Them lorries are goin te break teh road up if they keep goin up and down like that.' His long strides were closing in on Liam when he added, 'Five ev them big metal ones have gone up in teh last half hour. De yeh think someone is tryin' te build a new road teh Belfast or somethin'?'

'Could be, could be,' Liam replied, turning his head and shoulders out into the road. He knew the road through the old Ballyglass village was being widened for the buses and delivery vans that serviced the housing estate, but right now all he wanted to do was humour his friend so he repeated, 'Could be.'

'All them heavy trucks is going teh ruin teh village,' Brian moaned. He was eight inches taller than Liam, and as they walked along the narrow pavement into the village he stayed on the outside, near the kerb. When they met a mother with a pushchair he stepped into the road to let her pass. After the third pushchair had passed them, Brian stayed close to the kerb and walked on in front, believing that the women wouldn't raise their heads to see his swollen face if he didn't have to move to let them pass.

A village, for Liam, was a place where there were shops, a church, a pub, a bank, or a post office. There had to be roads to bring people into and out of it. He couldn't understand why Brian was always complaining about the plans the Dublin Corporation was proposing for all the new roads needed for the housing estates.

But then Brian read the newspapers, and books, so Liam respected his friend's opinions. He decided that if he could encourage his friend to get involved in a discussion about the pros and cons of building new houses for city dwellers that were currently cramped in the tenements Brian might forget about the pain in his face.

They walked on in silence for a few minutes. When they had crossed a narrow road that gave access to the back of an old pub, Brian shrugged his shoulders towards the building and said, 'Look at that place.'

Liam didn't need to look at the old pub. He knew every brick and piece of wood that held the place together from spending many hours at the bus stop on the other side of the road with nothing to do but stare at the wretched place. 'I see what yeh mean,' he lied. He grew to hate the sight of the several tall, narrow windows that stood like scruffy soldiers on top of the three wide black ones. But it wasn't the pub he hated. It was when he had to go down to the self-service grocery shop three times a week. He knew his mammy saved money because the self-service was cheaper than the shop on the corner, or using the van with flat tyres that never moved from the corner at the top of the road.

Liam didn't mind carrying the bags home, and it wasn't so bad when one of his young sisters came with him and picked out what was on the list. But his mammy wouldn't always pay the bus fares for two, and when it was raining he went for the shopping on his own.

It wasn't raining now so Liam forgot about his shopping days, more concerned with keeping Brian talking about the village so he would forget about the bruises on his face. He raised his face to the long sign that was over the front of the pub and said, 'I love that fancy writin, and teh gold paint they use fer te paint it.'

The pain made Brian cringe again when he raised his head to look at the sign over the Beggars Lodge public house. 'The whole place needs te be done up.' He stepped into the road and looked up at the sign again before he said, 'Yeh know, Liam, I'd love te work on restorin' places like this.'

Liam felt his heart sink a couple of inches into his stomach. He had to pull his friend's mind away from staying in Ballyglass and saving the village. He needed Brian to come with him. 'I was wrong,' he said.

Brian looked down at his friend's bowed head. 'Will yeh take a look at teh paint on teh windas upstairs, fer God's sake,' he said stepping back up on to the pavement. 'Teh bricks are grand all right, I'll grant yeh that.' He didn't want Liam to feel stupid.

'No, Brian, I didn't mean that,' Liam shot off his reply while he pulled his hand out of his pockets and hitched up his jeans. He flapped his hands in front of his chest. 'Yer dead right about teh Beggars Lodge,' he said, 'I meant what I said about me bein teh youngest.'

Brian smiled with his eyes. 'I keep fergettin about yer Cathy,' he said. 'She doesn't look like teh rest of yez at all.'

Picturing his twelve-year-old sister with her hands on her hips and her thick dark curly hair blowing around her face and neck, Liam wondered what Cathy would say if she was walking with them. 'Not many people ferget Cathy,' he said.

'I didn't ferget her,' Brian lied, 'I just didn't count her in me mind right now. He knew that Liam was very fond of his two youngest sisters, but he thought that Joan was his friend's favourite. It was the sister that used to work in the shoe shop that Brian remembered the most. He looked down at his feet.

Recalling the day when his mammy bought his shoes for

his confirmation Brian said, 'Is the short one with the curly hair in England or America?' He remembered Liam's sister had opened every box on the children's shelves in the small shop, then with tears in her bright blue eyes she informed his ma that she would have to buy a man's shoe.

'That's Pauline,' Liam replied relieved that Brian's attention moved away from staying in Dublin and renovating old buildings. 'She's in Canada.'

Chapter Six

When the friends were at the crossroads of the old village there were six or seven shops on both sides of the main road, and cars or vans parked everywhere, so Brian couldn't continue to walk in the kerb so he walked behind Liam.

'Have yeh everythin ready fer yer party?' Brian asked the back of Liam's head, taking advantage of not having to look at Liam as he said, 'I won't be joinin yeh.'

'As much as I can fer now,' Liam called over his shoulder. 'Yeh can always pop in fer a drink if yeh feel like it.'

'And what would that be?'

'The marquee, and the beer is ordered,' Liam said smiling at the memory of his brother Maurice's face when he asked him for ten quid towards the cost of the beer.

'How many people have yeh got comin?'

'I have asked all the football club,' Liam said continuing to smile. This smile was for his brother Donal who had given him twenty pounds for the beer.

'Did yer sister know the football team?' Brian asked as he tried to remember if he had ever seen any of Liam's sisters at any of the matches when the team played.

There were no other pedestrians coming towards them now so Liam moved to the inside of the pavement so that Brian could walk beside him. 'Te tell yeh truth, Brian,' he said, 'I don't know who Maura knew when she was livin' at home, but there will be enough with the family and a few cousins so I don't think she will notice who else is there.'

'Jesus, Liam, how did yez all manage fer sleepin' in three bedrooms?' Brian asked as he tried to imagine twelve people living in a house the same size as his own.

'Te tell yeh te truth, I don't know, and I don't know how we're goin te manage this time because we're all much bigger now,' Liam said turning his head to his friend. 'I can promise yeh one thing though. I'll not be sleepin in teh same bed with Una and Pauline this time.'

'Are yeh sayin' that yeh slept with yer sisters?'

'Only Una and Pauline,' Liam said, stretching his legs so he could keep up with his friend's long strides and added, 'As often as I could.'

'Yeh did?' There were four in Brian's family. He knew that in some large families, boys and girls slept in the same room. But liking to sleep with them in the same bed was different; he had never heard of that before. He recalled how his ma wouldn't let himself or his da go into his sister's room, even to close the windows when it was raining heavily. 'Why?' he asked.

'Because Una always had sheets on her bed,' Liam said. He couldn't remember how his family had managed in a three-bedroom house when they were all living at home but he continued, 'Una put her foot down with teh sheets. I hated sleeping with me brothers, because of teh sheets.'

'The sheets?'

'The sheets,' Liam repeated. He wanted to laugh at the be-wildered expression on Brian's face, but he was afraid that his friend would think he was laughing at his bruises, so he said, 'Yeh see, Una was teh one fer teh mendin'.'

'Yeh mean, like sewin' on patches and buttens?' Brian asked.

'Una done a lot more than teh buttens and patchin,' Liam

said combing his hair back from his face and recalling how the doors in the bedrooms only opened halfway because of all the beds. 'Yer right though te wonder how we managed. We had five beds but we didn't have enough sheets fer them all, all the time. Una done her best te keep up with teh patchin' and hemmin'.'

'Yeh wanted te sleep with yer sisters because ev sheets?'

'The boys beds were teh first te go without teh sheets, or had teh ones with teh tears still in them,' Liam said. He wanted to scratch his bum with the memory as he continued, 'Jesus Brian, but I couldn't sleep half of teh time with me brothers because ev me feet gettin tangled in teh sheets, or teh blankets makin me arse itchy all night.'

'Una is teh one with teh red hair?'

'And teh temper.'

Still smiling, Brian patted his sore face and asked, 'What did Pauline do?'

'Pauline made teh best rissoles and apple pies in Dublin.'

The clouds were still chasing after each other across the heavens when Brian looked up into the sky. 'Six sisters,' he said as if he was asking for six young girls to drop down from heaven. 'I can't imagine havin six sisters.'

'I never ordered them,' Liam replied as they walked past the last couple of shops on the main road. He called out in a friendly way to some of their neighbours they met while they crossed the road, so that they wouldn't have the time to stare at Brian's face, until they came to an old two-storey house. 'The studio and everythin' is upstairs,' he said pushing in the door, and holding it open for Brian to follow him into the dark hall.

'Is this a studio?' Brian asked frowning at the cobwebs hanging from the ceiling.

Liam depressed a switch and a dim electric bulb came on. 'Up yeh go,' he said, then closed and bolted the door behind them.

Chapter Seven

Adamp musty smell oozed from the walls in the small square hallway. Liam knew it well. The studio was near the bus stop and people often stood in this little room when they needed to shelter from the rain. There was enough space for four adults to stand comfortably.

On a number of occasions when the bus was late, Liam had been more than glad to be one of the seven or eight people that had been squashed together. As he started to mount the stairs, he imagined he could feel the thickness in the air and smell the damp clothes.

Daylight fell on the landing when the door opened slowly after Liam knocked a tune on it with his knuckles and called out, 'Patrick?'

'Liam. It's yerself?' Patrick sang, leaning his head back so he could see through his glasses. 'Will yeh come in out of teh cold?' he roared, bowing his head to the tall man behind Liam. 'Yer in grand time.'

Brian followed Liam into the small untidy room.

'This is me friend,' Liam said turning to Brian.

Holy mother of god, Patrick thought when he saw the bruises on the tall lad's face. He was used to taking photographs of people to make them look pretty or handsome. Now he had to use his lights to show every mark on the lad's face.

'Like I told yeh on teh phone, Patrick,' Liam said, 'Brian was beat up by a couple ev corner boys.'

Brian smiled down at Liam's short stout friend and shrugged his shoulders. He then cast his eyes around the small office again. He thought the shelves along one wall were ready to cave in from the weight of the faded blue and pink folders that were stacked on them. He wanted to sit down so Patrick wouldn't have to look up at him, but the two chairs beside the desk were laden with papers. The fabric on the short bench against the wall facing the shelves was torn so badly that it looked like a pile of ribbons.

'Go straight in.' Patrick pointed over to a heavy red curtain that covered part of the wall facing the desk. 'Just pull it back,' he added, when Liam looked at the curtain but didn't move.

Behind the red velvet curtain Brian scrutinized the dull studio. There were three windows along the wall where he could hear the traffic coming from. Running his eyes along the ceiling, he decided that the office and the studio were two rooms that had been made into one, and then a section taken away for the office. As he watched Liam walk about the room and examine old flowerpots, vases and bunches of paper flowers, he wondered why there was so much old furniture, frames, and other junk.

'I'll be two minutes,' Patrick called over to Brian then set about sorting through a bundle of electric cables and flapped them around the floor.

Brian smiled a reply with his eyes because the cables reminded him of curling snakes he had seen in a film.

'Sit down in teh mother's corner,' Patrick said pointing to a couple of chairs near the door.

The basket chair creaked when Brian sat down. He watched Patrick move frames about the room, fix bulbs and shades on the tops of them, and pull different coloured curtains back and forth along rusty rails. The rails creaked and squeaked like torture birds. Brian wanted to go home to get some oil or Vaseline. 'All them cables around teh floor like that is dangerous,' he said to Liam raising his head to the ceiling. 'If the fire brigade come in here, he'd be fined.'

'Do they work durin lunch hour?' Liam asked, thinking of his sister Una. She would either clean the place up or burn it down. He moved his head closer to Brian and whispered, 'The place needs te be pulled down.'

Although the room was almost dark, Brian could see the moulding around the ceiling and plaster decoration around the original lights. 'It could be renovated,' he said.

When Patrick saw Liam and Brain stretching their necks to see down the room he switched some lights on.

'Yer a right awl fraud, Patrick, de yeh know that?' Liam said when he saw some old furniture and statues at the other end of the room.

'Most ev us are, some of teh time,' Patrick said switching on the lights he had fitted. 'I won't need any ev them down there fer us,' he continued and made some adjustments to the lights, and then placed a chair in front of a blue velvet curtain. 'In yeh go,' he said to Brian.

Liam inhaled when Patrick's camera puffed out the first soft explosion. The flash was short and sharp but it was enough to show all the colours on Brian's face.

For the five minutes while he clicked away with his camera, Patrick prayed that his skills were good enough to capture the pain in the face of Liam's friend. He appeared to be comfortable enough, so instead of asking Brian to turn his head, Patrick moved his camera and his lights.

The big lad reminded Patrick of a photograph of Victor Mature he had seen in a film magazine. Patrick couldn't remember the name of the film, but it was set in biblical times and the Romans had beaten up the star.

He didn't believe that the lad had been in a fight with couple of corner boys, and started to wonder why Liam was so concerned about getting the photographs of his friend's

26

bruises. Brian didn't look like a bousey, but just the same Patrick wondered if Liam's brothers knew he was so friendly with a lad that been beaten up so badly.

Patrick knew Liam as the younger brother of Maurice and Donal Malone, and had seen him at the football club a few times. He had met Liam's mother once. She came into the studio fifteen minutes before her appointment and insisted that her photograph be taken immediately because she had a taxi waiting. She left without paying or even asking when the photographs would be ready.

A week later, a small young girl of about twelve years old had called in and asked for the photographs. It had been raining all day and the child was soaking wet. She had removed her spectacles to dry them, when he had told her how much the photographs were. She told him that her mammy never said she needed to bring any money. The cast in her left eye made Patrick think she was talking to someone behind him when she asked if he could give her a bill because her mammy needed the photographs to get her passport. He had felt so sorry for the young girl that he gave her the photographs and a bill that had yet to be paid.

Chapter Eight

By two o'clock Liam and Brian were in the chip shop. Liam stood in the queue while Brian stayed at the door and held it open, and smiled broadly at the sympathetic stares of his neighbours as they came in and go out of the shop.

The two boys were nearly finished eating their chips by the time they had walked back up the Ballyglass road to the church.

'What time is it?' asked Brian.

Liam glanced at his watch, then bent his head back and poured the remaining crispy bits of his chips into his mouth. He then rolled the empty bag into a small ball and walked over to the kerb. He waited until a car came up the hill then threw the bag under it. He stayed standing at the kerb trying to recall what the three of them had talked about when they were in Patrick's studio.

'We've plenty of time,' Brian said joining Liam at the kerb. 'I don't have te be there till four and it can't be long after two.' He squashed his own empty bag and rolled it into a smaller and harder ball than Liam had made. He waited until a lorry came up the hill before he fired it under the back wheel. 'Are there any coppers in yer brother's football club?' he asked when the lorry had passed.

'There is one on teh committee if that's any use te yeh,' Liam said frowning as he added, 'He's Peter Carey's father.'

'Paul Carey?' Brian said the name like it was a question and smiled at Liam's frown. 'Peter and Paul, two good names from the bible.' He moved back from the kerb to be away from a dirty tractor almost touching the pavement as it came roaring its way up the hill.

'I'm goin te learn te read,' Liam mumbled to the vibrations from the engine that was spitting from the tractor. This was the first time he'd had to depend on someone, and although he was fond of Brian he was worried with having to need him.

'I was thinking,' Brian said, waiting until Liam was walking beside him, 'if we knew a policeman and we gave him teh pictchers then he might go round and show them te me da.'

'Do yeh mean unofficial like?' Liam said kicking at a stick as they turned into the housing estate at the traffic lights. 'Are yeh sure that yeh want Carey te know? I mean with him bein' the father of the sly little git in school.'

'That's teh whole point,' Brian said raising his head to the clouds. 'I think me da might stop teh hittin if he knew fer definite that Carey knew. Me da'ed be too worried about meetin' Carey if he done it again. And I think he'd finally have te believe that teh whole road knew.'

The two boys bowed their heads to avoid the grit blowing into their eyes from the trucks and tractors thundering along the dirt road as they make their way towards the building site, 'It's certainly worth a try,' Liam said, elated that Brian was still going away with him.

'Yeh know yerself when women just stare at yeh with icy eyes how yer knees nearly bend under yeh,' Brian continued, 'An with me da bein a bus conductor, he'll be meetin some of them every day.'

'When we get teh pictchers, we'll show them te Donal and see what he thinks,' Liam said nudging his friend in his arm. 'Come on, let's get over that little hill over there and get yeh that job on the building. Yeh'll need some money te keep yeh goin' till we go away.'

'Why Donal?'

'Because fer one thing, I like him teh best.' Liam didn't trust his other two brothers not to tell his mammy what he was going to do. 'Donal,' he shouted over the wind, 'talks teh least but he thinks teh most.'

'What about teh one that's married?' Brian thought that Donal was too young to know what to do. He looked over at the mountains while he tried to think about Liam's brothers but decided after a few seconds that he didn't know them very well. The tall one, Maurice was never friendly, but the other one with the thin straight hair, Donal, was always very nice. And Liam was right: he didn't say very much.

'I suppose yeh mean me brother Sean.' Liam zipped up his jacket. He didn't know his eldest brother as well as he knew Donal and Maurice. It was four years since Sean moved into a small flat with his new wife. He came up to the house three times a week, since his daddy died, but he was always more interested in Cathy and Joan. 'Sean's all right too, but he's not there all teh time like Donal is.'

'De yeh think that Donal be all right then?'

'Absolutely,' Liam replied quickly. 'Absolutely,' he repeated then turned his back on the wind and walked backwards in front of Brian. 'Jesus, Brian, are yeh sure yeh want teh work on this building site? Teh wind and teh rain will cut teh eyes out of yeh.'

The crunching roar of the tractor struggling along the road only added to the pain in Brian's face when he laughed. He watched Liam's thin curly hair blow about his head and his small ears flap in the wind like stiff little flags. 'Teh money's good,' he said, 'and it's not always this windy.' When he looked up over Liam's head towards the mountains he saw tiers of grey brick walls with timber beams growing out of the tops.

He was still gazing at the wooden stumps when he said, 'De yeh know how many houses they're putting up over there on that lot?'

'I don't,' Liam replied, turning to face the wind. He held his head down and counted his steps. He didn't care either, but he knew that half of Dublin knew, and that they cared, and he felt sorry for them. These were the families that lived in the remainder of the old tenements in the city, and some were even young married couples living with their parents. They were all on the housing list.

'Five hundred,' Brian shouted over the wind. 'If they keep on goin' like this they'll be at teh bottom of the mountains in three years. There's another school goin' up as well.'

'I hope they put in better teachers than they gave us,' Liam said, feeling the breeze blowing around the tops of his legs. 'I thought I'd never get out of teh place and I can still barely read. All that catechism and Irish.' He ran forward a few paces and kicked at some stones. 'And fer what?' He continued to kick at the stones until they had reached the end of the pavement.

Brian ran past his friend and picked up a few stones.

Liam sat down on a pile of bricks and watched Brian throw the stones into the distance. 'What's yer plan with teh pictchers?' he asked. He needed to be sure that Brian was coming away him by the weekend, because he wanted to tell his sisters, Pauline and Una about his plan for going away. After all, it was Brian's idea in the first place, and Brian had sent away for the forms and Brian knew how to fill them in.

While Brian threw the stones into small puddles of water among the mounds of earth and mud, Liam sat on the bricks and struggled with his thoughts. He had to get Brian to go to the Garda with the photographs, just as he had promised yesterday. He worried that Brian was right. Donal was only nineteen and he wasn't at all forceful. Maurice was only a year older than Donal and he was much more forceful. But Maurice wouldn't do, because Maurice would tell his mammy. He always told her everything. By the time Brian finished throwing his stones and came to sit beside him, Liam had decided that it would have to be Donal or the Garda.

Brian sat beside Liam and leaned his body forward, rested his elbows on his knees, and twisted the stone round in his hand for a few seconds then gestured with his head towards the old village and said, 'When Patrick was movin' all his stuff about and teh lights were on I saw me face reflected in one of his lamps.'

'The lights showed up the colours worse than they really are,' Liam lied.

Maybe, Brian thought as he said, 'Liam, I was frightened meself when I saw teh colour of me jaw.' He raised his face towards the housing estate and continued as if he was talking to the half built houses. 'I'm goin te stop him. I don't care anymore if he goes te jail.' He patted his sore jaw, and then raised his voice. 'Me da's not goin te do this te me sister. And me not goin' away wouldn't stop him.'

Liam squeezed his eyes against the grit still blowing around them, but now he closed them tighter against the memory of the light shining on his friend's damaged face. 'What do yeh think Carey can do that'd be different te goin te teh Garda in teh village?' he asked.

Brian sat up straight and ran his eyes along the grey concrete wall that enclosed the housing estate where both he and Liam lived. 'I don't like Peter Carey, but his da is all right, and I think that he'll do teh job and get me da te sign the papers.'

Those five last little words lifted Liam's heart. He studied the dirty earth and gravel at his feet for a few seconds. 'It'll be hard leavin' yer sister, just teh same.'

Brian knew that Liam's ma didn't hit her children, but she was a hard and snotty-nosed old bitch. Although there were more of them to miss, there were more of them to look out for each other. 'It'll be hard fer teh both of us,' he said.

'What'll yeh do if yer da doesn't sign teh papers, even after yeh show him teh pictchers, and old Carey goes te see him?' Liam asked. His ears didn't feel so cold now.

'I'll go to teh Garda in teh village,' Brian said, throwing the stone out into the dirt road imagining he was aiming it his da. 'Me da is goin te stop teh beatins, or he is goin te jail.' He sat up straight again and gripped his knees with his hands. 'What about yerself? Have yeh asked yer ma yet?'

Liam stood and ran his eyes over the concrete blocks, rubble, mounds of earth and pipes as though he was admiring the housing estate. 'I won't be askin' her,' he said, shoving his hands into his trouser pockets. 'I'll be tellin' her.' He had never talked about his mammy to Brian before, but he felt privileged that Brian had told him about his da. 'She'll do it,' he said, 'she'll do it fer teh money. It won't be much but if she doesn't sign she won't get anythin.'

Chapter Nine

When the train pulled into Holyhead, Josie was confident that the longest and worst part of her journey was over. She used the money Mike had given her and secured a porter to carry her suitcase onto the boat. She proudly produced her sailing ticket so she avoided standing in a queue and she was one of the first passengers to board the boat for the three-and-a-half hour sail to Dublin.

After the eight hours sitting on the train Josie looked forward to rambling around the deck like she always did on the boat on her journeys across the Irish Sea, and Eileen loved to be wheeled around in her pushchair. She had expected the sailing time to pass quickly.

Unfortunately, the pushchair caused problems. Josie found one door that was wide enough to get the pushchair through, but mail boats had not been designed with child access in mind and she needed help to lift it over the fender. Her stroll on the deck was short because the wind blew in circles everywhere she went. A steward helped her to lift the pushchair over the fender again when she was going back into the lounge, and told her about the mother-and child room.

After twenty minutes in the room Josie could hardly tell who was making the most noise: the fighting children or the screaming mothers. By the time she had left this room the boat was already well out to sea.

The boat rocked and swayed more than Josie had ever

known before. She started to feel dizzy so she sat down on the edge seat of a row of six low upholstered chairs, and turned the pushchair around in the two-yard passageway between the chairs and a wall. Still she convinced herself it was worth it for the three hours. The money she was saving travelling on the boat instead of the plane would help her mammy with the extra food when all her family would be home.

Fifteen minutes later Josie's fragile peace was interrupted when three women and seven children set up their temporary home in the other five seats. Even if she had had somewhere else to go Josie knew she would have been sick the moment she stood up. Instead, for the next two hours, she was forced to endure stories of confinements, evictions, council housing, bingo wins, and job hazards. God, she thought, why do all Dublin women have to tell everyone their business?

The way the women talked also irritated Josie. She knew she had a Dublin accent, but like her older sisters she finished her words. She thought briefly about when her mammy used to correct their speech. One of the few criticisms she allowed herself to have against her mammy was that she had never bothered to insist her brothers and her young sisters speak properly.

Chapter Ten

While Josie was suffering her voyage on the Irish Sea her brother Liam and Brian enjoyed the wind at their backs as they made their way over to the Ballyglass housing estate.

'It must be only four,' Liam said looking at his watch.

'Ten to,' Brian said then raised his voice. 'Why don't yeh get yerself a proper watch? Yer always lookin at that thing and yeh know it doesn't work.'

Liam raised his hand and shoved his cuff back to gaze fondly at his wrist. 'It's goin all right,' he said, 'it's just that it's a bit slow some ev teh time. I don't wear it enough and it needs teh electricity in me arm te keep it goin' all teh time.'

'Most ev teh time is not good enough.'

'A few of yer prayers might help,' Liam said tapping the watch gently as though it was a pet dog, then raised his head to his friend and winked.

Brian smiled then lifted his shoulders as though a weight had been taken off them. He turned back to the building site as if to make sure it was still there. He had been hoping to get that job, but he was still surprised it had been so easy. He wondered if they would teach him how to drive a tractor. 'Are yeh still sellin' yer bike?' he asked.

'No,' Liam replied quickly, 'I'm givin' it away.'

'Yer what?' Brian shouted. He stopped walking and watched Liam continue to saunter on for a few steps then shouted after him, 'After yeh spent yer money and yer time puttin on teh new tyres? If yeh do teh brakes, it'll be as good as new.'

'It was me daddy's bike and I couldn't sell it,' Liam shouted back enjoying the wind at his back.

'Jesus, Liam, I never thought I'd see yeh waste yer money like that,' Brian said as he caught up. 'Yeh said yerself that yer brothers won't use it because it was yer da's.' When Liam quickened his steps, Brian shouted, 'Yer not changin' yer mind about comin away are yeh?'

'No, I'm not changin' me mind.' Liam stopped walking. 'And I didn't waste me time, or me money and yeh can do teh brakes yerself because I'm givin' yeh teh bike. Yer goin' te need it if yer te get up here fer eight, and especially if yer still goin' te go te seven o'clock mass every mornin'.'

'Thanks, Liam,' Brian said smiling back glancing at the spire of the church over his friend's head. 'I'll pray every morning fer teh watch.'

Chapter Eleven

As Liam turned the corner into Plunkett Road, his nose caught the whiff of newly cut grass and he inhaled deeply. Seeing the small, wiry body of his neighbour Angie Dolan at her rose bushes, he crossed the road.

'Teh grass all right, Angie?' Liam called out opening her gate.

'Grand, Liam, grand.' Angie smiled and continued to pull at a small tool.

'Yer scissors stuck again?' Liam asked holding his hand out.

'I've told yeh before Liam, it's not a scissors. It's a sickators, and yes – it's stuck again,' Angie said, shoving her glasses back up her nose. She glanced at her bushes. 'I just thought I'd get teh roses nice and tidy fer when Una comes.'

'And quite right too.' Liam nodded at the green bulbs that were ready to open and smiled down at the top of his friend's head. 'Una likes a nice garden, and she's lookin forward te stayin with yeh fer teh two nights.'

'It'll be grand fer yez all te be tegether fer a while,' Angie said pushing her glasses up her nose again.

Liam nodded agreement and said, 'I hope we'll see more of Una with her stayin' nearer the house this time.'

'It's not easy in a large family to give a couple a bedroom on their own,' Angie said.

'That was true the first year when Una came home,' Liam

said. 'But when Josie, Pauline, and Maura left we could do what we are doing now for Maura and her new husband.'

'What's that?'

'Move over a bit,' Liam said. 'Just because a girl changes her name it doesn't mean she has changed her family.'

'Yeh have an answer fer everythin', Liam.'

'I'll do er own lawn again before Maura and Pauline come,' Liam said, raising his head from disentangling the tool.

'Yeh'ed better book the mower then,' Angie said tossing her head backwards to the other end of the road from where the whirring of a lawn mower was coming from. She turned round to Liam and smiled.

Liam raised the heels of his feet off the ground, followed Angie's gaze and saw a body bent forward, moving slowly up and down the front garden of a house about five houses along from where they were standing.

'That's the third one since three o'clock,' Angie said raising her shoulders and bowing her head respectfully towards her lawn mower. She folded her arms across her flat chest and laughed.

'Angie,' Liam shouted draping his arm around her small shoulders, 'yer not goin, te tell me that teh neighbours are all doin' their gardens because me sisters are comin' home.'

'I am, Liam.' Angie continued to laugh and patted the rolled up ponytail on the back of her head. 'We've never had a party on teh road before. And one with a massive big tent in teh back garden an all.'

'Cathy,' Liam chuckled, glancing over at his own house again. 'And what else has she been tellin' everyone?'

'Apart from teh fact that there's over a hundred people from all over Dublin comin', and teh marquee'll be teh full size ev yer garden, and as everybody knows, it's as big as a ballroom, I don't think she's said anythin' worth mentionin',' Angie said.

'I'll be over fer yer mower at ten in teh mornin' and when I've done er front, I'll clean yer windas after I've done ours,' Liam said, removing his arm from around Angie's narrow shoulders.

'That'll be grand, Liam. That'll be grand,' Angie said, removing her glasses and picking at the thread she was using for a hinge on one of the sides.

'They need a drop of oil,' Liam said, pulling at the old small rusty tool for a few more seconds and then, taking the secateurs in his hand, started walking towards Angie's gate. 'I'll bring these back when I've had me tea.'

'Sure, there's no hurry, Liam,' Angie said, pointing to the roses. 'I've done them fer now and it's only April. The petals won't be fallin off until teh end of May.'

Chapter Twelve

As Liam closed the hall door behind him his youngest sister, twelve-year-old Cathy, came out of the kitchen. She waved a fistful of knives and forks and gave her brother her usual bright smile while she crossed the hall and went into the living room.

'All right, Joan?' Liam called into the kitchen.

'Grand, Liam,' Joan said smiling over to her brother from where she was standing at the sink.

Joan was small, gentle, and kind, and even though Liam had always seen her as an angel, for a second he thought she had grown wings because her elbows were sticking out from her back. 'Leave it,' he called out when he saw she was about to lift a pot of potatoes from the cooker.

Joan wore one of his mammy's old aprons over her best pink dress. She was thinner than his mammy, and after she had wrapped the apron around her hips she could bring the strings back around to the front to tie in a bow.

'I'll do them,' Liam shouted into the kitchen removing his jacket and draping it on top of the three others on the knob at the bottom of the banisters.

'Thanks for bringing in the washing,' Joan said, handing her brother the potato masher.

'All part ev the service,' Liam said, making his sister laugh imitating movements with his chin and arms, like some wrestlers he had seen on the television. He plunged the masher into the pot.

The kitchen reeked with the smell from the oven and the potatoes. They were having baked beans with mashed potatoes and a meat pie.

'Are yeh early?' Joan asked removing two tinned meat pies and some dinner plates from the oven.

'I make it ten past six,' Liam replied, suspecting she wanted to know whether to plate up the dinners yet, and he felt angry that she should have to get the dinner ready for them every day. He banged the side of the pot with the masher.

Joan looked at her brother's watch and laughed.

Liam opened the top of the window over the sink to allow the steam from the potatoes to escape. 'Plate them up anyway,' he said because they'll be in soon, and yeh can put Maurice's and Donal's back in teh oven if they're not.' He balanced the heavy pot of mashed potatoes on a corner of the table and watched Joan spread out the six plates.

'They're comin in the gate,' Cathy called from the doorway, smiling at her favourite brother. She fiddled with the belt around the waist of her new green and blue check patterned dress, and pulled at the bodice to try and make the skirt shorter. 'Mammy said not te ferget about Josie,' she reminded her sister, casting her eyes over the plates and counting them. 'She's comin home this evenin,' she said, stretching up to the shelf above the table for another plate.

'Now how could any ev us ferget Josie?' Liam sang, banging the side of the pot with the potato masher. The whacking sound bounced off the wall of the small kitchen as he added, 'I expect she is having a rough crossing today and she won't be wantin anythin te eat.'

Physically the girls didn't look the least bit like sisters. Cathy with her mass of dark brown, nearly black hair, her wide mouth and her freckles could almost be taken for a gypsy. With a firm and agile body, she looked as though she might have been working since she was three years old.

Often referred to as a 'mouse', because she was so quiet Joan had fine light brown hair. Liam knew both of his young sisters were as much afraid of his eldest sister as they were of their mammy. Right now he felt sorry for Josie. He banged the side of the pot with the masher again and wondered if anyone in the family liked her, even his mammy.

Chapter Thirteen

Maurice walked into the house in front of Donal and continued down the lobby so he would be first into the toilet. Donal put his head into the kitchen and said, 'All right, Joan?'

'Grand, Donal,' Joan replied, looking up from the meat pie she had taken out of the oven and returned her tall brother's smile. 'Dinner is on the way,' she said.

'No hurry,' Donal replied, combing his thin hair back from his face. On hearing the click from the toilet door, he looked down the lobby as Maurice went into the bathroom, then walked down to the toilet.

While Joan cut the meat pie, Liam spooned the potatoes onto the plates. He hoped that in the future when he came home, in a few months time, all of his family would be looking forward to seeing him. He knew that his mammy had meant Joan to keep some dinner for Josie, but he also knew that Josie would never eat the meal Joan had made. 'Josie'll give yeh a break from doin' teh dinners,' he said, smiling, thinking about the lovely dinners they would have while Josie was here.

Cathy made space on the table for another plate.

'No, Cathy,' Liam said, 'Josie may not be in till after nine, and that's far too long te keep a dinner in teh oven. It'll just be a waste ev gas. Put the plate back.' He nodded to Joan and said, 'Leave some ev teh pie in teh tin fer her. I'll tell mammy that I told yeh.'

Cathy put the plate back on the shelf.

'Have we any eggs?' Liam asked.

'A dozen,' Cathy replied, pointing over to the set of shelves that were behind the door and said, 'Mammy sent me out fer them when I came home from school.'

'Josie has always liked eggs,' Liam said. He emptied the rest of the mashed potatoes into the Pyrex dish that was on the top of the cooker. He nodded at Joan and added, 'Leave some of teh pie in teh tin anyway.'

While Liam and Joan were plating up the dinners Maurice walked into the living room. He was surprised to see his mammy sitting by the fire watching the television. She always went into town, or down to her friend in Arbour Hill on a Monday. He also worried when he felt the room was very warm because it meant that the fire had been lighting all day. He made a mental note to answer the door on Thursday evening when the coal man came for his money. The last time the coal man called he had to give him two pounds because his mammy hadn't any money.

Scenes of the destruction the high winds had wrecked on the coastal towns came on the screen. 'It's a good job we don't live near the coast,' Maurice said, patting the pockets of his jeans to check again that he hadn't left any of his small screwdrivers in them.

Sheila stood walked over to the television and turned it off. She closed her eyes at her tall handsome son, then sat down in her chair again.

Chapter Fourteen

Huge green apples the size of dinner plates printed on the red tablecloth glared at Liam when he pushed in the door of the living room. Just as he put the two plates he was carrying down on the table, in front of his older brothers, his mammy rose from her easy chair beside the fire and sat down in her usual place at the end of the table, facing the door.

Liam didn't really want the dinner, but he wouldn't hurt Joan by not eating it. He knew she did her best with what their mammy gave her to cook with. Cathy came in behind him with two more dinners. She put one in front of her mammy, smiled mischievously at Liam, then sat down with the other dinner.

It never mattered who sat down at the table first in the Malone family, but it was always their mammy that was served first. Liam assumed Cathy had seen he had given his brothers their dinner first so he grinned back at her. He prayed in his heart that she and Joan would become good friends, like Pauline and Una after he went away. He swallowed to clear the tingling sensation on the inside of his mouth, which wasn't from the smell of the meat pie. He was going to find it easier to eat his dinner than to leave his two little sisters.

'Has Joan kept some dinner for Josie?' Sheila Malone asked.

'No,' Liam replied, 'I told them te save yer money on teh gas.' He turned to go back to the kitchen to get the other two dinners when Joan appeared with the two full plates stretched out in front of her. She had removed her apron and Liam thought she looked very pretty in her pink dress. He thought of Una again and wondered if she knew how much pleasure she gave her two younger sisters when she made up these little dresses and posted them over.

'She won't be home fer ages yet,' Cathy said. She didn't care if her sister never came home. But then, she didn't have to make the dinner every day.

'I wouldn't be surprised if the boat is in already,' Maurice said.

'Why do yeh say that?' Donal asked.

'Because of the high winds we had today,' Maurice said looking impatiently at his cheeky young sister.

'Which way were they blowin'?' Cathy asked.

'What difference would that make?' Maurice snapped.

'It stands te reason,' Cathy said, 'if the winds were blowin' towards England then the boat could take days to get here if they keep blowin' like they were when I was comin home from Doreen's.'

Liam didn't want Maurice to ask Cathy why she was coming home from her friend's house instead of from school so he said quickly, 'I agree with Cathy.'

Donal sat up straight and moved his head around the table as though he didn't care who would answer him and asked, 'How many days?'

'About three or four,' Liam said, 'but she should be here in time for the party.' He winked at Joan who was sitting opposite him.

Cathy started to count the days on her fingers.

'Is that all you're worried about?' Maurice bellowed.

'I'm not worried at all,' Liam said, 'but I think that Josie will be.'

Maurice rested his hands on the table and his handsome

face was red when he chuckled, 'I should think she would be worried if she was stuck out in the sea on a boat fer a few days.'

'And with the wind blowin' as well,' Cathy said, 'she'll be starving when she gets home.' She winked at Liam.

'Maybe someone will go out in small boats and get them off?' Joan suggested.

'They could send helicopters,' Cathy suggested.

Donal suspected that Liam was annoying Maurice, but he saw his sisters were enjoying themselves so he said, 'I'm not sure if we have helicopters in Ireland.'

'They can get them from England,' Cathy said, looking at her mammy and continued, 'Did you see helicopters when you were in London for Josie's wedding?'

Sheila Malone kept her eyes on her plate while she put some potato into her mouth.

Enough is enough Liam thought when his mammy began filling her fork with potatoes again. He never worried when she displayed her ill-humour to Maurice or Donal. They were both old enough to stand up for themselves, but his temper came when she shunned his young sisters. He knew his mammy didn't want the party and he also knew she could have stopped the arrangements weeks ago. 'I am sure Josie will be home by Saturday,' he said.

Afraid Liam would take his joke about Josie too far, Donal asked, 'When will Maura be home?'

'Durin' teh week,' Maurice said, lowering his head to his dinner, expecting someone else to say something about his sister Maura and about the party that was planned for her birthday on the coming Saturday night. He had never liked Maura and he had always resented the fuss his daddy used to make of her. It would be another four years before he learned why Maura was spoilt but he never grew to like her.

'And Una is comin on Saturday mornin,' Cathy said, 'so

we will all be home for three days because Una is goin' back on Monday.'

Liam covered his meat pie with his mashed potato so he would be able to eat it. The activity helped to take his mind off being angry with his mammy. He hated the way she stayed silent, always waiting for someone else to answer. He put some food into his mouth and chewed for a few seconds, then looked meaningfully at his two brothers and said, 'Teh both of yeh make sure that yer here on Saturday mornin.'

Donal nodded his head in agreement and asked, 'How long will it take?'

Sheila raised her face to the window behind Maurice's head and stared at the clouds for a few seconds. Because he was sitting in front of her, Maurice watched tears begin to glisten in her eyes. He wondered if somebody was at the window so he turned round to see who it might be. There was nobody there and when he turned back again his mammy was standing.

'What time will they be here at?' Cathy asked while her mammy was walking towards the door.

'There will be plenty of time to get teh garden cleared up and move anythin' else to make room for teh marquee,' Liam said while his mammy was walking out the door.

As he was nearest to the door Maurice felt the draught on his legs first. 'I think Mammy is upset about something,' he said.

'And so will you be when your turn comes,' Liam said wondering how his selfish brother could be so stupid not to see that their mammy was throwing one of her tantrums. 'Anyway,' he added, 'Mammy is not upset she's emotional.'

'My turn for what?' Maurice asked, feeling the breeze on his legs again.

'For when all yer children are coming home at the same time,' Liam said, trying to keep from laughing. He pointed over to the door and added, 'Close that before we all get phnumonia or there won't be anyone here at all on Saturday.'

'Mammy is out in the garden,' Maurice said.

'I'm not,' Liam snapped, 'and mammy has every right to go out to her garden anytime she likes.'

'I'll close it,' Cathy said and got up and closed the door. 'She might stay out there until Josie comes and we can't keep the door open fer a few days if the wind is still blowin.'

Chapter Fifteen

Sean Malone gazed out into the Irish Sea and watched the boat from Holyhead grow larger as it came into Dun Laoghrie harbour.

He hooshed his young son Brian up onto his shoulder as high as he could so that the three-year-old boy could look out into Dublin Bay. He pointed to the greyish white object, swaying far off in the waters. 'Look, out there,' he said, 'yeh see yer Auntie Josie's boat?'

When Brian turned his head away from the sea and buried his face in his daddy's neck, Sean moved away from the harbour wall. 'I think yer right,' he said, 'teh breezed blow yer eyes out.' He gulped a nose full of the strong, salty seaweed pumping up from the waves and crashing against the harbour wall, and turned his back on the angry water.

He put his son down on the ground and let him run towards the brown-haired woman wearing a similar knitted Fair Isle jumper to his own. His wife Flo was holding the smaller boy, Kevin, by his hand.

'It's early,' Flo said nodding to the boat and closing her eyes against the wind. 'The storm must've blown it over.' She turned her back to the sea and looked at her watch. 'It's not even seven yet.'

'L-let's get these t-two into teh car fer a while,' Sean said, picking Kevin up before a fresh gust of wind could knock the child over.

While her brother was ushering his young sons into the back of his small car Josie sat in a comfortable chair near the exit door. While she listened to the rumblings of the engines grow louder as the boat reduced its speed, she hoped her Aunt Sue would be meeting her.

As the boat rocked its way into Dun Laoghrie harbour, Josie wondered why anyone would endure the same journey three or four times a year with two or three children. As the boat grated underneath, and vibrated harshly as though in agony, the thought of repeating such an arduous day made her feel sick and dizzy again.

Edging towards the harbour wall the groaning of the boat grew fiercer and the pushchair began to shudder so Josie stood to hold it. She cast her eyes around the nearly empty room. She didn't want to get involved with any more conversations about the voyage, or Ireland.

Evidence that the storm had played havoc around the shores of Dublin Bay was everywhere when Josie emerged from the customs shed. She scowled at the overturned bins, and stepped over a carpet of sweet wrappers. When she saw her brother Sean walking towards her she stopped walking and let go of the suitcase.

Because the gaffer had told Sean it had been a very rough crossing he expected his sister's face to look as green as her anorak but she looked as lovely as if she had stepped off an aeroplane. He was disappointed she didn't look pleased to see him.

'I take it yeh had a rough day then,' he said and knelt down to his young niece. 'I see yeh h-have curly hair like m-meself,' he said.

'No, I didn't,' Josie lied, still furious at having been forced to allow a strange man to rummage through her case and to search Eileen's push chair. 'It's only the car that the customs have searched before,' she moaned, avoiding saying anything about her journey. She wasn't going to admit she had made the wrong choice in coming by boat.

'Y-yer all r-right now, Josie,' Sean said. He was four inches shorter that his sister so he had to raise his arm to drape it around her back. 'T-teh car is n-not too far away.' He put his hand out for the holdall and motioned with his head towards the large concrete tract with bright white rectangles painted all over it then reached down and picked up the suitcase.

'They make us walk far enough,' Josie whined, scowling as she cast her eye over a small group of people waiting for other passengers off the boat.

'Is that r-right?' Sean said although he had no idea what she was talking about. He had never made the crossing him-self.

'Are you on your own?' Josie asked, bending over the pushchair to make sure that Eileen hadn't taken her hat off again. When she straightened up she glared at the boat, then started walking.

'Flo and teh b-boys are waitin in teh car,' Sean said, falling into step with her.

Sean loved all his siblings, but he knew his younger sisters more than her knew his older ones, and Josie he knew least of all. He had no memories of her playing out on the street, and she didn't laugh like Pauline and Una.

'I've never known winds as strong as this before,' Josie moaned as a strong breeze blew her hair across her face.

'It m-must'hev been teh gale t-that got yeh in s-so early,' Sean said, forcing his thoughts to remember she must have had a hard time on the boat. It would explain why she hadn't shown she was pleased to see him. 'I take it that y-yer woman w-was all right fer yeh,' he said looking down at the little girl in the pushchair.

'If you mean Eileen, of course she was,' Josie returned, closing her eyes against the wind and her brother. The expression 'yer woman' annoyed her. Eileen was a child, and her daughter. Compared to everyone else, she was never any trouble.

Used to being chastised by his eldest sister Sean said, 'That's grand,' and quickened his steps to keep up with her.

Josie had known, from the very second she had held the baby in her arms, that she would be the perfect mother. When the doctor had told her that she was pregnant, three years after she was married, she had been both surprised and disappointed.

Mike was surprised that she hadn't been pregnant sooner when Josie had shown him her private little calendar. Then she had shown him the article that she had cut out from a magazine.

'I'm going to have a baby then.' Josie said after Mike explained the difference between her menstrual month and a calendar month. She didn't tell husband she wasn't happy about the pregnancy and he hadn't asked her if she was.

Nevertheless, from the day that Mike had taken his two treasures, Josie and Eileen home from the hospital, Josie had enjoyed eight hours of sleep every night. Mike did all the early morning feeds, and walked the floor during the night when Eileen was cutting her teeth.

Along with his job in the city, Mike attended to the accounts for Josie's salon. He employed an extra cleaning woman and encouraged Josie to use her for cleaning the flat and doing anything else that would help her with looking after Eileen.

Nursing his disappointment that she hadn't said it was good to see him Sean said, 'I'm g-glad that yer here Josie.'

Josie increased her height when she raised her heels off the ground to look at all the cars while she walked across the car park, trying to find a black Volkswagen.

'There yeh are, Josie,' Flo called out.

Six years of living in England made Josie cringe at the sound of Flo's voice. She wished she was away from hearing people say such stupid things like, 'there yeh are' and 'is it yerself?' and 'everythins grand'.

'Isn't it grand that you're in early, Josie?' Flo called out as her grim-faced sister in law continued to look around the car park.

Flo had straight brown hair, grey eyes, a small nose and a wide mouth. But unlike most girls of her age, she didn't wear make-up. Una thought that Flo should use lipstick because it would show off her lovely white teeth.

Josie nodded her head for a smile, though her mood changed little at the sight of the car and Flo's hair blowing all over her face.

Sean put the case down on the ground, opened the car door and called into the back, 'Here's your Auntie Josie.' He beamed proudly as his two young boys scrambled out of the car and smiled at their daddy before they looked up at the tall lady glaring down at them.

'They grow quick, don't they?' Josie said, managing a thin smile, noticing that both of Sean's boys had thick, slightly ginger curly hair like their daddy.

Sean was pleased to see Josie smile a little, though he thought she might have shown more interest in his sons.

But Josie had never been impressed with children. Children had surrounded Josie all her life and she had never seen anything 'cute' or 'winning' about any of them.

'Y-you two get settled in with teh c-children,' Sean said, worried about the size of his sister's suitcase. 'I'll t-take care of all teh stuff.' He moved over to the boot of his car and took out several stretchy, coloured ropes with hooks on their ends and started to sort through them.

Torn between waiting to see if Sue and Fred would arrive and getting into Sean's car out of the cold, Josie looked around the car park again, but there was sign of her aunt and uncle. The wind caught her in the face when she deliberated between her case and the small car.

'G–go on, I'll manage,' Sean insisted. He took his sister's elbow and led her to the door. 'I'll g–get everythin' in, d–don't you worry.'

Though Josie was glad to get out of the breeze, she contemplate taking a taxi when she listened to Sean and Flo struggle to get the pushchair on to the roof rack. Every time there was a thud on the roof, the boys ducked and she squirmed.

Chapter Sixteen

While Sean was strapping the pushchair on the roof of his car, Cathy was folding the red tablecloth, and Donal was pushing the table back against the wall, their mammy was seated comfortably in her easy chair watching the television.

Expecting her brothers would be going off to play football like they usually did on a Monday evening, Cathy said, 'Yer football stuff is in yer bag under the stairs, Donal,' then walked out of the room.

Donal followed Cathy out to the hall and gave her a pound. He was pulling his bag out from the small cupboard under the stairs when Maurice came in from the back garden with a shovel of coal. 'Are yeh goin te football?' he asked.

'Why not?' Donal said.

'Just wonderin,' Maurice returned gruffly and walked down the hall and into the living room with his shovel of coal. 'This'll keep yeh warm fer teh evenin',' he said to his mammy as he brought the shovel of coal towards the fire. Just as he tilted the shovel Sheila Malone stretched out her feet.

Terrified he would spill some coal on his mammy's slippers Maurice said, 'Could yeh move yer feet back fer a second, mammy?'

Instead of pulling her feet back, Sheila Malone raised them, and kicked the shovel. Half of the coal scattered over the hearth. Maurice spilled the remainder of the coal onto the fire. His good sense told him his mammy had deliberately kicked the shovel, but his heart would not accept it so he said, 'Did yeh hurt yer foot, mammy?'

'No,' his mammy replied and got out of her chair and walked out of the room.

With tears in his eyes Maurice swept the coal off the hearth, and threw it onto the fire. He could hear the draught sucking the flames and smoke up the chimney and he wondered if Josie was really stuck out in the Irish sea on the boat and wouldn't get home for a few days. He wasn't worried about her, but his memory told him that she was the only one of his siblings that was able to pacify his mammy. He didn't want to be in the room when his mammy came back so he quickly returned the shovel to the coal shed and fetched his football kit from under the stairs and left the house.

Chapter Seventeen

After twenty minutes, and with the pushchair strapped onto the roof and the boot tied down with the suitcase jutting out Sean drove along the Rock Road towards the city.

Josie assured her brother she was fine, and that she had plenty of room for her legs. She just wanted to get home.

'We'll be grand w-when we get te D-Dorset Street,' Sean said worried about the weight his small car was pulling.

'What's in Dorset Street?' Josie asked.

'We'll only have te get o-one bus if teh c-car packs up,' Sean said moving out from the kerb to allow a man on a bike enough room.

Josie closed her ears to the stories of days at the seaside that Sean and Flo exchanged as they drove along Merion Strand. Sean and Flo reminded her of the women on the boat.

God, Josie thought; people who talk and talk never listen. She didn't want to be reminded of anything. She stared at the traffic ahead and prayed that the car would get them home before the pushchair fell off the roof.

Less than ten minutes after they had left the coast, Sean pushed his head back. 'This is it,' he said, slowing down the car because they were joining the traffic into the city.

'What is?' Josie asked.

'The traffic.' Flo bowed her head so she could see out of the side window.

'It's w-worse on a F-Friday,' Sean added quickly when he saw Josie pull her chin into her neck and heard her inhale through her nose.

'Fridays are always busy,' Josie volunteered, closing her eyes. She wasn't thinking about traffic. Mike always thought about the traffic. But Josie knew about Fridays, and they were nearly as busy as Saturdays. She half-turned her body to the back of the car so that both Sean and Flo could hear, and she raised her voice and she gave them a rendition of her weekend and how she had organised her business so that she could manage to be away for the two weeks she had planned to stay.

As they made their way around the edge of the city, Sean told Josie how their brothers and sisters were getting on. She didn't ask about anyone in particular or comment on anything he said.

The tall lanky windows and the bright paint on the wide hall doors of the old Georgian houses didn't lift Josie's mood. Instead she felt mortified when the boys waved out to other drivers and some pedestrians, on her side of the car, as they made their way up Amiens Street.

The overcrowded car reminded Josie of when their Uncle Fred used to take them all out to the seaside in Donabate when they were children. There were only eight of them the last time they went, and they were still living in Arbour Hill at the time. The car was bigger than this one, but she was sure that her brother's one must be nearly as old.

No matter what time it was, or how busy the traffic, there were always a few people that seemed to have a death wish. Sean was so busy watching his driving, with people scampering across the roads between moving cars, that for a while he was able to ignore his sister's sighs and long face. 'Not long n-now,' he sang when they had reached the main road into the Ballyglass estate.

Ballyglass was one of half a dozen new housing estates

developed or enlarged on the north and west side of Dublin since the 1950s. Many of the tenements and older houses in the city had collapsed, or were being pulled down because they were old.

The Malone family were one of many that gladly moved out of the city and enjoyed a third bedroom, a front and back garden, an indoor toilet and a bathroom. 34 Plunkett Road on the Ballyglass estate was the second house they had lived in since leaving the city fourteen years earlier.

The results of the wind were visible everywhere. Sticks, stones, even bricks and clothes could be seen on the roads and in the gardens. Some tin containers were lying on their sides on the pavements.

'Not much change here,' Josie moaned through her teeth; she had never liked Ballyglass and she often wished the family were still living in their purchased house in Ballymore.

'B-bin day is teh same everywhere,' Sean cut in. He didn't want to hear Josie list the faults of the housing estate. He knew she had never been happy with the move to Ballyglass. For the few years she had been living there she never stopped complaining about the children playing out on the road, and she had never made any effort to be friendly with the neighbours.

When the family moved to Ballyglass Sean was in his last year at school, and was looking forward to starting an apprenticeship as a bricklayer. At the time he wasn't interested in building anything, he just wanted to leave school.

He hated the bus ride to school so much that he always let everyone else on first, hoping it would be too full for him; then he could then go back home again. His daddy would be gone to work, and his mammy never minded: she always found a few jobs for him to do, and she would save on the bus fare.

But Sean's plan rarely worked for him. The bus conductors

knew the value of education for youngsters living on the Ballyglass Estate, and when they saw Sean hang back, they made
sure to create room for the stocky ginger-haired lad who kept
a tight grip on his satchel. They thought he was so well man-
nered because he never pushed past anyone.

Chapter Eighteen

The wind had died down and there were no debris in the garden when the Skoda slowly rolled to a stop outside 34 Plunkett Road. Josie pulled on the door handle on her side of the car as Sean raised the hand brake.

'Take yer time,' Sean shouted at his sister, using the elbow on his right arm to push his door open. His temper cooled when he saw his sister Joan walking down the front path. Her shy smile always made him think of a nun and reminded him that he should think the best of everyone. When he walked round to let Josie out of the car, three young boys of about eight years old were peering into the back seats and waving at Brian.

'I'm fine. I'm fine,' Josie whimpered, shoving Sean's arm away. She lowered her knees from under her chin and planted her feet on the pavement.

'Happy birthday,' one of the boys called out to Josie when she was getting out of the car.

'That's not teh one,' interrupted the other boy looking at the stern face of the tall woman. 'It's teh young, small one with teh white hair. Isn't it, missus?'

'Yeh'll have te wait till Wednesday.' Sean said.

'When is her birthday then?

'She doesn't have them any more,' Sean answered,

'Sorry missus, I didn't know,'

'Don't worry about it,' Josie returned, looking in amazement over the young boy's head as though she was seeing an apparition. Her mammy was walking down the path like she was a model strolling down a catwalk showing off her outfit.

Sheila was wearing an old cotton circular skirt that Una had made for Josie fifteen years ago. It was almost down to Sheila's feet in the front and only came to her calf at the back because it was too small at Sheila's waist and she could only zip it half way so she held it together with a pin.

Josie recognised the cardigan her mammy was wearing because she had bought it for her daddy about eight years ago. She assumed her mammy had cut the cuffs off because they were too long. 'Get my bag out of the car,' she said to Joan.

The bright smile on Liam's face didn't add any cheer to Josie's mood when she saw him standing in the doorway. She recalled snippets of things her mammy had said on the phone over the past few weeks and she stiffened her resolve: Maura would have a good party. As she lowered her head to find the first step on the path up to the house, she told herself again that her mammy was right. Joan was too young to tell her brothers what to do.

'This is your granny,' Josie said to Eileen when she met her mammy halfway up the path.

Sheila fixed her mouth in a tight smile.

Eileen buried her head in her mammy's neck.

'I think she is tired,' Josie said as her granny turned and walked back up the path.

'Can she not walk yet, Josie?' Cathy said when she saw Eileen wriggling in her mammy's arms.

'Of course she can,' Josie retorted, glaring at Cathy's knees and frowning at the uneven bottom of her sister's dress. She changed her mind about putting Eileen down on the ground when she saw the grass was hanging over the edges of the path. She struggled to hold her daughter because Eileen was leaning over to Cathy.

'There yeh are, Josie,' Liam called out as his mammy walked past him and went into the house. He had his arms stretched out to give her a hug, but Josie's arm was tired, holding her struggling daughter so she was glad to let her brother take her.

'In yeh go, Josie,' Flo said holding out the holdall bag. She had seen the weak greeting her mother-in-law had given Josie, and although she didn't like her sister-in-law she felt sorry for her. 'Joan is helping Sean with the pushchair.'

Cathy was already kneeling in the hall when Liam put Eileen down on the floor beside her and Josie walked in.

'Josie, yer little girl is beautiful. A perfect addition to teh family,' Liam said.

'I can do it,' Cathy said, pushing Josie's hand away. She removed Eileen's anorak and handed it to her sister then closed her arms around the little girl's body while Eileen pulled on the neck of her young aunt's dress.

'Josie, I think that yeh'ev brought Cathy home a little sister,' Liam said, smiling at the joy in Cathy's face as she cuddled Eileen.

'Don't be ridiculous,' Josie retorted, sliding her hands under her daughter's armpits. She didn't show any concern for Eileen when her daughter started to cry. Eileen was still crying and looking back into the hall for Cathy when Josie walked into the living room to present her daughter to her mammy again.

'Where are they sleepin'?' Sean asked from the doorway waving his brother's hand away as he continued to shove Josie's case in front of him. 'It's okay, Liam, I can manage. I just w-want te make sure that I p-put it in teh right room.'

'They're in teh back room on ther own,' Cathy said, tucking the skirt of her dress into her belt and walked towards the hall door calling over her shoulder, 'Liam, if Joan's lookin' fer me, will yeh tell her that I'm down in Doreen's.'

'I'll tell her,' Liam said, following her. He stood in the

doorway and watched his little sister jump over the rail into the garden next door like she was a small heavy horse. By the time Cathy had disappeared into a house down the road he had rehearsed again what he was going to say to Donal when he heard the living room door open.

'You can close that door now,' Josie snapped.

Liam didn't say goodbye when he stepped into the path and closed the door behind him.

Josie didn't notice Liam had gone because she was walking around the right-hand side of the ground floor of the house as if she needed to assure herself that it was all still there since the last time she was home. She frowned at the decorating that needed doing, but she noticed the small table in the hall had been dusted.

The last room Josie wanted to be in was the kitchen. She always hated this small room. The yellow quarry tiles on the floor made the room feel cold in the summer and freezing in the winter. And when she wasn't able to smell the grease from the cooker, she could smell the drain from the sink. She frowned at the Fray Bentos steak and kidney pie in th tin on the top of the cooker then went into the living room to get Eileen ready for bed.

Chapter Nineteen

The living room was warm and stuffy when Josie walked in so she opened the small top window in the front of the house. She didn't see her mammy turn round and scowl at the shouts and cheers of children playing on the road because she was now searching through her holdall bag for the jar of dinner she had brought with her for Eileen. She removed a small jar, opened it and sniffed at the contents.

Flo could smell the carrots in the mashed-up dinner. 'Do you want me te warm that up for yeh, Josie?' she said, holding her hand out. She was more pleased to get away from her mother-in-law than she was to help Josie. When Josie hesitated she suspected that Josie was worried that she would pour it into a pot without washing the pot first so she said quickly, 'I will stand it a pot of cold water and stir it until it is warm enough.'

'Yes please, Flo,' Josie said, giving Flo the first smile since they had met in the car park when the boat came in.' She returned to sorting through her bag for night clothes for her daughter.

Cathy was sitting on the floor playing with Eileen. Sean and Joan sat the table watching the two of them and Sheila was watching the television.

Sean was used to his mammy ignoring his two boys but he was annoyed she was showing no interest at all in Josie's little girl. After all this was the first time she had seen her. 'Is e-everythin' all right fer S-Saturday so far?' he asked and walked over to the window to see if his sons were still in the garden.

Half a minute passed while his mammy stared at Josie. 'As far as we can, for now,' Josie said picking Eileen up off the floor. She didn't know what arrangements were made because her mammy had avoided telling her anything.

'Liam has arranged for the marquee and the record player,' Joan said.

'I should hope so,' Josie snapped putting an apron around Eileen's neck.

Sean knew about the marquee and the beer. He looked between Josie and his mammy and asked, 'Is Sue and Fred still goin out to the airport to pick Maura and Carl up?'

'Yes,' Sheila Malone said pulling her eyes away from the television and glancing at Josie with a twist of a smile on her face then went back to the television.

Flo came in with Eileen's dinner and handed it to Josie. 'We'll be off now and let yeh get Eileen down,' she said, 'I'm sure that yeh must be exhausted from yer journey, Josie.'

'Not in the least,' Josie said quickly. She didn't want to be left on her own with her mammy.

'Just teh same, Josie, yeh have had a l-long day,' Sean said. He pulled his car keys out of his pocket and waved them at Joan and added, 'we'll be up at about f-five fer yeh on Thursday.'

'Why?' Josie asked. 'What's so important about Thursday?'

'She's comin out to teh airport with us fer Pauline,' Flo said smiling at Joan. 'We'll be off, now, and let yeh get Eileen down.' She wasn't concerned about Josie she wanted to get away from the worst humour she had ever seen her mother in law in. As she was walking towards the door she wondered if this time Josie would be able to cope with the selfish bitch.

Half an hour later Joan stopped writing and turned her face up to the ceiling in the kitchen from where she could hear Josie walking around the bedrooms. After a couple of minutes, when Josie hadn't called her to complain about the beds, or some cleaning that needed doing, she finished her homework. She then tidied the kitchen before leaving to go over to a neighbour's house, where she was going to baby-sit and sleep for the night.

Josie was so absorbed with checking out the bedrooms for where they would all sleep over the next few days she didn't hear Joan close the hall door, or the front gate. But then Joan never banged doors or gates. After she had counted the sleeping places, and checked the rooms were in order Josie found she was too tired to remember who would be staying on what nights so she went back into the room that she would be sleeping in.

A quick scan of the small back bedroom assured Josie that she would be comfortable. Though small, it managed to accommodate a double bed, with just enough space to open the doors of the built-in wardrobe that went over part of the stairs. There was also a little table beside the bed.

With the bed against the wall, Josie decided she could keep the case on the bottom where Eileen would sleep. For tonight, her mammy and Cathy were sharing the front room, and the boys the large one. She would sort everything out tomorrow before Maura and Carl arrived on Wednesday.

Josie had only done housework when she had to. Una, Pauline and her daddy had always kept the house clean. She didn't know that curtains, doors, and skirting boards needed washing until she had moved into her own flat after she was married. She didn't like to think back either, but now while she stood on the quiet landing she could feel the emptiness in the house. She walked into the big bedroom where she used to sleep with her sisters. The three beds were all made, but she noticed the old cotton candlewick bedspreads were baldy, and in places torn.

The room was cold, and even though there was a window at both ends, and the evening was still bright it was dark because the drapes were only half drawn back. Josie stretched her hand to pull back the one that on the window at the back and found it wouldn't move. The strings from the tape were knotted, and only half of the hooks had rings to slide on. A job for Una, she thought as she crossed the landing and went back into the room she would be sleeping in. She liked the room dark when she went to sleep so she tried to pull the drapes across, but they wouldn't come. The drape still didn't move when she pulled it harder, but the end of the cloth swept along the windowsill and knocked a tin of talcum powder on to the floor.

When she bent down to pick up the tin she noticed a black line along the top of the skirting board. Another job for Una she thought, then sat on the bed facing the window. She covered her face with her hands when she noticed the small rectangle on the net curtain where the small window opened was black. As usual Josie obliterated her worries from her mind by dwelling on something else so she convinced herself that the party for Maura was more important than housework.

Chapter Twenty

It was nearly ten o'clock when Josie walked back down the stairs after settling Eileen. The sounds from the living room over the quietness of the rest of the house prompted her to wonder what her mammy used to do before they had a television. On the very rare occasions when Josie wondered what her mammy did with her time when she wasn't in town, or sitting in her easy chair rummaging through her handbag, or watching the television she promptly dismissed the thought from her mind.

Until now Josie had never needed to know why her mammy was so work shy because Una, Pauline and her daddy had done all the housework. Her short tour of the house forced her to think about the cleaning and decorating that was needed now. When she walked into the living room she noticed the beige background on the drapes were streaked with brown like an outside wall that was stained from a rusty leaking gutter.

To the right of the large window in the corner the ironing basket stood four feet tall. The lid was resting on a protruding bundle of white fabric like a ghost with a straw hat on sideways.

Ironing was a chore Josie had always avoided, she left that to Una and Pauline. As if the ghost with the straw hat had spoken to her she remembered she hadn't phoned Mike. 'I must phone Mike,' she said to her mammy. 'I won't be a minute,' she added quickly. I just want to let him know that I have arrived.' She left the door open when she went out to the hall.

Sheila Malone sighed, sat back in her chair, raised her face to the ceiling and whispered, 'Stupid girl,' as she listened to Josie telling Mike that the sea had been a bit rough but it certainly wasn't a gale.

Returning to join her mammy after her phone call Josie decided she would get Joan to wash the curtains in the living room, and with the toilet off the lobby there would be no need for anyone to go upstairs on Saturday. 'Do the boys do their own ironing?' Josie asked her mammy as she was dragging the second easy chair around to the fire. She saw a little glaze in her mother's eyes as she announced proudly, 'Mike does all the ironing.'

Sheila Malone gazed into the fire as if she was contemplating taking some embers out and handing them to her daughter.

Josie continued, 'Una showed him how to iron his shirts.' She wondered if her mammy was getting a cold because she sniffed, but she continued anyway: 'I'll get Una to show Donal how to iron before she goes back.'

'Cathy does the ironing,' Sheila Malone said.

'Even so,' Josie returned. She wasn't thinking about ironing now, she was seeing the dirt on the doors, the windows, and the skirting boards. She raised her voice and said, 'Cathy can do other things.'

Sheila closed her eyes and sniffed. She had more important things to think about than ironing, or housework.

The news was over on the television and while a man waved his hands over a map of Europe while he read the weather Josie imagined she could feel the train gently rocking and the boat heaving, but she couldn't close her eyes or pull them away from the flames in the fire grate, or prevent her thoughts from going back to the last time she had seen Una.

She was about to question her own behaviour when the hall door rattled and Maurice walked into the room.

'There yeh are, Josie,' Maurice said from the doorway.

Josie shoved her chair back from the fire and faced her tall handsome smiling brother. 'Hello Maurice,' she said startled at how much like her daddy he looked, and wondered why she had never noticed the resemblance before. Then he rarely smiled at her and it was two years since she had seen him.

Encouraged by the warm look in her eyes Maurice said, 'We were worried that you would be stuck out in the sea from the wind.'

Surprised and pleased with his concern Josie said, 'Well I'm here.'

Sheila stretched her leg out rubbed her shin.

'Are yeh all right, Mammy?' Maurice asked.

'I think she's getting a cold,' Josie said, 'and I think she should stay in bed tomorrow so that she can get rid of it for the weekend.'

When Maurice saw the light from the fire shining in his mammy's eyes as she turned her head up to him, he felt he was her favourite child. When he heard her inhale through her nose he thought she was sniffing. He didn't see the anger or frustration in her eyes. But then Maurice only saw what he wanted to see. 'Yeh should have said somethin' earlier,' he said.

'I wasn't here earlier,' Josie snapped back.

'I was meanin mammy,' Maurice said, his smile fading.

'Even so.' Josie said, thinking that maybe Maurice would be better than Donal for doing the ironing. After all, he was an electrician so he would be able to fix the iron when it broke.

'Will I make yeh a lemon drink?' Maurice asked looking between his sister and his mammy again. He didn't want to upset either of them, and he didn't want Josie to snap at him again while at the same time he knew his mammy wouldn't answer him with Josie there.

Josie smiled and said. 'Not for me.'

'We don't have any lemons,' Cathy called out from the doorway.

Startled by the whacking noise their mammy made when she slapped her hands down on the arms of her chair Josie's head shook and her back teeth touched. Maurice felt faint, and Cathy walked out of the room.

'Mammy doesn't like lemons anyway,' Josie said as the sound of the whack her mammy had made with her hands rang her ears. She didn't need to be smacked or hit to imagine the pain. She swallowed her fear, and her disdain at the grey matted hair when she watched her mammy bend her body forward to get out of her chair.

Maurice had no idea what his mammy liked to drink but he smiled with relief and said, 'That's right.' For a few seconds he had seen himself walking around the village searching for one of the poky little shops that would be still open to buy lemons.

'I'll warm some milk for her,' Josie said dragging her chair back from the fire. 'Mammy can stay in bed tomorrow,' she said snapping her head in a sharp nod that was her usual sign to show she would take care of everything. 'I'll get your breakfast in the morning,' she said to Maurice, delivering another nod.

'Do yeh want me te stay home from school and mind Eileen fer yeh, Josie?' Cathy smiled hopefully coming back into the room.

'Certainly not,' Josie returned sharply glaring at her young sister's dirty white socks. 'You can watch her for me while I'm making the toast.'

'Other than bread and milk, we only have eggs,' Cathy said curtly; she thought Josie would know that their mammy never bought rashers or sausages for their breakfast. She then tossed her head back and walked over to the door.

Eggs were fine by Maurice. There were times when he was lucky if there was enough jam to spread over his margarine. He worried that Cathy would snap at Josie again so he said quickly, 'I like eggs.'

'You can all have scrambled eggs or make your own breakfast.' Josie said and walked out of the room. If she hadn't already been anxious about her mammy's behaviour she would have screamed when she saw the dirty bag on the floor at the bottom of the stairs. She guessed it belonged to her brother so she turned back towards the living room and shouted, 'Maurice, put that away before someone falls over it.'

Maurice was sitting in his mammy's easy chair when Josie came back into the room. His face was already a bright pink from the heat that came off the fire; when he saw Josie staring at his feet it turned red. The warm feeling he was enjoying towards her froze in his heart when he saw the disgust in her expression. While leaning over the fire so he could undo the laces of his shoes he had felt pleased and relieved that Josie was home. If his mammy were going to be in bed, then Josie would look after her. And when he remembered that his mammy liked eggs he thought about Josie's omelettes.

'I hope you don't intend to leave those shoes there all night,' Josie snapped, glaring at three of her brother's long toes moving like huge worms poking out of his socks.

During the silence Maurice heard the water gushing into the cistern in the toilet. He intended to leave his shoes in the hearth all night, just like he always did. They were usually damp from walking through the field coming home from the football club, and the remains of the fire dried them for the morning.

'It's a filthy habit,' Josie said, pulling a clean tea towel from the hot press and leaving the room.

Maurice stared at his sad-looking damp shoes. He didn't look at his mammy when she came back into the room and asked him to move, so that she could get her handbag from under the chair. He thought he would cry if he did.

'Will you tell Josie that I want cold milk. And I want plain bread and butter, not toast.' Sheila Malone said to her sad son as she picked her handbag off the floor and left the room.

The smell of toast went down into Maurice's wet socks when he was in the hall. He watched his mammy climbing the stairs. He knew that her skirt wasn't really shorter in the back than it was in the front. It just looked like that because the bottom had a lot of sideways pleats in it, and it was always like that when she had been sitting down for a while. When he saw his mammy's feet he wished he had some slippers, even if they weren't the same colour.

'Josie, Mammy said that she wants cold milk and she doesn't want the toast either. She wants plain bread and butter,' Maurice shouted into the kitchen. By the time his sister poked her head into the hall, he was on the landing opening the door into his bedroom.

Chapter Twenty-one

Maurice didn't turn on the light when he walked into the bedroom. He never did when he wanted to look out the window. At eleven o'clock every evening, all the young people that lived on the road were coming home from the pictures, or from other places where they had been for the evening. He was still standing in his usual place brooding over his eldest sister, and his damp shoes when he heard Josie come up the stairs with his mammy's supper.

He was now more interested watching some of the young girls that were walking along the road than he was in Josie or his mammy. Maurice let his mind take a five-minute holiday from his wet shoes and watched a girl walk down from the bus stop then walk up the path and go into Angie Dolan's house. He saw Cathy jump over the fence. He moved away from the window when he saw Donal and Liam walking in the gate.

The hall door opened when Maurice was at the bottom of the stairs. Cathy came out of the kitchen with a plate of toast in one hand and a mug of drinking chocolate in the other. When she saw Maurice scowling at her plate as though she had stolen the toast she said: 'Josie made them fer mammy and then mammy didn't want them she said fer me te have them.'

'I didn't know that we had drinking chocolate,' Maurice said staring at the brown liquid in Cathy's mug.

'We don't,' Cathy said walking over towards the door into the living room. 'Josie had some in her bag fer Eileen and she gave it te me.'

'Well in that case, yeh'ed better drink it all up,' Liam sang as he pushed in the door for Cathy. 'Yeh know that er Josie is worse than er Una when it comes to wastin' food.' He turned to Donal, 'And quite right too, so we have te do all we can te keep her happy.'

'Why?' Donal asked frowning.

'Because Josie is a better cook than Una,' Liam said.

Chapter Twenty-two

Josie strapped Eileen into her pushchair and wheeled her down to the front gate so she could watch some young children playing on the pavement. She inhaled the smell of the freshly cut grass as she walked up the path to cook the breakfast for her sisters, Carl and her mammy. She left the hall door open so she would hear Eileen if she cried. It was gone eleven and she was hungry. She didn't want to cook for herself, then cook again, and she didn't want to eat on her own so she went upstairs to see if her sisters or her mammy were awake.

As Jose was climbing the stairs, Pauline moved her legs in the bed and found the sheets were cold. She couldn't recall Cathy or Joan moving, but she had slept on the inside of the bed nearest the wall so they wouldn't waken her when they were getting up for school. The bed she was in was just inside the door with the top under the window. There was another double bed in the centre of the room with one side along the bottom of the one Pauline was in.

She raised her head off the pillow and looked around the room. The other double bed was empty so she assumed that Josie was up. She guessed the small bundle in the single bed under the window was her mammy. She turned her head to the door when she heard it open.

For a second Josie thought she was looking at Sean. Pauline had the same light curly hair but in the half light Josie didn't see it wasn't as ginger as her brother's, but Pauline had the same round face and bright blue eyes.

'Are you awake?' Josie asked.

Pauline threw the blankets off and she said, 'Enough to know I need a wee.' She had been so tired when she had come home the evening before that she only pulled her nightdress out of her case. She didn't want to waken her mammy so she picked her jacket off the bottom of the bed and put in on over her nightdress and followed Josie down the stairs.

'How did you sleep?' Josie asked Pauline when she came out of the bathroom.

'Not too bad,' Pauline lied. She knew it wasn't Josie's fault the old mattress was lumpy and the springs were sagging in the middle. 'I was so tired,' she said, 'I think I would have slept on the floor.'

Josie smiled and ran her eyes over Pauline's hair.

'What time did Mammy get in at?' Pauline asked, combing her hair with her fingers.

Josie pushed in the door to the living room and said, 'The fire is lighting.'

Pauline saw the table was pulled out and was set for five. She also noticed the net curtains on the two windows were bright white, but there were no drapes, and the wallpaper was faded. 'What time did Mammy get in at?' she asked again.

Josie looked at the clock, and then tossed her head to the ceiling and said, 'It's time the others were up.

The ceiling Josie tossed her head at was under the floor of the room where Maura and Carl were sleeping. 'Do you want me to wake them up? Pauline asked.

'Give them another half hour,' Josie said and walked over to the front window. 'Liam said he would be back by lunchtime and we can all eat together.'

Pauline followed her sister and saw her little niece in her pushchair in the garden. Eileen was watching three children of about three or four playing on the path. 'What about Mammy?' she asked again trying not to show her disappointment that her mammy wasn't in the house when she came home last night. 'What time did she get in at?'

'You can bring her up a cup of tea,' Josie said.

'Did you hear come in last night?'

'No,' Josie lied, 'I went to bed shortly after you. She walked away as she said, 'I'll get Mammy's tea.'

Pauline was about to climb the stairs with a cup of tea for her mammy when all the light disappeared. The tall body of Carl had come out of the back bedroom and covered the small window on the landing. He scowled at Pauline as he brushed past her and made his way down the lobby like a wild animal was chasing him. She had her foot on the first step on the stairs when the toilet door banged shut.

The light coloured unlined drapes didn't darken the room so Pauline could make her way over to the single bed under the window at the front of the house without falling over the other two beds or the case on the floor, 'I have brought you a cup of tea,' she said to her mammy who had turned round from facing the wall.

'Where is Josie?' Sheila Malone said, raising her head off the pillow.

'Downstairs,' Pauline replied expecting her mammy would recognise her voice and say something. 'Will I pull back the curtains?' she asked.

'Tell Josie I will be down in a minute,' her mammy said.

'Do you want your tea?' Pauline asked, again hoping her mammy would know the voice wasn't Joan or Cathy.

'Leave it there,' Sheila said.

Thinking that her mammy couldn't see in the poor light Pauline placed the cup of tea on the floor beside her mammy's bed, pulled the curtain back on the window then turned round to her mammy and said, 'It's Pauline.'

'I know who it is,' Sheila replied and turned her body away from the window towards the door.

Even in summer the room was always cold. Pauline was used to the cold in Canada, but right now she imagined the room had turned to ice. She was too stunned to ask her mammy if she had received her letter so she stood for a few seconds and stared at the small body under the blankets then left the room and went downstairs.

In the hall she found Maura pacing the floor. Pauline was used to seeing Maura in the mornings without her make-up but this morning she thought her younger sister looked very pale and older than her twenty-one years with her small skinny body curled over holding her flimsy housecoat closed. She also wanted to go to the toilet. 'I can't wait,' she said recalling when they were all living at home with only one toilet in the house, so she went out to the garden and found a rusty old bucket and brought it into the coal shed and peed into it.

'Mammy said she will be down in a minute,' Pauline said to Josie when she came back in.

'That could be an hour,' Josie replied, 'but I'm going to do the breakfast now. I can bring hers up if she isn't down.'

'She didn't know me,' Pauline said.

'I'm not surprised,' Josie lied again, recalling when she had come downstairs at three o'clock to go to the toilet and found her mammy sitting by the fireplace in the dark. Her mammy was drunk. 'She probably has a little hangover,' she said.

Pauline felt some comfort. She had never seen anyone drunk but she thought it must be the same as taking too many drugs and there were mornings when Harry didn't seem to know who she was. 'I didn't know Mammy drank,' she said.

Neither did Josie, but she didn't want to talk about their mammy's behaviour during the week so she said, 'A good breakfast will cheer us all up.'

By the time Maura had made up her face the smell of

bacon, sausages and fried eggs filled the kitchen, the hall and the bedrooms. Pauline was crossing the hall with the second plated meal when her mammy came out of her bedroom. She continued into the living room and put the plates on the table. She had returned to the hall when her mammy was at the bottom of the stairs. 'Hello Mammy,' she said.

Sheila looked at the floor, raised her head, closed her eyes and said, 'Hello.' She then walked down the lobby to the toilet.

Pauline went upstairs, sat on the bed and cried. She thought about the letter she had written to her mammy in February and tried to recall if she had written anything that would have upset her. It was a short letter and easy to remember. She went over every word. She felt even more desperate now than when she had written and wanted to believe her mammy had got her letter so she wondered if she had written the right number of the house on the envelope.

Shrieks of children laughing out on the pavement brought her attention to the window. They voices reminded her of when Cathy, Joan and Liam used to play out. She went over and stood looking up and down the road. Years rolled back for her now and she recalled when Una had come home from England for her wedding that her mammy wasn't home and her mammy hadn't been pleased to see her either. She saw Liam walking up the path with a large box. She thought she knew what was in it so Liam must have got her letter and it had the same number she had written on her mammy's. With hope in her heart that her mammy would talk to her about the letter when they were alone she went downstairs for her breakfast.

Josie came out of the kitchen as Liam opened the hall door and Pauline was at the bottom of the stairs.

'What on earth is that?' Josie demanded, staring at the box.

'A safe to keep all me money in,' Liam replied winking at Pauline.

'Your breakfast is in the oven,' Josie said curtly and walked into the living room.

'Did you get my letter, Liam?' Pauline asked, ready to cry again if he said no.

'That's what's in the box,' Liam said smiling. 'Did you think I wouldn't get it for you?' He noticed her eyes were red. 'Don't go getting a cold before we get a chance te use now,' He said.

'I wondered if I wrote the right number of the house,' Pauline said sniffing then feigned a sneeze.

'It wouldn't have mattered because there is only one Malone on the road and the postman knows the number,' he said shifting the box so he could hold it out in front of him and moved towards the stairs. 'I'll put this under the bed,' he said then climbed the stairs.

Pauline went into the bathroom and washed her eyes in cold water.

Chapter Twenty-three

I was about to call you,' Josie said to Pauline when her sister walked into the living room. She was sitting at the end of the table with her back to the door facing her mammy who was in her usual seat at the top of the table. Maura was sitting beside her mammy with her back against the wall and Carl was sitting facing her beside her mammy. Liam was sitting beside Maura. Pauline sat down in the empty chair beside Carl facing Liam. 'Sorry,' she said, 'I wanted to check I put my passport away safely.'

'You won't need it for a couple of weeks,' Maura said.

'Even so,' Josie cut in, 'it's best to look after it.' She had heard Pauline and her mammy in the hall and was worried because her mammy hadn't shown any pleasure in seeing her. She recalled her mammy hadn't shown she was pleased to see Maura either, but at least she was in the house when Maura came home. She raised her head to Maura and said, 'I would have done the same.'

'Have you got your passport in a safe place?' Carl asked smiling at Josie'

'I don't have one,' Josie replied.

'You will if you go to Canada,' Maura giggled.

'I have no intention of going to Canada,' Josie returned sharply.

'Don't you need a passport to get into the UK?' Carl drawled.

'I don't go to the UK,' Josie retorted, 'I go to England.'

'We don't need a passport to go to anywhere in the British Isles,' Liam said.

Josie didn't know the difference between the UK and the British Isles and to prevent a discussion about them she said, 'Mammy has a passport.'

'You can't use Mammy's passport,' Maura said spurting another giggle.

'I know that,' Josie snapped. 'If I want a passport I will get one.'

'You said you didn't want a passport,' Maura said giggling again and looking pleased to have irritated her eldest sister.

'No she didn't,' Pauline cut in, 'Josie said she didn't want to go to Canada.'

'And there is no reason why she should either,' Liam said tired with Maura picking on Josie every chance she got. He was going into town with Brian in half an hour so he said, 'While we're all here can we also decide about showing the movie?'

'What movie?' Josie asked frowning.

'Harry made a movie of our wedding,' Maura giggled triumphantly.

'And you brought it with you,' Josie said flicking her eyes between her two sisters and asked, 'from Canada?'

'Yes,' Pauline said.

'What are you going to show it with?' Josie demanded looking at her mammy.

Surprised that Josie didn't know Pauline said, 'Liam has borrowed a projector from his friend.'

Maura giggled a smile at Josie and shrunk her head into her neck.

'Mammy asked me to bring it,' Pauline said as though she was apologising to Josie. She looked at her mammy to agree with her.

Josie smiled at her mammy and said, 'Let's decide on the best time then.'

Sheila Malone left the door open when she walked out of the room. She opened the hall door, left that open and stood under the concrete shelf while her daughters and her son decided when they would show the film.

Chapter Twenty-four

Sheila Malone swallowed her sleeping tablets as her daughter Una was boarding the boat for Dublin at Liverpool with her young son Shea. Una made her way over to the tiny room with her two small cases. 'They will be all right there until morning,' she said and gave Shea's hand a gentle tug.

'Somebody might take them,' Shea said, using his other hand to point to the two cases his mammy had placed on the shelf.

'Nobody will take them, darlin', because the man will lock the door,' Una returned and tightened her grip on her son's hand. 'We have to go down the stairs and your daddy isn't here to carry them.'

Unlike her older sister, Una didn't enjoy walking around the boat, and she preferred the shorter train journey to Liverpool, and the night sailing into the North Wall. Jack always booked a cabin and they slept through the sailing. Because it was cheaper than a cabin, Una booked a berth in a dormitory.

Most of the other passengers stayed on the deck to see the boat pull out, but Una went straight to the cabins after she had left her cases in storage. She wanted to get a good berth, and get settled down and asleep before the noise from the engines of the boat started rumbling and grating when moving out of the harbour.

Holding Shea firmly by the hand, Una followed the directions written on the narrow bars that jutted down from the ceilings of the passageways and made her way down into the bowels of the boat to find the cabins.

As they went through the narrow passages Una met fewer people. She thought she could only bear one more set of stairs and then they would have to turn back. She was sure they were already under the water; she could feel the vibration of the engines getting stronger through her shoes every time she ventured down a set of stairs. Much as she wanted to get home to see her family she didn't want to drown.

After they walked into a large rectangular room that served as the women's dormitory, Una realised she had no idea of what a good berth would be like. There were six sets of two-tier bunk beds on both sides of the wall to the left of her and six sets going to the right. There were two sets of toilets and washrooms just outside the door.

Una cheered up a little when she felt a chill in the room; there must be air getting in somewhere. They weren't below the water line after all, so if the boat started to sink they could get out through one of the windows. They wouldn't have to go back up all those narrow passages and up all those stairs. Her case could go with the sinking boat as long as she could get out with Shea.

'This is grand,' Una said, bending down and kissing her son. She dropped her bag on the floor. She continued to hold Shea by the hand while she appraised the cabin. Every bed was made the same and taken together; they reminded her of a warehouse that sold grey blankets. They looked so smooth and soft that she had to go over and touch one of them.

On patting the third blanket, as though it was a pet kitten Una thought a top berth would be the safest; nobody would try to get up the ladder and take Shea, or her money. On the other hand, the top ones were quite high and Shea might fall out and break his neck. Even though she could hear the humming of the engines, the room felt deathly quiet. When she bent to kiss and rub Shea's hand she noticed two small bags on one of the lower berths.

'Are yeh all right there?' The sharp tone of a woman's voice called from the doorway.

Turning round, Una saw a woman was looking at Shea. She was short and thin with a sharp, pointed nose in her lined face, and her head was wrapped in a navy woollen hat. She wore drainpipe trousers, boots, and an old anorak. She reminded Una of the older women she used to work with in the garment factory in Dublin; widows in their forties or fifties. Una used to be afraid of them. They always stuck together when they were complaining and they shouted when they talked.

But Una admired the widows because they worked so hard for their children. 'I don't know what berth to take,' she said apologetically. She didn't want to offend or upset the woman because she knew how tough she might be. 'This is the first time I've had a berth in a cabin like this,' she said, casting her eyes around the bunk beds to avoid looking at the woman.

'Yeh take what yer given,' the woman said, lowering her eyes from Una's red hair to her trench coat. 'What number is on yer ticket?'

Una looked at her ticket. 'Seven,' she said, feeling stupid because she hadn't thought to look before.

'A or B?' The woman asked, smiling with her eyes at the young boy. 'Teh bottom one would be better fer teh little fella when teh boat starts rockin', and especially if he's sick.' She shoved her hands into the pockets of her anorak and walked over to the berth with the bags on it, and stared at them as though they were evidence at a crime scene.

'I never thought about that,' Una said, deciding she would sleep sitting up on the outside of the bunk.

'I'll swap with yeh, if yeh like,' the woman said, lifting the heels of her feet off the floor and nodding her head to the lower bunk. She removed one of her hands from the pocket of her anorak and showed Una her ticket and said, 'This one is mine.'

Una felt her mouth start to itch. Clearly the woman was older than her mammy. And even though she walked with more agility than she had ever seen her mammy do, she thought that it just wasn't right that she should climb up to a top berth and at the same time she didn't want to argue with her so she said, 'That's very nice of you.'

'The top ones were all gone on Wednesday when I bought me ticket,' the woman said, taking her bag up off the lower bunk as if she was expecting the swap to take place.

'Are you sure you want to swap?' Una said. She thought about her mammy again and no matter how angry she had ever been with her, she would never have allowed her mammy to climb a ladder to get into bed.

'I wouldn't offer if I didn't,' the woman said, picking up her bag and slinging it up onto the top bunk like she was playing basketball and throwing the ball into the net.

Una recalled how proud the widows she had worked with used to be. She also knew that they were always trying to prove they were as good as all the young girls because they needed to keep their jobs. 'Thank you,' she said.

When the woman had left the cabin, Una removed Shea's jumper and trousers and settled him down in the top end of the berth. She lay down herself at the other end, with her feet on the outside to protect him from falling out. She then secured her own small bag, under her bum.

Shea fell asleep straight away. Una lay awake listening to the rumble and grating of the boat pulling out of the harbour. She read Angie Dolan's letters again from her memory and tried not to worry about her youngest sister.

When the boat started to list a little Una prayed she would

have a safe crossing and as always when she prayed she said one for her mammy. She smiled into the semi-darkness of the cabin and wondered if her mammy ever prayed for her.

Unlike her sister Josie, Una could read her mammy's behaviour. She recalled when after she had read Pauline's letter telling her she was coming home she had phoned her mammy and told she would also be coming home. Every time she had phoned since then her mammy was either out or in bed. Clearly her mammy wasn't pleased she was coming home.

By one o'clock in the morning Una knew why the woman had been so keen to swap berths with her. The bottom berths were nearer the floor so they suffered more from the vibrations from the grating engines. She also had to endure the other young children running up and down the passageways, and getting in and out of any berth that had an empty space. However, the other women proved to be a friendly crowd and helped each other to get the children settled and asleep.

Convinced that her fellow sleepers had enough children of their own, without wanting to snatch her son, Una closed her eyes and thought back over her day.

Like Josie, this was the first time for Una to make the journey on her own, and with a child. It had been an easy journey. Jack had taken her to Euston and seen them onto the train, and with everything booked she had no problems. She would do it again on her own. She knew it was the only way she would be able to spend time with her own family.

Every now and then the sound of snores seeped through the rumbles of the engines. They reminded Una of her father -in-law and the nights she couldn't get to sleep because she could hear him snoring so loudly she thought he was in the same room. Never again will she stay there, she thought guiltily because at the time she had welcomed the change from staying with her mother.

When the mattress on the bed above Una's head trembled

she expected it was the woman she swapped with moving. She wondered how many children she had and if she was kind to them and if they were married did she like their husband or wives, or if they liked her. She recalled that her mammy had never like her granny Malone, and she didn't like Jack.

Chapter Twenty-five

This Saturday morning was the first time Sean had watched the boat from England come up the river Liffey, and although it wasn't as breezy as Dun Laoghrie he missed the salty taste of the sea. After one more sniff, he quickened his step away from the stink of the oil fumes and waited with Pauline. 'W-we're all home now,' he said when he saw Una and her son walk out of the customs shed.

'Are yeh tired? D-did yeh get any sleep at all?' Sean asked when Una walked into his arms.

'A good five hours,' Una said pulling her scarf from the pocket of her trench coat. She glanced into the customs clearing area to check that Pauline was still holding her son's hand. 'Just the same, Sean, thanks for coming down for me. It's great not having to make for the bus, especially with Shea and the cases.'

Una's bright and happy face helped Sean to forget the grumpy and sad face of Josie. He always felt very short when he was standing beside both of them. He raised the heels of his feet off the ground but he still had to look up when he smiled into Una's grey-green eyes. He noticed again that her front teeth needed the attention of a good dentist.

Una lowered her head to fold her scarf. She knew why her brother was trying to raise himself off the ground because she had seen him do it many times. 'Two inches won't make much difference Sean,' she said. She enjoyed teasing him.

'Y-yer g-goin te have t-te l-learn s-some m-manners,' Sean stammered. 'T-that t-tongue ev yers'll g-get yeh inta r-real trouble one ev t-these d-days.'

'It already has, Sean, and I daresay it will again, but I can't help it.' Una said. She was sorry she had made him stammer, so she put her arm round his shoulder and hugged him again.

'I mean real t-trouble, and not just makin' people laugh.'

'I know,' Una said, recalling the last time she had spoken to her father-in-law. 'Anyway, I always speak the truth,' she said, tying the scarf around her head.

'And yer man?' Sean nodded, his head towards Shea.

'The full ten hours,' Una said, turning to Pauline who was fussing with Shea's anorak.

Pauline's blue eyes shone with tears on seeing her sister. She had forgotten again that time hadn't stood still in Ireland while she was away. She bent down to Shea as if she needed to assure herself that she was holding Una's son's hand. When the wind came their way again, she put her hand on the little boy's shoulder and pulled him into her legs as if she would prevent him from blowing away.

'You look great,' Una lied.

'I'm still too fond of chocolate,' Pauline said, patting her stomach.

'Aren't we all?' Una laughed. 'Still, we keep the dentist in work.' It wasn't her sister's weight Una noticed. She found some grey hairs in Pauline's hair, and lines on her forehead.

'He's a real Byrne,' Pauline said, smiling down at Shea's blond hair.

Una returned Pauline's smile as she said, 'He is like Jack.' She laughed lightly and added, 'All the children so far are like their fathers, and from the photographs you sent me your two are like Harry.'

'Harry's sister,' Pauline said, recalling the third time that Helen had offered to mind her twin daughters. Harry's three sisters were all married and living in Canada and Helen was the only one she felt comfortable with. Although she missed her little girls she was content to know that Helen would look after them. Over the last couple of months she learned enough about Harry and his family from Helen to worry about her daughters. She needed to talk to someone who understood what Helen had told her. Helen told her she should talk to her mammy.

There were times when the ten months difference in ages of the two sisters felt like ten years to Pauline. Una always knew what to do when they were in trouble. Pauline never saw that if her sister hadn't broken rules, invented games and found lots of interesting things to do, then neither of them would have been in trouble in the first place.

'We all inherit features Pauline,' Una said but we grow to be ourselves,' She smiled down at Shea's blond hair and blue eyes and thought; thank God his daddy is not like his own father, and so far none of her siblings were as selfish as her mammy. She was to change her mind about that before she went back to London.

Chapter Twenty-six

The docks were grey, drab and hard. Pauline and Una walked behind their brother towards the car park. Watching their overweight brother as he trundled along with his shoulders dipping and rising with the suitcases and his curly hair blowing in the wind, Una said, 'With your hair short the pair of you look like twins.'

'Do I really look like the trunk of a tree?' Pauline laughed, frowning at her brother's short legs.

Fearing she had hurt her sister's feelings, Una said quickly, 'No, you don't. But you would if you were married to Flo.'

Pauline frowned.

'Flo likes cooking and Sean is fond of his food. I think she's trying to make up for all his hungry days in Arbour Hill.'

The memory of Arbour Hill made Pauline shut her eyes. It was a lifetime away. She imagined the pages of a book flicking rapidly over. It was full of pictures of her life until the day she met her husband Harry. She wanted to sit down and look at them all, but she knew that if she did she would cry. 'I didn't know him, or Joan, when they met me on Thursday evening,' she said softly as though she was apologizing. 'They have all changed so much.'

'Well, it has been five years,' Una said, bowing her head to the breeze. 'Young people change the most in that time. It's called growing up. Still I agree with you, I see changes when

I come home every year, and I find it hard to believe that so much can happen in such a short time.'

Una could list all the changes in the family over the last five years since Pauline went away. She would begin with Sean getting married, all the babies that had been born, Maurice and Donal working, Liam finishing school and looking for a job, the death of their daddy. 'Let's face it,' she said, 'if we can transplant hearts, enjoy the Beatles, and survive the death of Che Guevara, the assassination of Martin Luther King, a cultural revolution in China, and coup in Indochina over the last five years, then we should expect Sean to grow up.'

Pauline stopped walking. 'Una!' she shouted.

Turning back, Una said, 'Don't tell me that you haven't heard of the Beatles.'

Pauline's thick jumper hid her laughing, shaking body. 'You haven't changed a bit in all that time,' she said. She knew her sister was having fun with her, but she was thankful for the breeze that was blowing Una's coat around her legs, because she could blame the wind for the tears in her eyes. 'Yes,' she said, 'I have heard of the Beatles,' and started to walk on and tried to remember some of what her sister had said, but she could only remember another name. 'Is that who you called Shea after?' she asked.

'What are you talking about?'

'The garva bloke you just said. What does he sing, anyhow?'

'No, Pauline,' Una said waving her head, 'I didn't call Shea after Che Guevara.' She turned her head away from the breeze, 'But I might have if I had known about him at the time.' She smiled picturing the face of Jack's father if she had called his first grandson after an Argentinean rebel and said, 'He sings rebel songs.'

That didn't surprise Pauline. 'Six years, and six grandchildren,' she said in a tone that sounded like she was giving away a secret.

Una was looking at the assortment of boats and junks that were parked along the wharf of the Liffey. 'Less than four years for the children,' she said, 'If Mammy is fifty now and she has six grandchildren every four years, how many will she have when she is seventy?'

Pauline let go of Shea's hand and stopped walking again. She inhaled deeply then shouted, 'I don't know, and I don't care. And I don't want to know, and I don't want to care.'

'Thirty,' Una shouted back.

'Boys or girls?'

'If we all had ten children each, Mammy would have to buy a hundred birthday cards a year.'

'But Mammy doesn't buy birthday cards.'

'So your two don't get any either,' Una said thinking back four months to the row she had had with Josie before Christmas. 'Eileen had her first birthday just before Christmas and Josie bought her a card and pretended it was from Mammy.'

'Why did she do that? The child is only a year old.'

'For her friends and customers to see, I should imagine. I know she did because I saw the little W. H. Smith tab on the back of it,' Una laughed. 'She picked out the very same card that I sent.'

'How do you know that Josie sent it?'

'Because we don't have W. H. Smith in Ireland.'

The ground started to vibrate.

Pauline saw the huge moving machine before she smelt the petrol fumes. The metal beast was taller and longer than a double-decker bus. She stood with Una and Shea and watched the monster make a wide turning, then move off down the quay, recalling her granny Malone used to send them all birthday cards.

'Now, that was some treat, wasn't it?' Una said, hugging her young son.

'I thought the ground was going to open up,' said Shea.

Panic replaced the tremors Pauline had felt in her body from the vibrating of the machine. She had read about people being swallowed up in earthquakes. She wondered if if anyone would miss her if she disappeared into the ground and if Helen would look after her daughters if she never went back to Canada.

'How are your two?' Una asked as they came close to Sean's car. 'I'll bet you and Harry have enjoyed a few sleepless nights.'

'No. Harry hasn't, but I have.' Pauline said. She walked around to the far side of the car and helped Sean put the two cases in the boot.

Chapter Twenty-seven

The sky was bright blue when Sean stopped his car a few houses up from where Una's in laws lived.

When Pauline got out of the car she was amazed at how much the place had changed. The road looked much older now with cracks in the concrete. All the hedges had grown thick and the trees had grown taller. The almost white pebble-dashing on the houses had faded to a light grey.

When Una saw Pauline counting the houses up from the corner she assumed that her sister was trying to find her old boyfriend's house. 'If you're looking for Billy's Ryan's house,' she said, 'it's still there but Billy has moved away.'

'Where to?' Pauline asked.

Billy Ryan was Pauline's first boyfriend. He used to come up to their house nearly every evening when they lived on the road around the corner from where they were standing. They were both sixteen. Pauline was working and Billy was still going to school.

Remembering Billy's bright blue eyes and blond curly hair, Una smiled. Josie used to cut his hair for him, and Billy used to do the washing-up for Josie. 'His mother still lives there,' she said, 'but Billy went to South Africa two years ago.'

'So his mother is still alive,' Pauline said smiling and waving her head in disbelief. 'Is she still sick?'

For the first time Una made use of the gossip Betty Byrne enjoyed relating to her about the neighbours she used to know when her family were living around the corner. 'Apart from the Asian flu we all had about ten years ago, Peggy Ryan never suffered a day's illness in her life,' she said. 'Why do you ask?'

'It's a long story,' Pauline said, smiling again, recalling the last time she had seen Billy. 'I will make the time to tell you before you go back,' she added when she heard Sean's footsteps behind her.

'Were you in love with him?' Una asked.

Pauline thought for a few seconds. 'No,' she said, 'but I loved him.'

'We all did,' Una said.

'It's v-very quiet around here,' Sean said looking at the houses as though he was thinking about buying one.

'All housing estates become quiet when the children have grown up,' Una said as they walked on, the three of them looking at the houses and each of them remembering different people they used to know. As they arrived closer to the Byrnes, Una saw the curtain move in the small room over the hall door. When she opened the gate she heard the sound of wood rattling, and when she looked towards the hall door she saw Jack's young teenage sister Freda glare at her briefly, then flee inside.

The little bitch, Una thought as she pushed in the hall door and called out, 'Anybody home?' She felt embarrassed and angry when nobody answered after she had called twice. She was about to turn away when she saw the short and tubby body of Betty Byrne coming down the stairs.

Just as Betty reached the bottom of the stairs, her father-in-law's lanky frame appeared in the doorway of the kitchen that was facing the hall door. Jim Byrne lowered his face to his wife's slippers, then closed the door into the kitchen. He then stretched his right hand out and closed the door that led into the other back room in the house. He nodded to Sean and Pauline and indicated with his hand for them all to go into the front room.

Una didn't want to go into the awful cold front room. She didn't want to leave her son with her father-in-law either, but she knew that Betty would look after him for the two days. She let go of Shea's hand and stepped into the hall. 'Hello Betty,' she said smiling at her mother in law's hairnet.

It was nearly a year since Una had upset her father-in-law, and it hadn't bothered her that he hadn't spoken to her for the rest of the time she had stayed in his house. She looked at his bald head and small mean eyes and said, 'We won't be stopping long.'

'You won't want a cup of tea then,' Jim Byrne said, indicating again with his hand for her to go into the front room.

Una moved the suitcase with Shea's clothes to her other hand and said, 'I'll take this upstairs for Betty.'

While Una was upstairs explaining to Betty why she had brought every item of clothing for Shea, Sean and Pauline were sitting on a hard plastic-covered couch facing the pristine tiled fireplace in the cold front room.

Jim Byrne stood at the window behind the net curtains swivelling his head so he could scan the road as if he was looking for a police car. When he seemed to be satisfied he shifted his tall skinny body to the shelf beside the chimney-breast and moved a couple of ornaments as though he was counting them in case Pauline or Sean had stolen one while his back was turned.

By now Sean was uncomfortable sitting in the silent room. Other than at Una and Jack's wedding he couldn't remember ever talking to either Jim or Betty Byrne. Everything about the room was cold. The wallpaper was beige with dusty green leaves running down in stripes. He could smell the polish on the brown inlaid lino. He tried to imagine Una staying in the house for two hours let alone two weeks.

Unable to endure the silence any longer, Sean nodded to the fireplace and asked, 'Did yez get a new one?'

'No, we haven't,' Jim retorted as if Sean had said something rude. He bent his lean body and moved the gleaming handle on the poker that was sticking out of the grate, then walked out of the room.

Pauline felt as though she was sitting in the front room of Billy Ryan's house with her feet on the same brown lino that Billy's mother used to polish every time someone had been in the room. She even thought the beige half-moon rug with the pink roses in front of the fireplace was the one Billy's mother used to have in her front room.

Sean had a vague memory of his daddy papering the top part the hall with the same paper in the house when they lived in Arbour Hill. He remembered the leaves also made a pattern that had to be matched and kept straight. He ran his eyes over the top to see if the pattern was the same on all the strips when he noticed a square on the wall that was lighter than the rest of the paper. He wondered what photograph had been taken down off the wall.

'Do you think someone cleans the back of the fireplace?' Pauline asked her brother.

'Maybe,' Sean said although he didn't believe it. He was a bricklayer and he knew about building materials and what could and couldn't be cleaned. He wondered if the fire had been lit in the grate more than half a dozen times. He could hear footsteps on the ceiling, and spoons rattling in the hall. He thought that Jim Byrne was making tea for them so he tipped Pauline on her shoulder and stood as he said, 'We will wait outside.'

Una Betty and Shea were at the bottom of the stairs when Pauline and Sean came out of the front room. At the same time Jim came out of the kitchen.

Una pulled a small card from the pocket of her coat and

checked she had written the correct number on it, then handed it to Betty and said, 'If Shea is not well or you need me just give me a ring and I will be down in ten minuets.'

Jim Byrne stretched his long arm out and took the card. 'I think we have that number in the book,' he said then walked over to a small table and picked up a small book that was beside the telephone.

'You can still keep the card,' Una said, 'so you can find it quickly.' She kissed her son, then walked over to the door and opened it. Pauline and Sean followed her and they were making their way back down the driveway of his house before Jim had closed his little book.

Una was the only one to turn back at the gate and the only reason she did was to wave to her son who was standing at the door with Betty. If Shea hadn't waved to her she would have gone back and taken him with her.

'Sorry about that awful man,' Una said when they were crossing the road.

'It's not your fault,' Sean said.

'He was pleasant at your wedding,' Pauline said, 'but I thought Betty looked afraid of him.'

'He's nothing but a tall lanky mean bully,' Una said, 'and it's her own fault for putting up with him. She's not his child.'

'What can she do?' Pauline asked.

'Say no when he asks her to butter a slice of bread for him,' Una returned, smiling at the memory of the day when he had asked her to polish his shoes and she had said she was allergic to polish.'

While Sean was stretching across to open the doors for them Pauline said, 'Jim Byrne reminded me of Mammy when he walked out of the room.'

Una smiled. 'Usually it is the other way around,' she said. 'Jack walks away from him, and it is about time we did the same with Mammy.' She smiled again because Pauline had opened her eyes so wide with surprise that she looked like an owl.

'But then Jack is not living there any more,' Una continued, 'so he can walk out and never come back if he wants to.' She opened the car door. 'However it is more important to say no to Mammy and walk away from her if we are still living at home with her.' She looked back at her in laws' house and waved to Shea again. 'Including Josie,' she added, then got into the car.

Chapter Twenty-eight

Walking in the gate of her family home in Plunkett Road, Una could hear voices coming from the open window of the living room. She had never known Josie to talk to herself so she was pleased that she didn't have to face her sister on her own for a while.

The smell of cut grass made her think of hay and it reminded her of the country, so she looked down the road and over to the Dublin mountains. They were clear and smiling at her like they were welcoming her home.

As soon Una stepped into the hall, Liam's arms moved towards her. She kissed him twice on his ear and was looking over his shoulder when she saw Joan walking up the lobby from the bathroom. When she put her hands on the small shoulders of her young sister, she wondered if Joan was eating enough she was so thin.

'There yeh are, Una,' Cathy called out, coming down the stairs. Her hug was firm and strong.

Liam put his hand on Cathy's back and moved her down the lobby. 'Stop yer worryin,' he said, and ushered her out to the back garden. 'Look over all that's there and make yer mind up what yer goin' to pull out.'

A cocktail of smells assaulted Una's nose when she walked into the warm living room. This came from the turf briquettes on the fire, the freshly made toast, freshly cooked sausages, and cigarette smoke.

Both sides leaves of the table were extended, it was pulled out from the wall, and covered with a white cloth. Una smiled at her mammy who was sitting at the top of the table with her back to the window. 'Maura,' she said to her sister who was sitting with her back to the wall on her mammy's left.

Sheila returned Una's smile, then glanced coldly at Pauline who had walked in behind Una.

Maura looked down the table to her husband like she was showing Una a prize possession that was sitting on the same side of the table between Donal and Maurice.

Carl made to stand but his chair was against the wall and the table was pressed against his chest.

'Stay where you are,' Una said holding out her hand. 'Welcome to the family,' she added feeling his large soft hand close over her own.

'Looks like I won't be lonely,' Carl drawled, smiling broadly.

'Una, I'll take your coat,' Josie said, holding her hand out and hoping her sister would have forgotten about the row they had had before Christmas. She desperately needed Una's sewing skills before the party. 'Take my chair,' she said, 'I'll make a fresh pot of tea.' She was also glad to move away from sitting in front of Carl.

Una sat in Josie's chair and smiled at Carl. He was certainly handsome she thought. He had a square chin and forehead, and a wide mouth reminding her of a drawing from a comic. She also thought he was older than Jack, and was surprised his skin was a light brown because it suggested an outdoor job like a builder, but she thought he couldn't be because his hands were so soft.

Liam opened the door and called out, 'It's here.'

'It c-can wait until I've f-finished me s-sandwich,' Sean said, scooping a couple of sausages from the plate in the middle of the table and placing them on a slice of bread.

'Yeh can take yer time,' Liam said, 'I'll clear teh hall and teh lobby so we can bring teh whole lot through in one go.'

By now Maurice had given up any hope he had that the party wouldn't take place. He looked over at his mammy, then nodded his head to Maura and said, 'We'll have it all up, and pegged down in a couple ev hours.'

Sheila lowered her eyes to her hands, and Maura giggled.

Josie came in holding out a fresh pot of tea as though she was carrying the world cup. She filled an empty cup with the fresh brew and put it in front of Una, then sat down in the chair beside her mammy.

Three minutes after Una had asked Carl how he was adjusting to the Irish rainy weather, she wondered if her older sister was studying the tides and the oceans because while Carl was explaining why Alberta had colder winters than Toronto he didn't take his eyes away from Josie. And he didn't seem to notice or care that all the time he was talking, she was reading the label on the marmalade.

When the shouting and the banging from the hall grew louder, Carl did what a good preacher would do – he raised his voice and went on to recite what he knew on Niagara Falls.

God Almighty, Una thought, I didn't really want to know: I was just being polite. She lowered her head to the table to hide her smile when Donal picked up the jar of marmalade and began reading the small print on the label.

Despite the fact that it still irritated her, Una grew used to her mammy twisting her cutlery when she sat at the meal table listening to her children talking. When she saw that both her mammy and Maura were rotating a knife, she wondered if one of them was contemplating using it on Carl's throat.

'Is that right,' Maurice said. He wasn't asking a question. He always said, 'is that right' when someone was talking and he was bored.

Five minutes was enough to be polite, and Una decided that listening to her husband retell the history of the English Labour Party was a delight compared to the Canadian drawl instructing Josie on the climate of North America. She picked up a fork, then stretched her arm into the table and lifted a sausage from the dish that now had enough room for another four pounds and said, 'I must remember to bring some of these back with me on Monday.'

'They are lovely,' Josie agreed nodding her head to the dish of sausages, 'Liam cooked them.'

'They won't keep that long,' Maurice said, then looked at his mammy expecting her to be pleased with him for almost telling Una she was stupid.

'I don't mean these particular ones,' Una retorted shooting her brother an impatient glance. 'I'm talking about buying some on Monday.'

'Do they not make sausages in the UK?' Carl drawled.

'They make everything in the UK,' Una replied sharply.

'Can you get corn bread there?' Maura asked, knowing that the bakers didn't make corn bread in Ireland and to annoy Una for talking so sharply to Carl.

'They wouldn't eat corn bread in England,' Josie said.

'That's because we don't need to use corn for bread Josie,' Una said. She had no idea what corn bread was like, but she knew that some of her West Indian and Pakistani neighbours bought different breads. 'England produces the best wheat in the world so we don't need to use corn for bread.' She smiled at Maura's bright pink cheeks. 'We haven't used corn for bread since the famine.'

'What about corn flakes? We eat plenty of them,' Maurice cut in nervously, wondering why his mammy was smiling at her hands when Una was being very rude.

'You do,' Josie snapped. Her knowledge of farming and geography was limited, but she knew about cooking and nutrition. 'Una is right,' she said, 'and anyway porridge is much better for you than any of the packet cereals.'

'I like pancakes for breakfast,' Pauline said, thinking she should say something nice about Canada. She agreed with Josie about the porridge, and she didn't like corn bread.

'With all that maple syrup?' Josie hollered.

'I do beg yer pardon,' Sean said, his loud belch breaking the silence. He rubbed his belly and drank in the glances that were shooting at his smiling face. Me sisters are home he told his heart as he folded his arms across his chest and sat back in his chair to enjoy his sisters' argument.

The door opened. 'I hope yeh'ev got all yer nappies dry, Josie,' Liam called into the room, 'because we're goin' te take teh line down now.'

'I hope so too,' Josie said shoving her chair back. 'I told Joan to put them out two hours ago,' she said, walking over to the window at the back of the house.

'Would you get me a glass of water, Pauline?' Sheila said.

Pauline left the room and went upstairs to look out the bedroom window to see what Cathy was doing.

Poor Joan, Una thought, picturing Josie giving orders to Joan and Cathy for the past week. She joined Josie at the window. 'What on earth is Cathy digging the garden now for?' she demanded.

'I'll go out and see what she's doin',' Donal said, pushing the table from his chest.

'I don't care what she's doing,' Josie snapped. 'I want to know where Eileen is.' She walked out of the door before Donal was able to get out of his chair.

Curious about what Cathy was doing, Una went over to the window and looked out at the large back garden that was like an untended field waiting for a cow to come in and eat the tall grass. There were a few rose bushes that hadn't been looked after along one of the low breezeblocks sidewalls that separated it from the neighbours. She saw her young sister rummage through a patch of large-leaved plants that were growing along the end wall.

Because Cathy was bending over she could only see her bum, but Una could see her pull some of the leaves out of the ground and throw them over to the side of the garden. She though she knew what Cathy was doing but so she could get a better look she went upstairs to see from the bedroom window.

'What is she doing?' Pauline asked Una when she came into the bedroom.

'Are you thinking of making rhubarb pies today, Pauline?' Una asked as she watched Donal make his way down the garden with two cardboard boxes.

'Me! Rhubarb pies? Today?' Pauline asked, her face like an owl with her eyebrows raised and her eyes smiling.

'That's what I thought,' Una said. She saw the red stalk on the end of the leaf that Donal had picked up. 'Good God, she did it.' She laughed, 'I should have known that she would.' After a few seconds, she tapped Pauline on her arm, moved back from the window and said, 'Come on. I think Cathy could do with a hand out there.'

There were so many bodies in the hall that Pauline thought they would probably find it quicker to get out to the back garden if they climbed through the window. She smiled at the memories that passed across her mind when she eased her body behind Josie towards the back door.

'Did you get Mammy her glass of water?' Josie asked looking up from strapping Eileen into her pushchair.

'No,' Pauline said and continued down the lobby.

Eileen's pushchair was taking up most of the space in the hall. Sean and Maurice were standing at the open hall door talking to two strange men.

Liam stood with his back to the lobby as though he was on

guard duty. He caught Una's wrist as she was sliding past him. 'Will yeh stay here and keep Josie from goin' out to teh back fer a few minutes?' he asked.

'Not now, Liam,' Una said, wrenching her arm free and nodding her head to the back door. 'Cathy needs a little help out there.'

Liam smiled into his sister's face. 'Yeh'll need that te cut teh tops off,' he said, handing her a knife.

Una welcomed the cold air on her warm face when she walked out to the garden, but she could have done without the dank smell of manure that came from the tall scraggy grass.

The short broken concrete and rubble path that ran under the clothesline was just about visible. Three other pathways had been made from beating down the grass. Una was trying to decide which of the three paths to use so she could get down the garden when she heard Cathy shout out, 'We need another helper fer te do teh cuttin'.'

'Take this,' Una said, handing Pauline the knife that Liam had given her. 'You help Donal and I'll help Cathy.' The smell from the grass became sweeter as she stumbled her way down to the bottom of the garden.

After ten minutes, with Una helping her to pull the rhubarb Cathy stood up and rubbed her back. 'I think that'll do fer now,' she said.

Una shoved her arm into the plot of younger red sticks. 'You will be able to pull the same again in a week,' she said. I'll take some of it back with me on Monday.'

'It'll cost yeh,' Cathy said, throwing her head back like she was a proud peacock and walked over to Donal.

By the time Donal and Pauline had filled the two boxes with eight-inch rhubarb stalks Liam stuck his head out of the back door and called down, 'Are yez all right, or do yez need a hand?'

'We managed,' Donal called back.

Pauline rubbed her damp hands together, and inhaled the sweet smell coming from the box. 'There's enough rhubarb in both of the boxes to make twenty pies,' she said. 'What are you going to do with it all?'

Cathy stretched her hand out and slapped her brother lightly on his back and said, 'Thanks Donal.' She smiled at Pauline and added, 'I'm goin' te give them away.'

But Cathy wasn't going to give them away and Donal knew it. And even if she were, he would still have sat in the back of the dirty van with the horse dung because his sister had asked him to. He picked up one of the boxes when he saw Maurice coming out of the back door.

'What on earth are you going to give them away for?' Pauline asked in a tone Josie would use.

Before Cathy replied, two men came out and began stamping their feet into the earth. Liam knew they were measuring the garden for where they would put the poles for the marquee. He picked up the other box. 'We had better get movin',' he said. While he held the box with one arm he put the other around Pauline's shoulder and looked at his wild young sister. 'Go on, Cathy, he said, 'it's time that yeh told us all what yer givin' them away fer.'

'Well, they're small, but they're firm, juicy and sweet so I thought that I would give them away fer three pence a stick,' Cathy said combing her thick hair with her hands.

Chapter Twenty-nine

Eileen was waving her arms and legs like fury when Pauline was helping Cathy to get the pushchair down the step from the front garden and onto the pavement. She held the pushchair steady while Cathy tied a shopping bag to the handlebar. Donal and Liam came out of the house with the boxes of rhubarb and walked over to Angie Dolan's house.

The big white van unloading poles and bags drew the children that lived on the road to see what was going on. Pauline stood in the garden with the children and watched two men throw their cargo over the low railings into the front garden. She had seen a marquee delivered and erected in the back garden before, so she wasn't as amused as the children were.

Both the hall door and the back door had blocks of wood jammed into the bottom of them so they would stay wide open. Pauline could see Maurice and Donal tramping through the grass, bending over and picking up lumps of things and putting them into large grey plastic bags.

'Twenty fresh sliced pans fer number thirty-four,' a man's voice bellowed.

Pauline turned round to the strange loud voice. A young man stood at the gate holding a large wooden tray about the size of a kitchen table.

'Put it down on the grass,' Pauline said, pointing to the tray.

The plastic-wrapped loaves jumped when the man plonked the tray down on the lawn.

The loud voice of her new brother-in-law coming through the open window told Pauline how she could bring the bread into the house without getting in the way of the men bringing in the marquee. She pulled the window open a bit more and called out, 'Carl, will you come out here for a minute? I need you to help me.'

Carl passed the loaves through the window and Pauline stacked them on the chairs. She was about to put the last two loaves on the only empty chair when Carl came back into the room.

'Carl is sitting in that chair,' Maura said, getting to her feet as though she had been given an order when her husband had moved his eyes from the chairs to the floor when Pauline was about to leave the loaves on the chair on which he had been sitting before she had asked him to help her.

Pauline was about to place the loaves on the table when Josie and Una came in.

'Una is going to need the table,' Josie said.

'Put them on the floor,' Una said, wondering why Carl wasn't out in the garden helping the boys to put up the marquee. 'If it's for ironing the curtains you're thinking about, Josie, don't worry about them. I'll manage with the ironing board.'

'They will be fine on the floor.' Pauline said removing the loaves from one of the easy chairs. 'We'll be making the sandwiches with them in an hour.'

Una nodded a smile at Josie's sad face and said, 'Pauline's right and they are all wrapped in plastic bags.'

'Take these two,' Maura said, holding out the loaves to Una and keeping her eyes on them as if was beneath her to handle them.

Furious because Maura didn't look at her, Una said, 'Drop

them on the floor.' She wondered if her sister had the strength to hold the two loaves for any length of time because she looked so thin. She reminded her of one of Lowry's matchstick figures.

Maura giggled and looked at her mammy. She left the bread on the table and sat down again.

'You help Pauline, Josie, and I'll set the iron up.' Una said.

'I'm not talking about ironing them, Una. I'm talking about making them,' Josie confessed. She wanted to die when she heard Maura giggle again.

'You're pulling my leg,' Una said, wanting to slap the giggle off Maura's face.

'I bought the fabric yesterday,' Josie said looking at her mammy with pleading eyes.

Sheila Malone lowered her eyes to the floor and picked up her handbag.

'I had better make a start then,' Una said, 'If I run out of time, Maura can iron them.' It didn't really make any difference to her whether she made sandwiches or curtains.

'Thanks Una,' Josie said smiling with relief. She wondered about Maura helping. She had never seen the spoilt little bitch with an iron in her hand.

Una nodded to Pauline, then left. Pauline followed her into the kitchen and she had put the kettle on to boil when Josie joined them. 'I just want to get Mammy a glass of water,' she said, picking up the only glass tumbler they had on the shelf above the table.

'Mammy likes ice in her water,' Pauline said as Josie was wiping the outside of the glass.

'Actually,' Una said, 'she prefers whiskey.' She had very little patience with Josie, but she wasn't cruel. When she saw Josie staring at the glass of water as if she was praying for it to change colour, or freeze in her hand she said, 'I'll take the water into Mammy, you sort out the bread.'

When Josie had left the kitchen Una poured out some of the water then topped it up with hot water from the kettle. 'Maybe next time Mammy will get her own glass of water,' she said to Pauline before she brought the water into her mammy.

Josie was busy moving the loaves of bread so that they wouldn't be in Una's way. Carl, Maura and her mammy were staring at floor in front of the fireplace as if they were waiting for the black marks to get up and dance when Una walked in with her mammy's glass of water. 'Do you want it now or will I leave it on the mantle piece?' she asked.

Sheila held her hand out and took the glass of water. She took a sip, then held it out over the arm of her chair in her right hand.

While Una was extending both ends of the table Josie was bringing the bread out to the kitchen.

'I'll have the fabric now, Josie,' Una said when her sister came in from the kitchen to get another armful of bread.

'Right you be,' Josie said happily returning the loaves she had picked up to the chair and making to walk over to the hot press in the corner of the room.

'Just tell me where it is,' Una said turning round in time to see her mammy jut her arm that was holding the glass of warm water in front of Josie as she passed her mammy's chair. The remains of the water flew across the room. In her hurry to get the fabric Josie didn't notice. Una picked up the empty glass and put it on the mantelpiece.

'The floor is all wet,' Maura said.

Una swallowed to keep her temper under control and said, 'If it is bothering you, Maura, than get a towel and dry it.

Josie was down on her knees with her head in the hot- press retrieving the fabric for the new curtains from under the boiler. She didn't know she had knocked the glass out of her mammy's hand. She had pulled her head out when she heard Una say towel. 'There are plenty of towels,' she said.

Maura glared at Una, then stood.

'While you are on your feet, Maura,' Una said, 'you can get Mammy another glass of water.

Chapter Thirty

Una didn't think much of the material Josie chose for the curtains but her sister had measured the windows and bought enough. She knew why her sister had chosen the four shades of dark green that were meant to look like leaves. It wouldn't show the dirt, and it was cheap.

The musty smell that spilled out every time Una unwound the roll told her the cloth was very old. She also knew from the dust that flew out when she was tearing the cloth into the lengths she wanted it would be like a rag when it was washed. But that would be a couple of years away. She started a bout of sneezing from the dust so she opened the window into the back garden.

'Everybody move back,' Liam shouted from the side of the garden. While her brothers pulled on ropes Una stood at the window and watched the big tent rise off its knees like a monster that was going to plod down the other gardens.

Perfect, Una thought when she waved back to her brother. He was too far down the garden to hear her say, 'That dirty brown green colour will make these curtains look bright.' Her smile faded when she saw Maura walk into the marquee behind her mammy. She gasped when she saw Maura tilt her head back like she was going to shout, then place her hands over each other on the top of her stomach just below her waist.

Maura's performance was such a perfect imitation of how her mammy walked into a room that Una wondered if her sister had inherited the pose, or she had learned to copy it. She used to think that her mammy copied a nun with the way she held her hands across her waist. Then when she saw Queen Elizabeth on the television she thought perhaps her mammy copied the way the royal lady carried her handbag.

Una watched her sister walk around the marquee dishing out smiles of approval to her brothers and the two men that were erecting the big tent. Her mammy turned her head away every time one of them looked at her.

With Maura smiling like a child as if she had been given a longed for present, and her mammy scowling like a bulldog, Una changed her mind about the pair of them being alike. Maura's dress hung on her like it was on a hanger; she was dressed up looking like she was going out on a date. Her mammy with her hair not combed, her trousers stretched like balloons at her knees, and her cardigan barely covering her bum at the back and almost down to her knees at the front — she looked like a dealer at a barrow selling vegetables.

Una had seen her mammy dishevelled before. She had also seen her mammy in some awful moods that had lasted for days. A bath and clean clothes would change her mammy's appearance, but she hoped something would happen to bring about a change to her mammy's temper before the party started.

'Have you enough material, Una?' Josie called out from the doorway.

'Plenty,' Una replied. She was about to turn away from the window when Pauline stepped down from the back door, and by the time Josie was standing beside her Pauline walked into the marquee.

The two long sides and one ends of the marquee were pegged down. The end facing the house was still open. Maura and their mammy were down at the bottom end. Josie and Una saw their mammy walk up towards Pauline, close her eyes and walk past her out of the tent.

'I have never seen Mammy look so scruffy before,' Una said. 'Are you going to do her hair before the party?'

'I offered to. But she said she will wait until I gave her a perm tomorrow,' Josie said.

'I hope she combs it and puts on some clean clothes before people start coming,' Una said, turning away from the window.

So did Josie hope her mammy would clean herself up but she wasn't going to say that to Una.

'Just the same, Josie,' Una said, 'bank the fire up in case she changes her mind. You know what she is like at the best of times. And right now this is not one of them.'

Josie nodded her head in approval and, with relief that Una hadn't said anything about their mammy closing her eyes at Pauline, said, 'You are right, Una.' She looked at the clock. 'We will all want to have a bath anyway.'

Chapter Thirty-one

Una, I'm really sorry,' Joan said, closing the door behind her.

'Whatever for?' Una asked, shoving her arm into the narrow neck of the ironing basket. She knew her quiet young sister wasn't capable of doing anything that she would be sorry for. When she turned round the first thing she noticed was the cast in her sister's eye. 'Where are your glasses?' she asked.

'They're in me school bag,' Joan said placing her hands on the pile of green fabrics. 'The curtains.'

'Don't you worry, Joan, I'll get them made in time,' Una said smiling, 'I'd rather make them than sandwiches.'

'It's all my fault,' she said. 'It was me that washed them.' She wasn't afraid of Una, but she felt it was her fault that her sister had to make the curtains so soon after she had come home. 'Josie told me to give them a good wash so I put them in very hot water.'

'You had me worried there for a minute,' Una said smiling, 'I thought you were going to say that you picked out this dreadful material.'

Joan laughed. 'What are you rummaging through the ironing basket for?'

'The curtain tape,' Una said pointing to the bag the fabric was in. 'It's not in there.'

'I don't remember seeing it,' Joan said, walking over to the hot press. 'It might be in this,' she said, pulling a plastic bag out from the floor of the press. 'I put all the things that were on the window sill into it when Josie told me to clear it before she took the old curtains down.'

Things haven't changed, Una thought, opening the bag. She wondered how many other bags were stuffed into the bottom of the press as she pulled an assortment of photographs, a hair comb, and a couple of brass ornaments out of the bag before she found a small bundle of letters. Two of them had logos on the envelopes. The ESB, and the Corporation. She read the rent hadn't been paid for three months. 'I thought Mammy carried all her letters around in her handbag,' she said, holding the letters out to Joan.

Joan thought back to Tuesday when she came home from school and Josie was taking down the curtains. She remembered her mammy had walked out and went up to her bedroom. She assumed that her mammy didn't want the curtains taken down, because she always walked out when anyone was going to do something she didn't want them to do. 'She usually does,' she said.

'What did Josie say when she saw these?' Una asked flapping the letters before she put them on the table. She continued to rummage around the bag to find the curtain tape.

'She didn't see them,' Joan said, recalling the weak smile on her mammy's face when she came back into the room and left the letters on the windowsill. 'Josie told me to clear the windowsill before she went out to the kitchen to get a stool, so she could reach up to take the curtains down. She didn't see Mammy put them there, and I had put them into the bag before she came back.'

'There's no curtain tape here,' Una said, stuffing everything back into the bag. 'Is there anywhere else it might be?' She moved some of the towels that were packed around the boiler and closed the door. 'If there is no tape, there won't be any curtains,' she said and laughed loudly. 'Do you think Josie will cancel the party if I can't get those rags up on the window?'

When the door opened again Joan and Una were still laughing. Josie closed the front window. 'What are you two so happy about?' she asked, glancing at the clock, then resting her eyes on the pile of curtain lengths. 'I suppose you want your sewing machine brought down now?'

'Actually Josie, I want the tape first,' Una said. On seeing her sister raise her worried face to the clock she said, 'Forget it, Josie. We don't have the time to get into town and back again.'

'Mammy never said anything to me about the tape,' Josie said, turning to Joan and asking, 'What about the village?'

While Una was trying to remember if there was a shop in the village that sold curtain tape Pauline came into the room with Eileen who was struggling to get down on the floor. 'What's the matter now?' she said.

'I forgot to get tape for the new curtains,' Josie said, 'and we don't have time to go into town and get some.'

Bare windows glared at Pauline. She sniffed the musty smell from the new fabric. 'What about the tape on the old ones?' she suggested. 'Can you rip that out and use it?' She smiled at Una. 'You have done that before now.'

'We can if we still have them,' Una said, bowing her head in approval.

'I hung them on a nail inside the door of the shed so we would have them for floor cloths,' Joan told her.

The memory of Maura smirking, and the way her mammy had walked out of the room encouraged Una's determination to get the curtains made. 'Get the old curtains, Joan,' she said and, 'Josie bring down the sewing machine.' She was about to say she would go out and get her mammy and Maura when the two of them walked in.

Pauline looked down at her mammy's feet and walked out.

Sheila walked over to the hot press opened it and began searching through the towels.

'If you are looking for the bag with your letters, Mammy, it's on the bottom,' Una said.

Sheila closed the door of the hot press sharply as though she was slapping Una, then sat down in her easy chair beside the fire and pulled her packet of cigarettes out of her pocket.

Maura rubbed her hand gently over the pile of cut fabrics like she was testing to see if they would burn her. She raised her face to Una and was about to burst into a giggle when Una said, 'They are lovely, aren't they?' She held Maura's stare of astonishment for a few seconds and added, 'They are Mammy's favourite colours.'

The giggle froze on Maura's face as Joan came back with the old curtains.

'I have a little job for the two of you,' Una said, holding her hands out to Joan. 'Josie forgot to get the tape for the curtains so while I am hemming the bottom and sides of the new ones you can unpick the tape off these.' She handed Maura one of the old curtains first.

Chapter Thirty-two

It was half past three when Sean stood in the doorway of the room. He ran his eyes over the doorframe a few times then said, 'Them risin h-hinges are g-great fer times like this, and teh d-doors are p-perfect fer puttin' all teh stuff on in teh marquee.'

'You have all done great, Sean,' Una said, smiling at her brother.

'I see yez are s-still busy with yer needlework,' Sean said, returning Una's smile. 'Yeh must have te have g-good eyesight fer t-teh see them small stitches.'

His mammy and Maura continued to unpick the tape of the old curtains.

'Actually Sean, it's long hard nails you need to pull the old threads out,' Una said, smiling smugly when Maura raised her head from pulling bits of thread out of the old curtain tape, and scowled at her brother.

Sensing the temper in Maura's face, Sean went back out to the marquee.

Una stood and shook the curtain she had just finished, and started drawing the strings to ruffle it up when Josie came in.

'Cathy must be exhausted.' Josie said, pulling the net curtain back so she could see out of the window. 'Apart from half an hour when she had some lunch she has been walking up and down the road all day with Eileen.'

Her mammy raised her head and stared hard at her eldest

daughter so Josie added quickly, 'I must say that we have all worked hard today.'

Una saw her sister's smile die from the cold stare her mammy had delivered. 'I also think that Pauline, Joan and yourself have worked wonders out in the kitchen getting the food ready,' she said. On hearing her mammy sigh, she raised her voice, 'And as for Cathy, well, I did tell you earlier that she's not the one to be doing sitting down jobs.'

'That's true,' Josie said, taking the dish of curtain clips to hold for Una. 'I'll put these in,' she said, 'while you finish the others. All we have to do now is get the curtains up and ourselves cleaned up. I won't bother to bath Eileen tonight and I promised Cathy she could feed her and get her down to bed.'

Jesus, Una thought, recalling when Josie, Pauline and herself used to try to avoid putting their younger siblings to bed. 'I suppose it is Cathy's turn to look after the younger children,' she said. 'I might bring her back to England with me as a babysitter.'

'Una Malone,' Josie said sharply, 'you do get the most ridicules ideas in your head.'

'What is so ridicules about having a live in baby minder?' Una asked, taking the curtain off Maura to finish unpicking the tape because she was waiting for it. 'We could share her. She could stay with you every second week.'

Maura left the room.

'Cathy is still going to school,' Josie said.

No, she isn't, Una wanted to say but decided not to because Cathy didn't know she knew. 'She could come over during the summer holidays,' she said, warming to the idea although she had been only joking and wanted to prevent Josie from asking why Cathy was walking up and down the road.

'We'll see,' Josie said, also warming to the idea. 'At least we will know where she is,' she added, recalling Cathy didn't come in from school until six some days during the week. She had said she had been in her friend's house. 'We'll see,' she repeated, handing the curtain to Sean to hook up on the rail.

Pauline came in. 'I'm going to have my bath now,' she said. She wanted to get dressed for the party before her mammy so that she wouldn't be in the same room as her.

'That's a good idea,' Josie said.

'I'll only use enough water to have a good wash,' Pauline said closing her eyes at her mammy and leaving.

Una finished sewing the tape on the curtain she had taken from Maura. She handed it to Josie and said, 'Ruffle it up and put the hooks in.' She took the last curtain out of her mammy's hands, finished taking the tape out and sewed it on the last curtain without bothering to remove the old threads and she was finished by the time Josie had put the hooks in the one she had given her. 'You go and see to whatever needs do be done in the kitchen Josie,' she said. 'I'll put these up before I go over to Angie's to get changed.'

Right now, there was nothing Josie wanted more than a long hot bath. She was always able to wash away her worries when she was in the small room on her own with the door locked. She knew they would have to share the hot water with everyone else so a long hot bath she wasn't going to have today. Still she was happier now than she had been all week. The curtains were made and everything was ready for the party.

'Go on, Josie,' Una urged. 'I'll get Sean to bank the fire up before he goes so there will be enough hot water for Maura, Carl and Mammy.' Her memory kicked in again and she suspected her mammy would take two hours to have her bath. The bitch had kept them all waiting before when she knew they were going out. 'Pauline has already used half of the tank so you should have enough hot water to get a good wash. With the fire banked up, Mammy will have enough water to have a nice long soak and the water will be hot enough for Maura and Carl. The boys can have theirs last. They won't take so long because they don't have to do their hair, or make up their face.'

'I'll bring your sewing machine upstairs first,' Josie said.

Sheila Malone slapped her hands down on the arms of her chair and stood.

Una walked out the room before her mammy. She met Pauline coming out of the bathroom. 'Go back in and bolt the door,' she said, 'I'll call you when Josie comes down.

Pauline frowned.

'Please,' Una said, 'I don't want Mammy to go in and spend an hour washing her hands. Josie is on her way down to have a bath.'

Pauline smiled and went back into the bathroom. 'I forgot to clean my teeth,' she said and closed the door.

Chapter Thirty-three

Refreshed after a hot bath, Una smelt the tea as she descended the stairs in Angie Dolan's house. 'Angie,' she said when she pushed in the door, 'that was the most welcome bath I have ever had.'

'Yeh should get a couple ev fellahs with that short skirt yer wearin,' Angie returned.

'No thank you, Angie I am more then happy with the fellah I have, but I wouldn't mind some new in-laws.'

'They both come with the one package,' Angie said pouring Una a cup of tea. 'Like families, some are big and some are small, some stay together, and some don't want to know each other.' She thought briefly of her own small family and the great loss in her life when her husband died. She sniffed to avoid a tear and asked, 'How many have yez commin to teh party?'

Una had no idea. 'An army, I should imagine,' she said, 'Josie made up twenty loaves of sandwiches.' She spooned some sugar into her tea. 'Are you coming over?'

'I might drop over fer an hour later,' Angie lied. She had never liked Maura, but Liam had asked her and she didn't want to snub him. She turned round to a shelf behind her, picked up a small parcel and held it out to Una and said, 'Will yeh give that te Maura fer me?'

Una fondled the parcel. 'I didn't get her a present,' she said, 'It's not something we were in the habit of doing when we were children because we never had any money of our own to buy each other presents.' She laughed as she added, 'Then there were so many of us we would have had to buy one every month.'

Hearing a group of voices laughing out on the road, Angie walked over to the window. 'Yer sister will have so many presents she won't miss a couple,' she said. 'I think her guests have started to arrive. Come and take a look.'

A group of eight young girls and two young boys stopped outside Angie's gate. One of the boys passed around a packet of cigarettes.

'Who are they, and what are doing?' Una asked.

Angie moved the net curtain, took her glasses off and squinted her eyes at the group. 'They are yer sister's party guests, and they are waiting for the next bus.'

'I didn't know Maura had so many friends,' Una said. She thought she recognised one of the girls who used to play out on the road. 'Why are they waiting for the next bus?' she asked.

'So they can all go in together,' Angie said, moving away from the window. 'Finish yer tea, Una,' she said. 'Liam will want yeh over there when they all arrive. Like yeh said, Maura doesn't have many friends.'

Una noticed the girls carried small parcels and the boys carried something in plastic shopping bags. 'Who are they all then?' she repeated.

'They are from the football club yer brothers belong te,' Angie said, shoving her glasses up on her nose. 'Yez won't be eatin sandwiches fer yer breakfast in the mornin'.'

Poor Maura, Una thought, piecing together many of the events of the morning. 'You knew all along, Angie,' she said accusingly, walking back to the table.

'Knew what?' Angie asked, struggling to hide her smile.

'The party isn't for Maura,' Una said, 'the boys are giving a party for their friends.' She laughed, picturing Josie's face when a stream of young people paraded down the lobby. 'Does Cathy know?' she asked.

Angie lit a cigarette. 'Probably,' she said. 'Finish yer tea and go over and give yer brothers a hand.'

Chapter Thirty-four

Pressure on the hall door told Una the back door was open. The hall door closed with a bang after she had stepped into the hall. She could see Pauline and Josie at the far end of the marquee bending over the cloth-covered door of the kitchen that was mounted on two beer boxes. They were moving plates of sandwiches about.

Gunshots coming from living room told Una the television was on. She wasn't surprised to see her mammy sitting in her favourite chair staring at the brown wooden box as she passed the doorway on her way down the lobby to the marquee. The smell of aftershave and talcum powder coming from the bathroom were drowned by cheese and onion when she walked into the marquee. She prayed that Angie was right when she had said that they wouldn't be eating sandwiches for their breakfast in the morning.

Joan was standing on a chair fixing a bundle of balloons to the ceiling. Maurice and Donal were moving some electric cables about.

Maura and Carl were sitting in the far corner holding hands. Carl wore a light blue suit, a pale blue shirt and a royal blue tie. Maura looked lovely in a lime green satin sheath dress, with a stand-up collar, and short sleeves.

'I'll give you a hand with those, Pauline,' Una said. 'I'll just find a home for my handbag.' Past experience of parties reminded Una to look after her handbag. She thought the safest place for it would be the hot press in the living room. As she had expected she found her mammy watching a film on the television. She was about to close the door when a plastic bag tumbled off the middle shelf. It was the same bag Una had seen earlier when she had been looking for the curtain tape. She moved it to the bottom where it wouldn't get knocked over and the contents spill out onto the floor.

'Sorry, Mammy,' she said as she closed the door. She noticed that her mammy hadn't changed her clothes.

'Would you like a tea or coffee, Mammy?' Pauline asked from the doorway.

'No,' Sheila Malone replied curtly, then picked her handbag off the floor and walked out of the room.

'I would love a cup of tea, Pauline,' Una said.

A breeze blew down the lobby when Pauline and Una crossed the hall to the kitchen. The hall door was open and Sheila was standing under the concrete shelf watching a crowd of young people crossing the road from Angie's house. They had reached the gate when one of the boys called out, 'Hello Mrs Malone.'

As if a herd of cows were walking up the garden path Sheila Malone turned and she was in the hall when Liam came bouncing down the stairs.

'Out the back,' Liam called out and pointed down the lobby to the back door.

Pauline and Una smiled and nodded hello to the stream of young people as they followed each other down the lobby and out to the marquee.

'Who are they?' Pauline gasped. 'There must be thirty of them.'

'Thirty-two,' Una returned.

'Who are they?' Pauline repeated.

'Maura's guests.'

'I didn't know Maura had so many friends.'

'I said guests not friends,' Una laughed. She pulled the tea cloth out of Pauline's hand, threw it on the table and said, 'Come on I want to see Maura's face.'

It was Josie's face that Una saw first.

When the crowd of young people walked in Josie looked up from searching through the records and smiled at the young people, as much from surprise than as a way of greeting.

One of the young girls handed Josie a small parcel and said, 'Happy Birthday.' Josie turned round to the far end of the marquee where Maura was sitting beside Carl. 'It's not me,' she said and pointed over to Maura.'

The young men gave their plastic bags to Liam. By the time he had stacked the cans and bottles of beer his friends had brought in their plastic bags on the last empty table Maura had her arms full of presents and Josie had returned to sorting her records.

Pauline and Una returned to the kitchen, and while Pauline put on the kettle Una went into the living room to get her cigarettes. 'Sorry, Mammy,' she said when she stood in front of television to get to the hot press. The same plastic bag she had shoved to the back on the floor fifteen minutes earlier came tumbling out when she opened the door. This time she rolled it up tight and shoved it far back on the top shelf. She removed her cigarettes from her handbag and had closed the door when Maura walked in with her arms full of small parcels.

'There's one on the hall table from Angie,' Una said.

'Bring it in,' Maura ordered, pulling a small card off one of her presents and stabbing her thumb into the thin coloured wrapping paper on one of the parcels.

Pauline was at the kitchen doorway when Una walked into the hall: 'If you don't tell me who that crowd are, and where they came from you won't get any tea,' she said.

The doorbell rang.

'Then I will have to make my own tea,' Una returned, 'because I don't know.' She opened the hall door as Josie walked up the lobby.

A smaller group of six boys and two girls stood in a circle around the door. Expecting them to be more of Liam's friends, Una smiled, then opened the door wide for them to come. The girls walked in first. 'Happy birthday,' they chorused to Josie when they stepped into the hall. When the boys walked in, Liam was in the hall, and Pauline was standing in the kitchen doorway.

'Out the back,' Liam pointed down the lobby.

Una handed Josie Angie's parcel. 'Take this in with you,' she said. When the last boy had walked down the lobby she caught her brother's hand and said, 'In the kitchen.' She shoved him to the end wall away from the door and asked, 'Who are all those youngsters?'

'Just friends from the football club,' Liam said, winking at Pauline as he added, 'We had to ask some people.'

'What about Maura's friends?'

'There is still plenty of room,' Liam said. He pointed to the remains of the food on the small table and added, 'and sandwiches.'

Maura was opening her seventh parcel when Josie handed her another six. 'I expect these are for you,' she said, placing the parcels on the table on top of a pile of torn wrapping paper.

Maura continued to rip the paper off the parcel she was opening. Tears came to her eyes when she found another pair of thick knitted gloves. She slapped them on top of the other four and started on the next present.

Josie wasn't spiteful, but she enjoyed a smile when she counted four knitted hats. She left Maura to her presents and went out to the marquee to start the dancing.

Chapter Thirty-five

When the dot faded on the television Sheila Malone drained the last of her whiskey and washed down her sleeping pill, picked up her handbag and left the room.

Music was blaring from the record player, and feet were thumping on the wooden floor of the marquee when Sheila closed the door on the small toilet. Five minutes later the music stopped but the singing continued.

Ten minuets later three young girls were waiting outside the toilet.

The smallest of the girls knocked on the door and called out, 'Is someone in there?' She put her ear to the door. 'I don't hear anythin', she said to her friends

'Jeasus Betty I'm burstin', the tallest girl said.

'Maybe whoever is in there has passed out?' the third girl called Mary said. 'I remember that happened to a woman on the road where I live and they had to get the fire brigade to break down the door. 'The woman was screamin' so much when they got her out that the ambulance men had to strap her down.'

'Why was she screamin'?' the tall girl who was bursting asked.

'She didn't want to go to the hospital,' Mary said. 'The woman said she had fallen asleep, but her husband insisted she go.'

'How long was she in fer?' Betty asked putting her ear to the door again

A young boy joined them. 'Is one ev yez waitin fer toilet?' he asked.

'We all are,' Mary said, 'and don't ask us what we want te do or I'll box yer ears.'

The boy smiled then made his way down the side of the marquee.

'Go on, tell us what was the matter with the woman that was taken off to the hospital,' Mary said.

'Nothin,' Betty said.

'Then why was she in hospital fer three weeks,'

Betty knocked on the toilet door again before she said, 'It's the reason why the window on our toilet is all loose and swingin.'

'Fer God's sake, Betty,' Mary moaned, 'I couldn't care less about yer toilet winda. Why was teh woman in hospital fer so long if there was nothin' the matter with her?'

'Because her husband kept tellin' them te do more tests,' Betty said, and that's why me ma had the window in er toilet loosened. And she made me promise that if she ever fell asleep I would get in the winda and wake her up.'

Mary raised her head as if she understood. 'I see now,' she said, 'she didn't want the door of the toilet broken down.'

'Me ma doesn't give a shite about the door,' Betty said impatiently. 'She didn't want me da teh send her off to teh hospital because she was afraid he would leave her there.'

'Speakin ev shite,' Mary said, 'give that door a good feckin' kick'

'Language girls, language,' Una said, walking out of the kitchen. She had heard everything the girls had said.

As if a nun had overheard her, Mary put her hand over her mouth. 'Sorry,' she said, nodding her head to the toilet door, 'I'm burstin' te go and somebody has been in there fer ages.'

139

Ages, Una knew, could mean anything from a minute to an hour when you want to do a pee. 'Can you estimate how long you have been waiting?' she asked, trying to remember how long it was since she had seen her mammy walking down the lobby. 'If it is only a pee you want to do there is a bucket in the coal shed and a roll of toilet paper on the door. One of you can stand outside for to make sure nobody goes in.'

'That'll do me,' the tall girl,' said.

'I'll watch fer yeh,' Betty said and the two of them left.

Una walked back up the lobby to see if her mammy was in the living room. She was about to climb the stairs to see if she was in bed when she heard the familiar click of the metal bolt on the door of the toilet. She looked down the lobby and saw her mammy walk into the bathroom.

Music blared in through the small window on the landing when Sheila was at the top of the stairs.

Josie came out of the small front bedroom. 'Would you like to sleep in my bed for tonight, Mammy,' she said. 'Eileen is fast asleep and she won't wake up until seven in the morning.'

'Close that window,' Sheila said, raising her handbag to indicate she meant the landing, then walked into the big bedroom where she had been sleeping since the night Pauline had come home.

Josie closed the window and returned to the party. Humouring her mammy was one thing, but missing the chance to dance was another.

The voice of Tom Jones singing "Delilah" was almost drowned out by the singers when Josie walked into the marquee. Three couples were waltzing to the slow tune, and small groups stood in circles, singing and waving their arms about.

Josie had joined Maura who was searching through the records when Carl put his arm around her waist and pulled her out into the middle of the floor. The young people moved back and sang while Josie and Carl danced. The young people were so impressed with the older handsome couple they clapped until the record was played again.

Liam nodded his head to Una who promptly tapped Josie on her shoulder and changed places with her. Liam then whispered to one of his friends and pulled Maura onto the floor. The whisper had gone around the whole group by the time Maurice took Josie's hand and brought her on to the floor again.

Una steered Carl down to the far end of the room and Liam steered Maura to the centre. Everyone sang the last line of the song, "Forgive me Delilah I just couldn't take any more", so loudly they drowned out the music. Liam lifted the needle off the record and called out, 'All together now,' and he started singing Happy Birthday to Maura.

The tears that burst from Maura's eyes were not from the clapping and singing. They were from jealousy of Josie, and hurt from her husband.

Chapter Thirty-six

Josie wound her small clock and checked the alarm setting was turned off.

Pauline crept up the bed along the wall and eased her body under the covers careful so as not to disturb Eileen. 'What time is it, Josie?' she whispered.

With singing floating up from the marquee and the drone of her mammy snoring in the single bed under the front window, Josie could see no need to whisper. 'Just gone four,' she said, sliding into bed. 'I should get about three hours sleep.'

'You stay in bed in the morning,' Pauline said. 'I'll get up with Eileen.'

A light sleeper since her babies were born Pauline dozed in between the sounds of her brothers clearing the marquee after their friends had left. Used to knowing the time now from the sounds out on the road since she had come, Pauline estimated it was getting on for eight when she heard the milkman changing the crates at the hall door.

Sensing movement, she lifted her head off the pillow and saw her mammy walking out the door. Eileen was still asleep so she gently crept out of bed and followed her mammy downstairs.

While her mammy was in the toilet Pauline put the kettle on and waited until her mammy walked into the living room then followed her. 'You didn't answer my letter, Mammy,' she said and sat down in a chair beside the table.

'What letter?' Sheila asked, removing a cigarette from her packet.

'I wrote to you shortly after Christmas,' Pauline said, 'asking you...'

'The only letter I have had from Canada,' Sheila cut in, 'was from Maura.' She stood.

Hurt and angry, Pauline also stood. She faced her mammy and said coldly, 'You need to write and tell Harry that because you should also have had a letter from him.' She walked away then turned back. 'Don't bother to tell him because I posted it, and I registered the letter. I still have the receipt and I will take care of it.' She had seen her mammy angry so often that she could bring a memory of the cold eyes and small tight mouth to her thoughts any time. But this was only the second time she had seen her frightened. She walked out of the room and went upstairs to bring Eileen down.

Pauline opened the door slowly so as not waken her sisters. Eileen was sitting up in bed playing with her mammy's hair. Josie opened her eyes.

'Stay where you are, Josie,' Pauline whispered, 'I'll look after Eileen.'

'She needs changing,' Josie said.

'I have done that before,' Pauline said, her heart melting with the smile on her young niece's face who also had her arms stretched out.

'Her clean clothes are on the top shelf in the hot press,' Josie said, and stretched her legs out, then turned over.

Pauline felt the breeze on her legs before she saw the hall door was wide open. Recalling the day years ago when Una had locked her mammy out, Pauline thought a smile. She was surprised to see her mammy sitting in her chair when she went into the living room.

'Close the hall door,' Sheila ordered when Pauline walked in.

'When I'm ready,' Pauline returned and walked over to the hot press. She felt the copper boiler and was pleased to find it was still hot. She pulled a towel down from the middle shelf, and the plastic bag that Una had shoved into the bottom came tumbling out. She retrieved Eileen's clean clothes, then used her foot to ease the plastic bag into the bottom of the press and closed the door. She then walked out of the room with Eileen still in her arms and went into the bathroom, closed and locked the door.

As always the small bathroom was cold, but it warmed a little when Pauline ran hot water into the bath. She lay Eileen on the floor and removed her dirty nappy. She put the nappy liner into a small bag that Josie has left on the windowsill; she then wiped her bum with the corner of the nappy. By the time she removed the rest of the little girl's clothes there was enough hot water in the bath for her to add some cold water and lift Eileen into it. Although she wasn't expecting to find any she searched every part of Eileen's body for bruises. By the time she had dried and dressed Eileen the toilet door opened and shut.

Expecting her mammy was in the toilet Pauline bundled up Eileen's clothes and unlocked the bathroom door just as the toilet door opened and Joan walked out. 'Where does Josie keep these?' she asked holding out Eileen's clothes.

Joan looked past Una into the bathroom and asked, 'Have you thrown out the water?'

'Not yet,' Una said, 'I thought I would get Eileen a biscuit to keep her occupied while I do them.

Joan took the clothes off Una, 'I'll wash them out in the water,' she said. 'The marquee won't be taken down until tomorrow, and if it rains we will have trouble getting them dried if we let them mount up.'

Una gave Eileen the clothes, then let Eileen down on the floor to run around. When she walked into the living room her mammy walked out. Pauline closed the door after her, pulled out the table and spread the tablecloth. She didn't know what time her family would get up, but she thought it would be nice for Josie if she set the table. She was about to bring Eileen out to the kitchen with her to get the cups and plates when the door opened and Cathy walked in.

Eileen let go of Pauline's hand and ran over to Cathy with her arms held up.

'Will you mind her while I make some porridge?' Pauline asked.

'Only if you make some for me as well,' Cathy said jokingly, picking Eileen up and kissing her.

The front door was open when Pauline crossed the hall and went into the kitchen. She found the oats on the shelf over the small table and a clean pot under the sink. Without giving any thought to how many she was making for she made a pot of porridge. Her mind was so far away thinking about what she would do about Harry and her babies that she didn't hear the door open or Joan walk in.

'Is there enough for me?' Joan asked sniffing the smell that was oozing from the pot.'

'We'll divide what's there between the four of us,' Pauline said, turning the gas off from under the pot.

Joan spread an assortment of dishes out on the table.

'Which one is Eileen's?' Pauline asked.

'It doesn't matter,' Joan said, stretching up to get another dish.

'Four is enough,' Pauline said dishing out the porridge. She was pouring water into the pot as she said, 'Will you go in and put Eileen into her chair, and put her bib on? Yourself and Cathy can sit down. I'll bring the porridge in.' The front door was still open when she walked across the hall. She was afraid to look but she prayed that her mammy would stay out in the garden until they were all sitting down to eat their porridge.

Unfortunately Pauline's prayer wasn't answered. Her mammy was sitting in her chair staring out the window into the back garden as though she was expecting the glass to smash at any moment.

Cathy was sitting on the chair against the wall nearest the door, and Joan was sitting in front of her with Eileen's chair beside her as though neither of them wanted to sit near the top of the table where their mammy usually sat. Pauline gave the smallest dish of porridge to Eileen and the other one to Cathy and left the room to get the other two. When she returned with the other two dishes her mammy was walking over to her usual place at the top of the table. She placed one dish in front of Joan and the other on the end of the table facing her mammy and sat down to eat.

Sheila rested her elbows on the table and waited. Her daughters continued to eat their porridge in silence. Both Joan and Cathy were curious to know why Pauline hadn't included their mammy when she served the porridge but they were afraid to ask. After a few minutes of silence heavy footsteps bounced down the stairs and Maurice walked in.

Pauline turned round to see who had come in.

'Stay where yeh are Pauline,' Maurice said, 'I'll get my own.' He liked porridge and he intended to serve himself a good portion. He returned immediately. 'Is the hall door open for anything special?' he asked.

'I didn't open it,' Pauline said.

'Neither did I,' Joan said.

'Me neither,' Cathy said.

'Will I close it then?' Maurice asked.

'Ask Mammy?' Pauline said.

Maurice wasn't going to ask his mammy anything so he said, 'I'll close it fer now,' and left the room.

Out in the kitchen he took down a large dish from the shelf over the table and turned to the cooker. There was no pot of porridge. He wanted to cry when he saw the pot in the sink and saw there was no porridge for him to fill his plate with.

Chapter Thirty-seven

It was gone eleven-thirty when Una closed the door of Angie's house to go over to her family home. She was crossing the road when two young girls about Cathy's age were walking up the path. 'Leave the door open,' she called when she was at the gate.

The two girls were running down the lobby when Una closed the door behind her. She heard water running in the kitchen and voices in the living room. Thinking Josie was probably in the kitchen, she went into the living room. If she hadn't smelt the cigarette smoke she would have thought Maurice, Maura, Josie, and her mammy were saying prayers because they all had their hands on the white tablecloth.

Except for a half-empty sugar bowl, a couple of teaspoons and some breadcrumbs the table was bare. 'I see everybody's up,' she said.

'Carl is still in bed,' Josie said, without turning round from sitting at end of the table with her back to the door.

Una didn't care if Carl was gasping for air while trying to get out of Cathy's rhubarb patch at the bottom of the garden.

Maura closed her eyes at Josie by way of showing her annoyance at her sister for saying her husband's name and said, 'Cathy and Joan are in the marquee with Eileen.'

'And Liam and Donal are playing a football match,' Josie cut in quickly.

'And Pauline, Una asked amused at the competition of her siblings to update her on where all the family. were

'In the kitchen,' Maura said.

'She's peeling the potatoes,' Maurice said, giving Josie a nervous and furtive look. He had given up hope of his eldest sister bringing his mammy out of her sourly mood, also his anguish over his mammy was shared with some worry over Pauline not making enough porridge for her.

Sheila Malone raised her head and stared at the front window and for a few seconds blinked her eyes as though she was finding it hard to see.

Another demonstration Una thought. 'I'll give Pauline a hand with the potatoes,' she said and left the room to make a phone call.

As soon as Una closed the door Josie went over to the hot press, opened the door and scanned the middle shelf to make sure she would have enough clean towels for the afternoon. She then felt the boiler and said, 'We will have to light the fire soon so we will have enough hot water for this afternoon.

'We don't have to light a fire in Canada to get hot water,' Maura said smiling at Josie as though it was her fault that the house didn't have constant hot water.

Maurice hated lighting the fire, and he knew that some people had emersion heaters fitted into their boilers. 'Neither do we,' he said.

'Yes we do,' Josie said.

'We could have an emersion heater fitted,' Maurice said,, smiling triumphantly at Josie.

'You could do that,' Josie returned, closing the door of the hot press. 'Mike hired an electrician to put ours in.' She suspected he was telling her to have the heater put in. She didn't think for one minute that he would buy one but he had been annoying her all week about what her mammy wanted. She stared into his red face and added, 'Make sure you put a timer on it. It is very expensive if it is left on all day. But for now,' she said, 'you can get the fire going.'

The door of the hot press didn't close because the catch was a small metal ball that was on the side of the door and this slid into a small metal hole that was on the doorframe. When Josie had opened the door the bag that Pauline had shoved in with her foot toppled forward. Josie picked the bag up and peered into it. The two letters were on the top so she pulled them to see what other things were in it.

Straight away Josie knew what they were. She glanced at the windowsill with the intention of putting them back then changed her mind thinking that Joan and Cathy could do it. 'These were on the windowsill,' she said. 'Joan must have put them into the press when I asked her to clear it when I was cleaning the windows.' She was about to return the letters when she noticed the logos. 'You will want these, Mammy,' she said and placed them on the table in front of her.

Maurice looked at the clock then left the room. His temper was slightly mollified when his nostrils caught the smell of meat roasting. He could hear Pauline and Una talking in the kitchen as he made his way down the lobby. Even before he had opened the back door he could hear the voice of Cathy over the other girls in the marquee.

When Joan saw her handsome brother she came up to him and said in her usual soft voice, 'Maurice can you help us to get the record player going?'

Joan was the only one of Maurice's six sisters that he would never refuse to do anything for. From where he was standing he saw the plug of the long flex he had made to bring electricity for the record player and some lights into the marquee. He had taken it out before he went to bed. He unhooked the rolled up end of the flex and brought it over to the window into the dining room and hooked it onto the nail over the window. 'Hold this,' he said to Joan and handed her its plug.

'Pass it to me when I open the window,' he added and went back into the house.

'I thought you were lighting the fire?' Josie said when Maurice came back into the room.

Maurice ignored her and walked over to the back window, opened the small one at the top and put his hand out and took the plug from Joan.

'What are you doing that for?' Josie demanded when he had inserted the plug into the socket on the floor under the window.

'The record player,' Maurice replied and walked out of the room again.

'What does he want the record player for?' Maura asked.

'He doesn't,' Josie said recalling that Cathy had asked her if she would teach her and her friend to dance. She smiled at the memory of listening to her cheeky young sister tell her friends that her eldest sister has so many medals for dancing that the drawer she keeps them in had to have steel put into it because it was so heavy.

Maura giggled, looked at her mammy and asked, 'What did he plug it for?'

Josie continued to smile, and stood. She looked at the clock then left the room. She met Maurice in the lobby. He had an old bucket and a battered shovel in one hand and a bundle of sticks in the other.

'I'll close the door, Maurice,' Josie said when she saw him raise his foot to kick it closed. She had walked backwards towards the kitchen to let him pass her when Carl came bouncing down the stairs.

The passage was so narrow that Maurice had to hold the bucket in front of him and to prevent his knee from hitting the bucket he had to walk slow.

'Get a move on, man,' Carl drawled.

Maurice put the bucket, shovel, and bundle of sticks on

the floor then walked back towards the door and went into the toilet.

Josie picked up the bucket and shovel and brought them into the living room. When she came back to get the sticks Carl was making his way down the side of the tent to the bottom of the garden. She had picked up the sticks when Maurice came out of the toilet. She smiled and handed them to him and said, 'I brought the bucket into the living room.'

Maurice gave Josie his first smile since she had come home and said, 'Do you want me to put a match to the fire now?'

'Yes please Maurice,' Josie said and continued down the lobby to the marquee to keep her promise to Cathy.

When Carl walked into the living room Maurice had cleared the grate of the ashes and was lifting the cushion on his mammy's easy chair to find a newspaper. When he pulled the top one off the pile he saw that it hadn't been opened and he recalled that he had been so busy with getting ready for the party that he hadn't looked in the evening paper so he sat down and opened it at the sports page.

'Reading the paper won't get the fire lighting,' Maura said.

Maurice looked over the top of the paper at his sister and delivered her as cold as stare as his mammy had ever given her and said, 'If you are in that much of a hurry you can roll the papers.' He looked at his mammy and was surprised to see her smiling at her hands.

'That will have to wait until she has brought me some toast,' Carl said.

Maura stood, glared at her brother and left the room.

Maurice continued to scan the paper for a few more minutes. Then with his mammy and Carl watching him in silence as though they were examining him on his skills as a competent firelighter he rolled, twisted and laid the papers in the bottom of the grate. He then laid the sticks in a cross pattern like Una had taught him when he was ten years old.

'You have done a good job, boy,' Carl drawled when Maurice had picked up the bucket of ashes.

Sheila Malone had listened to her children argue with each other since they could talk. She had never once known any of them use their fists. When she saw Maurice glare at Carl and tighten his grip on the bucket she stood. Much as she wanted the smile on her new arrogant son in law's face wiped off she didn't want be a witness.

Maurice walked out of the room in front of his mammy and made his way down the lobby to get coal to put on top of the sticks.

Chapter Thirty-eight

auline was leaning into the sink peeling potatoes when Una walked into the kitchen Fifteen minutes before Maurice started to light the fire,'

'Leave some for me,' Una, said opening the drawer in the table and withdrawing a knife. On hearing splutters from the oven she inhaled the smell of the pork. 'It's like old times,' she said, recalling when they were living at home and the two of them used to peel the potatoes on a Sunday morning.

'Lovely pots,' Pauline said moving to make room. Right now she didn't want to think about, or talk about old times.

Una had seen the pots before. She leaned over and gazed into the small one that was nearest to her, and was pleased to see it had been washed properly. Cathy only half-washed the pots, and Joan couldn't do everything. But right now she didn't care if they cooked the potatoes in a cake tin. She plunged her hands into the basin then raised her face to the window. 'Josie bought the pots the last time she was home,' she said. When she saw a young boy about the same age as her son walking up the garden path on the house across the road she wondered if she should have made her phone call. 'Josie is still very generous to Mammy,' she said, 'she always buys her something when she comes home. Or brings something with her.'

'What did she buy her this time?' Pauline asked, glancing at the big pot again.

The water was cold as Una moved her hand around the basin to find an unpeeled potato. 'I don't know and I don't care,' she said, recalling the row she had had with Josie at Christmas, and the telephone call in late January telling her that Maura was getting married. 'Why did Mammy change her mind about going out to Canada for Maura's wedding?' she asked.

'Mammy was out last September,' Pauline said, resting her wrists on the edge of the sink and dangling her fingers in the water while she thought for a second. 'I didn't know anything about her coming out for the wedding,' she said.

'Josie sent her the money for her ticket, and I sent her some spending money.'

'Did you ask Maura?'

Una raised her head to the window again and thought back to when Josie had told her she had sent her mammy the money for her ticket. 'Josie hadn't said that Mammy wanted to go to Canada,' Una said. 'But Josie seldom knows what Mammy is saying any more than the rest of the us. Mammy plants the idea in Josie's head and Josie runs with it.'

'Probably,' Pauline murmured, her mind on the letter she had written her mammy that her mammy said she didn't get.

The two sisters talked about the rest of the family that were living at home while the living room door opened and closed, and people walked up and down the lobby.

Music drifted into the kitchen when Maura opened the door and leaned the top part of her body into the kitchen as though she would dirty her dress if she came any further. She looked around the small room before she said, 'Will one of you tell Josie that Carl is down and he would like some toast?'

Una dropped a half-peeled potato into the basin, turned round to Maura and said, 'Tell her yourself—she's out in the marquee.'

Maura pulled her head back as if Una had slapped her across the face and left.

Una could hear Josie's voice shouting dancing instruction to the children before she closed the door.

The door opened again. 'Where's Josie?' Sheila Malone commanded from the doorway, delivering her daughters one of her cold threatening stares.

'She's in the marquee with the children,' Una said, 'I think she's teaching them how to dance.'

Three loud splashes burst from the meat in the oven while Sheila Malone opened the drawer in the table, and closed it sharply. She moved some packets and tins on one of the shelves in the corner of the kitchen, then walked out of the room.

'I'd better call Josie,' Pauline said, dropping the potato she was peeling into the basin.

Una caught her sister by her arm. 'You will do no such thing.' She felt a breeze around her legs and it told her that her mammy had opened the hall door and was standing waiting for one of them to fetch Josie. 'If Carl's toast is all that important to her then she can make it herself.'

'Do you think she would?' Pauline asked, dreading her mammy coming back into the kitchen.

'No,' Una said, 'and I don't think Josie will either.' She glanced out the window again and asked, 'Where did Maura meet the pain in the arse?'

Yes, Pauline thought, smiling. That's exactly what Carl is, a pain in the arse. 'In my back garden,' she said.

'What was he doing in your garden?'

'Levelling the earth and laying a lawn.'

'I thought he worked as a caretaker for a block of flats?'

'He does,' Pauline said, recalling when Carl was working on her lawn and Maura used to bring him out a cup of coffee every hour. 'He also does gardens during the day when he works nights.'

'And a romance blossomed?' Una suggested.

Pauline wasn't so sure about a romance on Carl's part. 'I think he is too old for Maura,' she said while at the same time she thought, at least he is younger than Harry's father who had been too attentive to her young pretty sister.

'More like Maura is too young for him,' Una said recalling Carl dancing with Josie at the party. 'What does his family think of Maura?' she asked.

The emotional pressure of pretending began to weigh heavy on Pauline's ability to devise answers to question from her family about Harry and Carl. She knew Una always followed unanswered questions with more demanding ones so she decided to tell her sister what she knew about Carl. 'He is an only child,' she said.

Una laughed. 'Did he know the size of our family before he married Maura?'

Pauline rested her wrists on the sink as though she had remembered something, then said, 'I have never had a conversation with him about anything.'

'Did he talk to Harry?' Una asked.

Pauline had to dig into her memory to recall when Harry had been at home when Carl was there. The effort was fruitless and she wondered now if Harry had avoided Carl or Carl had avoided Harry, but she recalled one incident very clearly and is if talking to herself she said, 'I mentioned to Harry that I thought Carl was too old for Maura.'

'What did he say?' Una asked.

'He said Maura would have a more secure life with a mature man than she would with a young man that would probably chase after other girls.'

'A good point,' Una said. 'What about his parents?'

Pauline didn't meet Carl's mother until the wedding and she thought the big fat woman was as big a bully as her mammy. 'I haven't met his father because he is away most of the time. He cuts down trees in different parts of the country and in South America.'

'Does Maura get along with Carl's mother?'

Pauline had no idea. Maura had never told her anything about Carl's parents. She thought briefly about Harry's family and how she hadn't known them before she was married. 'Maura hasn't said much about them,' she said, 'but his mother seemed pleased enough with her at the wedding.' To prevent Una asking her anything else about the Grants she said, 'Maura is married now so she will have to make the best of it.'

'No she doesn't,' Una said, searching the water for an unpeeled potato, 'she can always come home, or better still kick him out if she has a house.'

You could, and you would, Pauline thought. 'It will depend on whether she has children,' she said. Fearing she was getting too close to her own problem she moved the conversation back to Maura and said, 'What is the difference between Carl being to old for Maura and Maura being too young for him?'

Again recalling Carl dancing with Josie, and him watching her when she was dancing with others as though he fancied her, Una said, 'He comes over to me like he prefers older women.' She picked a potato out of the basin and before she put the knife into it, she rested her hands on the edge of the sink and thought for a few seconds then said, 'Unless Maura is pregnant.'

Pauline dropped the potato she was peeling into the basin as if it had burnt her hand and stared at her sister with her mouth wide open.

'She wouldn't be the first girl to be pregnant when she got married, and I doubt she will be the last,' Una said, trying not to laugh. 'However,' she continued, 'he didn't marry her for her brains, or her money.'

Shock at the notion of Maura being pregnant turned to near-terror in Pauline's thoughts, as for the idea of Maura having money… . Apart from the thousand dollars that Harry had given her as a wedding present as far as Pauline knew Maura didn't have a penny or a cent to her name. But Harry had and Maura knew he had. She swirled her hand through the water and said, 'All done.'

'I'll take the skins out to the bin, Una said. 'Liam brought one of them out to the front garden before they put the marquee up.'

As Una had suspected when she had felt the cold on her feet the hall door was wide open, but her mammy wasn't standing under the shelf. She was at the gate looking up the road. Una put the skins in the bin, slammed the lid shut, went back into the house and closed the hall door. 'I don't know how we used to manage in this small kitchen when we were all living at home,' she said, stealing a quick glance out of the window to see if her mammy had moved since she had closed the hall door.'

'It was certainly better than going back to Arbour Hill,' Pauline agreed. She hadn't known houses had proper built kitchens until she was sixteen and she walked into their lovely new home in Ballymore.

The kitchen in Arbour Hill had a corrugated roof that their daddy had built over a large brown sink outside the back door. They called it a scullery after he had built a draining board and put in a wooden floor, so they could put the cooker out there.

While drying her hands on a wet towel, Una recalled the day the family had moved from Ballymore to the small kitchen, her daddy and Uncle Fred tying their furniture on the lorry, and how they all prayed that it wouldn't rain until they had moved everything into the house in Ballyglass. 'I like the kitchen at the front though,' she lied. 'I have always liked that. You can see what's going out there all the time.'

'Only if you are tall enough,' Pauline said raising her heels off the ground towards the window. 'All I can see out there is the upstairs windows of the house across road.' Thinking she saw a small grey cat walking along the window ledge outside, she leaned on the sink and raised her body higher and saw it was the top of her mammy's head. She dropped her heels on the floor, pointed out the window and said, 'Is that Mammy walking up to the house?'

Probably, Una thought, as a hard knock sounded on the hall door. She closed the kitchen door, then looked out the window as another hard knock echoed through the wall. 'So it is,' she said smiling.

'Will you let her in,? Pauline said meekly.

'No,' Una said, picking up the kettle, 'Maura can let her in. I'm going to have a cup of coffee.'

The family had many plates, bowls, mugs, and pots, and the kitchen didn't accommodate much storage space for food so someone had to go to the shops every day. Sauces, gravy powder, and vinegar weren't replaced until the old packet or bottle was empty because there was nowhere to store them.

While Una was searching through a row of shelves that were screwed to the wall at the other end of the kitchen for a jar of coffee, Maura walked over to the window in the living room to see who was knocking so loudly on the door.

'God Almighty, Una whined when the knocking continued, 'some of this stuff has been here for years.' She moved small packets, bottles and jars about. 'The shelves are black with grease,' she moaned.

Afraid her sister would start cleaning the kitchen, and so to remind her of the time, Pauline asked, 'What time are you going down for Shea?'

Una still wasn't sure she was doing the right thing about her son when she said, 'I'm not. It will take too long to go and get him, and then bring him back and then come back again myself. The buses are dreadful on Sundays and Shea is too young for all that walking.'

'The buses were never great, at any time,' Pauline agreed as she saw the jar of coffee on the table behind the bowl of sugar. She was more relieved that Una wouldn't continue to search for it than pleased to have found it.

The door opened. Maura leaned the top part of her body into the kitchen and said, 'Someone is knocking on the door.'

'Then open it,' Una snapped as another hard knock sounded in the hall.

Maura hesitated then said, 'I won't know who it is.'

'Then call Mammy,' Una replied, casting Pauline a look to say nothing.

Maura giggled as she said, 'I think it is Mammy.'

'Please yourself, Maura,' Una said, struggling not to laugh, 'but I think you should open the door and let her in.' When Maura opened her mouth to say something, Una added quickly nodding her head to the cooker and the sink, 'We are finished with that end of the kitchen for a while so when you have let Mammy in you can make Carl his toast.'

Maura closed her eyes at Una before she left.

Chapter Thirty-nine

Maura opened the hall door and found her mammy standing with her back to her looking down the street. She also saw the key was in the lock.

'Sorry Mammy,' she said, 'I thought I heard knocking.' She left the door open and went back into the living room.

'That bloody hall door,' Una said, getting off her stool and opening the kitchen door. She had taken one step into the hall when her mammy walked in and continued down the lobby. Una closed the door and went back into the kitchen. 'At least she didn't come in here again,' she said when she sat down again.

The meat burst out a couple of fresh splashes making the small room reek with the smell from the meat. 'Did you lock Mammy out when you went out with the potato peelings?' Pauline asked, walking over to the oven and lowering the temperature.

'No, I closed the door, and the key was in the lock so she could have let herself in any time she wanted.'

Pauline rested her eyes on the oven as if she was determined to see the meat walk out when it stopped splashing. Her resentment towards her mammy was starting to be clouded with some animosity for Maura. The meat roasting reminded her of her eldest sister. She sat up straight on her stool as though she had woken from a dream and asked, 'Do you see much of Josie?'

'Usually once a month,' Una said, 'but I haven't seen her since before Christmas.'

'Do you miss seeing her?' Pauline asked wondering if Maura would bother to come and see her now that she was married, or if she wanted to see her again when they went back to Canada.

'Yes,' Una said, looking up at the window in response to the sound of a car on the road. 'I know I fight with her but I do love her. She has been generous to us all with her money, and if she hadn't given Mammy so much then we would have had to.'

Pauline nodded agreement.

'Just the same,' Una continued, 'Josie goes too far with pleasing the selfish bitch.' She started to recall the evening in December. She smiled, recalling how Josie's cooking always made up to Jack for having to listen to her talk about her customers. He was holding his plate out to Josie for a second slice of her Black Forest Gateau when she looked over at Una told her not to forget to post her money to their mammy the next day so that she will get it in time for Christmas.

Jack was reaching into the table for the cream when he asked her what money she was talking about. It wasn't the money Una assured herself again. Jack never complained about her sending money home. When she had told her sister she wasn't sending her mammy any, Josie had rested her chin in her fists, stared at her and asked why she bothered to go home at all because when she did she spent all her time with the Byrnes.

'What did you fight about?' Pauline asked.

Una thought for a minute. She didn't know whether the argument had been over money, or their mammy but the issue that had annoyed her most was when Josie had accused her of being more of a Byrne than a Malone. 'Mainly Mammy and sending her money,' she said. 'It doesn't matter what the fight was about because I have made my mind up that she is not going to bully me. I don't want to be as cruel to her as Daddy has been to Mammy.'

Pauline wanted to cry, but smiled and raised her eyes to the ceiling. 'Now what are you talking about?' she asked.

'Don't tell me you haven't noticed Mammy's behaviour over the weekend,' she said.

Pauline stared at her sister. She didn't know what to say.

Taking Pauline's stare as a yes Una continued, 'Daddy allowed Mammy to bully him and us.' She nodded over to the shelves in the corner of the room. 'There is so much cleaning needing to be done since Daddy died that it will take us all a week to do it. If Daddy had insisted that Mammy got off her arse instead of getting us to do so much she would manage on her own now. I dread to think how she will manage when we are all gone.'

Recalling when Una had said that they should all say no to their mammy Pauline said, 'Mammy would be different if we all stood up to her.'

'She might,' Una said, as Josie passed the kitchen on her way into the living room.

'When will the meat be done?' Pauline asked.

'I've no idea,' Una said, looking at her watch, then over to the cooker. 'We'll have to ask Josie. If you didn't put it in the oven, then she did, because I could smell it cooking when I came over from Angie's.'

Josie had left the back door open when she had come back into the house. The sisters could hear Perry Como singing, 'Catch a Falling Star'. Neither Pauline nor Una sang like birds. Pauline sang on a note so high that she sat up very straight or stood when she sang. Una sang on a note so low that when anyone was listening to her they always stared at the floor.

For the next two minutes, Pauline stared at the ceiling and

Una bowed her head to the floor as they harmonized along with the music that was coming into the kitchen from the marquee. They were clapping their hands when Josie stood in front of them.

'Have you two nothing better to do?' Josie chastised, looking very happy and excited. She picked a tea cloth off the draining board, glanced into the pot of peeled potatoes, then bent down and opened the oven door.

'Christ. Is it burnt, Josie?' Una said closing her eyes and waving her hands about as smoke gushed out of the oven even though she knew the smoke was coming from old grease on the bottom of the oven.

'No, it's not,' Josie snapped, embarrassed with the smoke and the dirty oven. She slid the meat back into the oven and turned off the gas. 'It's cooked, and the crackling is nice and brown. Just leave it to rest for half an hour.' She ran her eyes around the kitchen walls, then nodded to the cooker and said, 'Put the potatoes on now.' She pointed to the draining board. 'There's two tins of peas over there. Put them on when the potatoes have boiled but don't let them boil over.'

'Anything else?' Una asked pleased to see her sister was happy again.

'While you're waiting for the potatoes to boil, you can set the table in the marquee. There's a clean white sheet on top of the washing machine in the bathroom.' Josie returned happily handing Una the tea cloth, then left the kitchen.

Una stood. 'I wonder what has put her into such good form again,' she said, lighting the gas under the pot of potatoes.

Chapter Forty

The smell of roast pork had seeped into every corner of the house, five minutes after Una had taken it out of the oven.

There were so many bodies struggling for space in the small kitchen that Donal thought about removing the kitchen door again. Pauline wasn't the only one who was hungry so while Josie was feeding Eileen, Maurice carved the meat. Liam mashed the potatoes while Una strained the peas and set the plates out on the table and the draining board. It was getting on for two when Cathy and Joan were making their way down the lobby to the marquee with the plated dinners.

The entrance to the marquee faced the back door into the house. Sheila Malone sat like a mafia queen at the top of the long wonky narrow table that ran the length of canvas room. She watched in silence as her children scurried in and out of the tent with plates and dishes.

Maurice ran his eyes over the dinners on the table as he made his way down the side of the tent to put the plate of meat in front of his mammy. 'Are they all the same?' he asked. He was the eldest living at home since his daddy died, and he always expected to be given the biggest dinner.

'Yes,' Pauline said, 'so you can sit where you are, Maurice. Una and myself will sit at the end of the table so that we can get the dessert.'

But Maurice didn't want to sit where he was, because he

didn't want to be near Maura. However, he didn't have any choice because the only space left was beside Carl, and the seat was on the other side of the table.

Una was looking for space on the table for a dish of mashed potatoes when Maura shouted, 'You left out Carl.'

'No, I haven't,' Una replied, glancing down the table, 'we have only eleven plates and I have used them all.' She picked up the dinner that was in the empty space beside Carl, and placed it in front of him. 'I was leaving Josie to last,' she lied and smiled smugly at her mammy. She didn't know whether to feel sorry for her mammy because Carl was sitting at her right hand, or sorry for Josie because she wasn't sitting beside her mammy but was sitting beside Carl. She went back into the kitchen to get the last two dinners.

The loose floor shook and the tables vibrated when Josie made her way brusquely up to the top of the marquee as though she was afraid she would miss something. She inhaled the warm smell of the food and nodded a smile of approval at the spread on the table. 'She should sleep for a couple of hours,' she said smiling broadly at her mammy.

Walking down the two steps from the back door with Josie's dinner in her hand, Una saw that all her family had their hands close together over their plates still holding their knives and forks staring at Josie as if they were waiting for her to say grace before they could start eating again.

'It was me, if yeh must know,' Liam said while Una was placing her sister's dinner on the table.

'And what have you done now that's so terrible that your family aren't able to swallow their dinner?' Una asked.

'I let teh peas boil over,' Liam shouted out.

'No you didn't,' Una contradicted. 'I did. I always do.' Even though she was looking at Liam she could see the light green bubbles on the top of the pot when she had spooned the peas on the plates. 'All the skins were floating on the top of the peas when you came into the kitchen,' she said using her fork to stir some of her peas into the mashed potato. 'I always boil tin peas for at least fifteen minutes.' She cut her meat, then looked at Josie and said, 'I hate tinned peas.' She mixed more of her peas with the mashed potatoes. 'Anyhow why is it so important?'

'Mammy doesn't like her peas all mushy,' Josie replied.

Maurice had already tasted the peas before Josie had complained about them and he thought they were very nice. He looked at his mammy's plate and saw she had eaten some of her peas. He didn't know how she liked her peas cooked. He had no idea how his mammy liked any of her food cooked, but he worried about Una and Josie arguing.

Unlike his brothers, Maurice had never grown used to his two eldest sisters snapping at each other, and he always worried when their argument involved any reference to his mammy. Expecting he would be pleasing his mammy he looked down the table to Una and asked, 'Why do yeh cook teh peas then if yeh don't like them?'

'Because Jack likes them,' Una said, stretching her arm out for the gravy. She raised her face to her brother and smiled.

'I think teh dinner's lovely,' Cathy said. She didn't like Maurice, and she thought it was none of his business how Una cooked her peas. 'And anyway,' she continued, 'nobody cooks tinned peas. They are already cooked. That's the whole point of tinned foods. They are made especially for people who are too busy like Joan, or are too lazy to do their own cooking.'

Una saw Maurice lower his red face to his mammy's dinner plate. She imagined that he wanted to apologise to her. They both knew that on the rare occasions when their mammy cooked everything she served up came out of a packet or a tin.

To prevent Josie or Maurice telling Cathy off Liam looked at Una and said, 'why do yeh boil teh peas down so much?'

Una put some food in her mouth, and chewed it for a few seconds while she wondered about telling a lie. She had forgotten about the peas but she wanted to support Cathy. 'Jack brought them home when he did the shopping and I thought I would stop him from getting them again if I messed them up. Unfortunately he liked them all mushy and soggy.'

'Then it served yeh right,' Liam said, delighted to move away from talking about mushy peas. He was so pleased to be eating roast meat that he didn't care if he never got peas. 'You modern women,' he continued before Una could reply, 'have lost teh run ev yerselves since men invented teh vacuum cleaner and teh washin machine. And as soon as yez got teh vacuum cleaner yez wanted carpets. Then when yez got teh washin machine, yez wanted wardrobes so that yez could have somewhere te keep all teh clothes that yez had te buy so that yez could wash them in teh washin machine.'

Una laughed into her dinner.

Pauline asked, 'How do you know all this?'

'Me friend Brian Farley told me,' Liam said, winking at the confused expression on Donal's face.

'And how would he know?' Pauline asked.

'Because he reads a lot ev books,' Liam replied. He rested his elbows on the table, joined his hands over his dinner and slowly swung his head up then down the table as if he was a judge reading out a sentence and said, 'Ask Maurice, he reads teh whole paper every day.'

'So does Mammy,' Josie said, taking the opportunity to include her mammy in the conversation and hoping she would be more agreeable. She didn't read books but when she could find the time she read some of the women's magazines that she bought for her customers to browse through while they were waiting to have their hair shampooed. She cut out many of her cooking recipes from the magazines. Mike read books, and Mike knew everything, so Josie had respect for people who read books.

Cathy didn't read books or the paper. She knew that Maurice would talk for hours about what he had read in paper that morning so to prevent her brother from telling them about all the bad things that were happening in the country she said, 'Maurice is great with fixin teh washin' machine and teh hoover.'

'So is Jack,' Josie cut in, recalling she had been very grateful to her sister's husband a number of times when he had repaired the hair dryers in her salon. She remembered that he also read books because she had heard him talking to Mike about things he had read about. But she was sure that Jack read the wrong books, because she had seen Mike lend him books to read.

Piqued at being upstaged by Jack Byrne and annoyed with Josie for reminding him he wasn't the only electrician in the family, Maurice ignored his sisters' praising and comparing their labour-saving devices and enjoyed his mushy peas. He was less interested in washing machines and vacuum cleaners than his mammy who he noticed was also enjoying her dinner.

Chapter Forty-one

Revolting, Una thought, casting her eyes over the four mounds shivering on the plates. One was purple, another lime green, another pink and the fourth yellow. They shivered again when Pauline rocked the floor coming back after bringing the last of the dinner plates into the kitchen.

'Who wants what?' Pauline called out holding a large spoon over the mounds of Jelly and blancmange.

'Mammy will have port wine jelly,' Josie said.

'How do you know what Mammy will have?' Maurice asked.

'Mammy always has port wine,' Cathy said. 'It's her favourite. And she won't get drunk because it isn't really wine, and it doesn't smell her breath like whiskey does.'

Una smiled at her young sister and said, 'I hate the smell of whiskey.' She took the dish with the port wine jelly off Pauline and looked down the table to her mammy and asked, 'Do you want blancmange or custard?'

Dimples formed on Sheila Malone's cheeks when she closed her teeth tight as if she was afraid her thoughts would escape from her mouth. She raised her head then closed her eyes at Pauline.

'It's not custard,' Joan said, 'it's vanilla blancmange.'

'Mammy will have vanilla,' Cathy said.

'Mammy is capable of telling Una what she wants herself,' Maurice said.

Tempted to say that her mammy wouldn't say anything if someone would say it for her Pauline smiled at her brother and said, 'We will give everyone a bit of them all.' She cast her eyes over the ten plates that had a blob of the two jellies, then stood and picked up the empty plates that had held the jellies and left to bring them into the kitchen.

Sheila glared at Una.

Mammy will get the whole plate in her face, Una thought, if she looks at me like that again. 'What one do you want, Mammy?' she asked sternly, holding the spoon over the dish. She waited two seconds for her mammy to answer, then added, 'Think about it while I am dishing up the others.'

'I'll have some of both,' Sheila said.

Una handed Maurice the dish of dessert and said, 'Pass that down to Mammy.' She picked up one of the plates with small servings of the two jellies and began sharing the two blancmanges.

'I'll have the same as Mammy,' Maura said.

'You will have the same as everyone else,' Una replied, spooning the vanilla blancmange onto the plates. 'You can swap the lime jelly with someone for port wine, or the other way round,' she added handing the plate to Josie to pass to Maura.

'Not me,' Cathy said. 'I like the port wine.'

'I hope you don't get a taste for real port or wine for some time,' Una said, smiling at her young sister. She handed Cathy her plate of dessert and added, 'and I hope you don't go to parties with vodka in your handbag even if doesn't smell your breath.'

'I totally agree with you, Una,' Josie said passing a plate of dessert to Carl. 'I really don't know why any of you youngsters bother to take the pledge at all,' she continued, remembering the young men at the party who couldn't dance properly because they were drunk.

'We were never given a choice,' Maurice said defensively. He was eighteen when he enjoyed two half-glasses of stout after being told by a friend that a pledge is only binding when it is taken with the full knowledge of what you are doing.

'Even so,' Josie returned. 'A pledge is a pledge.'

'What's a pledge?' Carl asked.

'It's a vow we take when we make our confirmation,' Donal said, 'we pledge to abstain from drinking alcohol until we are twenty-one.'

'It's not a proper pledge if yer made te take it,' Liam said. 'I was only eleven at teh time, and I'd never taken a drop ev teh stuff.'

'I was only ten,' Cathy cut in, 'and I haven't broken it either.'

Josie sat up straight, glared at her youngest sister and said,, 'I should hope not.'

Pleased to see that at last his mammy was smiling, Maurice looked from Una to Josie and asked, 'Do neither ev you not drink then?'

'I do,' Una lied, recalling the day she had thrown up the two gin and tonics she had drank with her new friends before she left the pub on the Friday she had been given her first English pay packet. She never told anyone about her struggle to get home by tube before she was sick again. She was able to keep her embarrassment from Jack, for when he came home from the late shift she was fast asleep in bed.

Una knew the Cullens didn't drink so when she saw Maurice grinning at Josie, as if he had caught her stealing she wanted to slap him across his handsome face. She had no idea why the Cullens didn't drink, and she didn't care. 'Gin, sherry, brandy,' she said, imagining she could taste the two gins she had swallowed as if they had been iced water.

Liam wasn't the least bit concerned that his mammy was as miserable now as she had been before Josie came home, and he didn't care if he never saw her smile. He ceased to wonder why Josie tried so hard to please her, but he would miss her cooking when she went back to England. He felt he owed her for that alone. 'I agree with Josie,' he said, 'seventeen is too young fer girls te be goin' drinkin.'

Maura could find nothing amusing with her siblings bantering. Her jealousy of Carl dancing with Josie at her party was now magnified with jealousy of Cathy for the way she spoke her mind. She wasn't used to feeling jealous of, or had ever bantered with her siblings. When she was living at home she was used to getting all the attention she had ever wanted from them.

Every time Maura thought about the knitted scarves, hats and gloves Liam's friends had brought her, she wanted to cry. She recalled he didn't drink any of the beer at the party so by way getting back at him she called out, 'What liquor do you drink, Liam?'

'Maura enjoys rye,' Carl drawled.

'Does she eat it? Or drink it?' Una asked. 'I thought rye was bread.'

'The Americans make whiskey from rye,' Pauline said.

Until now Carl had nothing to contribute to the bantering of his new wife's family and he wasn't used to listening so he grabbed the opportunity to inform them about the manufacture of rye whiskey.

Like many of his countrymen when he was being attentive to a boring conversation Maurice said, 'Is that right?' Every time Maurice said, 'Is that right?' Carl raised his voice.

Donal was also bored listening to Carl, and he also agreed with Una and Josie. There were many occasions he saw young men stagger out of the pub on Friday evenings after drinking four pints, then cough them up in the street. He still couldn't understand why some of them would do the same again the following week.

By way of shutting his ears to Carl glamorising about the production of whiskey, Donal allowed his thoughts to dwell on his siblings. If he were asked to talk about his family he would say his two eldest sisters were very bossy. He would also say that they were very kind. Unlike his brother Maurice, he had never missed his mother's care or affection and he would always be grateful to his three eldest sisters for caring about him and the rest of his family when they were living at home. He never talked with them much, but then they weren't interested in football. He never interfered or took sides when his sisters argued with each other, but he wasn't going to tolerate his brothers making fun of them because they didn't drink.

A spoon leaped off the table and completed a somersault before it landed in Maurice's dish of jelly. Donal had hit the bowl of his spoon when he slapped his hand lightly on the table. Before Maurice realised what had happened Donal said loudly, 'It's teh drivin' that bothers me.'

'Driving what?' Josie asked.

'A car,' Maurice said.

'What's wrong with a woman driving a car?' Josie asked, pulling in her chin and glaring at Maurice as though he had been rude to her.

Una couldn't recall Donal losing his temper before and, taking advantage of his outburst, she asked, 'Is it women drivers or young drivers that bothers you, Donal?'

Donal had never given a thought to women drivers but he was concerned about the growth of young people driving and not being insured. They got insured for a month and didn't renew it when the month was up. He wiped the spoon on the side of the tablecloth and thought for few seconds then said, 'It's teh insurance, Una.'

'He's right,' Maurice agreed.

'Are you saying that women don't get insured?' Una asked,

finding it difficult not to smile watching Donal continue to polish his spoon.

Donal avoided arguments, and all he intended to do was stop his brothers from making fun of his sisters because they didn't drink. 'It's not women,' he said, 'but young people are drivin' and they are not all insured.'

'Young men and women are not paid as much as older ones, and women are paid less than men even when they are doing the same work,' Pauline said. 'And men of all ages drive cars without being insured.'

'Pauline is right,' Josie said. 'One of my customers had an accident and she had to pay for her car to be repaired because the man that ran into her wasn't insured and the driver of the car was a man in his forties.'

Maurice also knew a man that had knocked a bump in another car, drove away and bragged about it. However, he was enjoying himself now with Donal arguing with his sisters so he said, 'Women don't work as hard as men.'

Sheila Malone sighed loudly, rose from her chair and walked out of the marquee.

'Name one job a man can do that a woman can't,' Una asked, glaring at his smug face.

'A priest,' Cathy said.

'I mean can't,' Una said, 'by not being able to. I don't mean can't because we aren't allowed.'

Relieved that the conversation had moved from women drivers, Donal said, 'There's liftin' heavy things. Women are not built as strong as men.'

'They have machines for lifting these days,' Josie said, and trolleys for moving them.'

'What about bringin' in the coal?' Cathy said. 'I wouldn't like to do that.'

'Neither would I,' Josie said, 'but I suppose it could be put into smaller bags, and we could bring them in on a trolley.'

A light gust of wind rippled the walls of the marquee when Sheila Malone walked back into the tent. Una waited until her mammy had sat down and asked, 'What was it like to get a job when you were young, Mammy?'

The sides of the large tent rippled like a soft drum roll from another light breeze while Sheila Malone's children waited in silence for her to answer. She stared hard at Josie and said, 'Education was important.'

The bitch, Una thought. 'It still is,' she said, delivering her mammy a colder look than her mammy had given Josie.

Disturbed by the cold look her mammy had given her and terrified that Una would berate their mammy about the poor education she had allowed her children, Josie said, 'Schools are better these days.'

Una had seen the look their mammy had given Josie and she felt sorry for her sister. But she wasn't going to allow her mammy to bully her also so she said, 'A good education is still important in getting a decent job.'

'That depends on the job,' Pauline said, raising her head from her hands to her mammy. 'You don't need much of an education to work in a factory, or a shop.'

'Education is like being in a union,' Liam said.

Maurice laughed loudly, then sneered, 'Educated people don't join unions.'

'Yes they do,' Liam said, 'teachers join unions.' He regretted now that he hadn't tried to be more attentive in school. 'Union means united,' he said, 'and educated people stick together like flies around a heap of shite. More often than not doctors marry doctors and they never criticise each other. It's the same with solicitors.'

'There are more benefits to having an education than getting better paid jobs,' Una said. 'Lack of education keeps people ignorant and vulnerable to being bullied by their employers.'

'Not if you have yer own business like Josie has,' Cathy said.

Seething with jealousy at being reminded of Josie and her money, Maura raised her voice and said, 'Not everyone wants to have their own business. Some people are very happy to work for a wage. People with their own business need workers.'

'If we were all educated,' Cathy said, 'we wouldn't have any coalmen.'

'Or coal for that matter,' Liam said, winking at Una as though they shared a secret about child labour and continued, 'We would have to send the children down the mines again.'

Una knew that Cathy wasn't attending school, and she knew that Liam knew as well so she said, 'Not all children, just the ones that don't go to school.

For a second Josie felt weak. She had seen pictures on the television of children working down the mines. And as usual she closed her mind to them, telling herself that they came from another world. Imagining her daughter with a dirty face and bandy legs she said, 'That's ridiculous. Mike would never allow that to happen.'

Maura giggled. 'How could Mike stop it from happening?' she asked.

'He couldn't,' Una said. 'But it won't happen because education is better now, both for children and adults, and especially for women.' She smiled at Maurice and added, 'Who knows but in a few years women will be the top engineers and bankers. We will have better wages so we will be able to insure our cars.'

'Yez will never be President,' Maurice sneered playfully and laughed loudly.

'And why not?' Una snapped. 'What about Queen Elizabeth? And before her we had Queen Victoria. Tell me one thing that you can do that Josie can't.'

'And Catherine the Great ev Russia,' Liam said, silently thanking his friend Brian for his lesson on Russian history. He tapped the table in front of Maurice and asked, 'Apart from puttin on teh plugs that you do fer yer job, what can you do that Josie can't?'

'I can put a plug on,' Josie said, 'Jack showed me.'

'So can I.' Pauline said.

'There yeh go,' Liam said, jutting out his chin towards his cranky brother. 'Can you do a perm?'

'I do the perms,' Josie said.

'I can do a perm,' Una said, surprised Josie could put on an electric plug. However, she could paper walls and paint doors, so she added: 'And I can do decorating.'

'There yeh go again,' Liam said, nodding his head to Maurice. 'Er sisters can do electrical and buildin' work. Now what about you and doin' teh permin'?'

Relieved now that her young daughter wouldn't have to go down a coal mine, Josie said, 'Liam, there's no need for Maurice to be able to do a perm.'

Donal was enjoying the bantering but he had known his youngest brother to go too far with annoying Maurice. 'Yeh know yerself, Liam,' he said, 'there's more to bein' an electrician than puttin' on a plug.'

'I know there is,' Liam said in a slow and gentle tone like he was talking to a child, 'and you know, Donal, that there is more te bein' a hairdresser than doin' perms. 'There's cuttin' and dyein, and…'

'And setting, and bleaching,' Una continued for him when she saw her brother was struggling to remember what he had seen Josie do with hair.

'I do all those,' Josie said, sounding exhausted. She looked at Maurice and added, 'And there's absolutely no reason why you should be able to do them, as well.'

'That's not teh point, Josie,' Liam interrupted. 'All we are sayin is that women are able to do as many things as men and there is no reason why a woman couldn't become president.'

'Liam,' Josie said with the impatience she always felt for her young brother, 'you don't have to be a hairdresser to be become president.'

'I know that,' Liam shouted back. 'But it shouldn't stop yeh.'

'Even so,' Josie said, closing her eyes to the smiling faces of the rest of her family. Even though she now knew that Liam was having fun with her she said, 'I don't want to be president.'

'That's entirely yer choice, Josie,' Liam said gently, 'and no-body is askin' yeh te be.' He winked at Pauline. 'I suppose it's a good thing, too, because the country yer livin' in doesn't have a president. It has a Queen.'

'Even so,' Josie repeated. She smiled at Maurice and added, 'Don't you worry about learning to do a perm.'

Like her eldest daughter Josie, Sheila Malone never thought back over her life but now while she listened to her children she tried to recall what they used to talk about when they were all living at home. All she could remember now was her sons talking about football, and Josie talking about her customers. She also recalled her older daughters arguing.

Although she would probably not be able to name her method, Sheila used divide and rule to control her children. For the first time since she became a mother she worried about how friendly her children were now.

Charmed by her youngest brother's banter, and enthralled at his nerve to shout at Josie, Pauline thought how different Harry's family was to her own. She had never heard them laugh at each other. She thought it would be much easier to put up with her mammy's moods now if she came home for good. She looked down the table and smiled triumphantly at her mammy.

Sheila closed her eyes at Pauline, then lowered her face to the knife she was twisting. When she looked up again Pauline was still smiling at her. If she hadn't been worried about money she would have been stunned at Pauline's smug smile.

The sides of the marquee swayed, and the corners of the tablecloth flapped when a gust of wind blew in through the opening. Maurice was talking about the political structure of Ireland but nobody was listening. Sheila continued to twist a knife in her left hand, and Maura was rubbing her thumb around the bowl of her dessertspoon.

The droning of her brother's voice transported Josie's thoughts back to Kent. At least once every day since she had come home this time she had wished herself back in her own clean flat where nobody shouted at her, and she didn't have to worry about doing anything to please anybody. She was deep in thought about her driving lessons when she said softly, 'Eammon.'

'Who is Eammon?' Maurice didn't want to know but he thought his mammy did because she stopped twisting her knife and looked at Josie.

'His name is Eammon,' Josie repeated into her brother's blank face.

'Are yeh tellin' us that yer carryin' on with a fella called Eammon?' Liam asked.

'I haven't met him yet,' Josie told Maurice. 'I have seen him, though. He does the collection at ten o'clock mass every Sunday.'

'What's his other name?' Liam asked.

'I don't remember,' Josie said. 'It doesn't matter because Mike booked him.'

Maurice frowned deeply and tried to imagine what a man named Eammon, that Mike Cullen had apparently booked, had to do with all the houses that the corporation were going to build in Ballyglass, which was what he had moved on to talking about.

'To teach me to drive,' Josie said. 'I have my first driving lesson the day after I get back.'

'I'm ahead of you there.' Pauline said.

'Are you learnin' te drive as well?' Cathy asked.

'I've got my own car,' Pauline said. She smiled at Donal and added, 'and I am fully insured.'

'Yeh must have lashins ev money,' Cathy gasped. 'Cars are awful expensive.'

Jealousy was an emotion new to Maura and was inflamed further with the recollection that Pauline had her own house and car. She had enjoyed living in Pauline's lovely house and she had believed as Pauline's sister she was entitled to keep all the money she earned as a waitress.

'Do you have yer own car, Maura?' Cathy asked.

Maura continued to rub her thumb around the bowl of the spoon and stare into the gleaming surface as if it would tell her what to say. Unlike Pauline she was neither amused nor charmed with any of her siblings. When she had been living at home she had never wondered why she had always been given her own way. In the silence her thoughts went back to when the church bells were ringing and of Josie leaving the room. It was her first experience of being ignored by her mammy when her mammy had simply walked out of the room as Carl was telling her about the summer cabin he was going to build. Then when her mammy came back into the room again, she opened the back window and insisted they listen to Josie teaching the children to dance.

Though impatient with her now, Carl was used to Maura's sulky moods. 'Not yet,' he said, stretching out his hand to take hold of hers with the intention of lifting it to his mouth to kiss her fingers.

Maura handed him the spoon and went back to brooding

over Josie. She recalled that when Josie came back into the living room before dinner her mammy was pleased to see her. She blamed Josie for the decision not to show the movie of her wedding after tea.

Josie was able to turn her mind off for minutes at a time as if she could close a door on what was going on all around her. In her thoughts she would go shopping or cook. While her handsome selfish brother, and new brother-in-law pumped information about what car she should get she closed her ears so tight she didn't hear the doorbell ring or notice Liam leave the table.

With her eyes almost closed because she was squinting, Sheila Malone's sister Sue stood in the doorway of the marquee and smiled at her sister's children.

Sue was five feet four, and weighed around ten stone when she was careful with her diet. Her hair was dark grey, like Sheila's. Her eyes looked small because she squinted continually. She hated wearing her glasses and rarely put them on.

While Sue hugged her nieces, her husband Fred stood in the doorway looking over the marquee as if he was a building inspector. He was a couple of inches taller, and half a stone heavier than his wife. His dark wavy hair was grey at the temples, and he wore a grey double-breasted suit, a white shirt and a blue tie.

Josie had always believed she was her aunt's favourite niece. With all the excitement of getting ready for the party, and the more than usual efforts trying to please her mammy, Josie had forgotten about her disappointment at not finding her Aunt Sue and Uncle Fred at the boat to meet her. Right now she was especially pleased to see her because she would be away from her brothers teasing her, and she would get some relief from her mammy's scowling. She swung her leg over the bench and said, 'I will get on with perming your hair.'

Sue usually had to wait until Josie had washed, cut and put

the perm curlers in Sheila's hair first so she hesitated because she though that Josie meant her.

'Go on, Sue,' Una said. 'Maura, Pauline and myself will wash up.' She swung her legs over the bench and added, 'I'll make a start in the kitchen.' She was also pleased to get away from her mammy and she knew that the last place she would find her was in the kitchen.

Chapter Forty-two

The draining board was stacked with plates, cups, and dishes waiting to be dried when Pauline walked into the kitchen after leaving Carl sitting on his own staring at the bottom of the marquee like it was a work of art.

'Where is Maura?' Una asked, starting on the pots.

'Making a phone call,' Pauline said, wondering if she had heard correctly when Maura had asked Carl if five o'clock would be all right with him to visit her friend. She took a tea towel off the table, began to dry the plates and worried about Maura going out before tea.

Maura came in and looked around the kitchen. 'Where do you keep the clean tea towels?' she asked.

'I'll do them,' Pauline said. 'You can dry up after tea,' she added, hoping that Maura would tell her about visiting her friend, and that she would be back for tea.

'I won't be here for tea,' Maura replied curtly, then closed her eyes at Pauline as if it was her fault.

'Have you changed your mind about seeing the movie then?' Pauline asked.

'No but Mammy has,' Maura replied sullenly. 'Carl and I are going down to Nula's after I have had my hair cut.'

'Why?' Pauline demanded, changing her mind about picking up a plate to dry and stared at Maura.

'Since when do I need your permission to visit me friend?' Maura asked.

'I mean why has Mammy changed her mind about showing the movie today.

'I heard them talking about going to the Glen later on,' Maura said, moving around so that she could keep her back to both of her sisters.

'Who's going to the Glen?' Una asked.

'Fred, Sue, Mammy and Josie,' Maura spat out in a tone that sounded like she hated the four of them.

'When was that decided?' Una asked. She wasn't asking about the showing of a movie because she didn't know anything about it. She was thinking about Josie going to a pub.

Maura wasn't lying when she said, 'I don't know,' because she didn't, but in her heart she knew it was her mammy that had decided the movie wouldn't be shown. She was upset about it and blamed Josie. 'You had better ask Mammy, or Josie,' she said through her teeth, then walked out of the kitchen.

The wet soapy cloth Una slapped on the top of the cooker sizzled because one of the rings was still burning. She switched off the tap. 'What movie is Maura talking about?' she asked, turning round in time to see Pauline throw down the teacloth and walk out of the kitchen.

Una sloped the cloth around the cooker and wondered what the hell was going on.

Chapter Forty-three

Pauline was so hurt when she left the kitchen she knew she was going to cry. With her head bowed she was about to climb the stairs when she heard the living-room door open behind her.

Glancing under her arm, Pauline recognised the new slippers. When she turned round her mammy lowered her face to the ground and walked over to the hall door. Her eyes started to sting from the breeze that came into the hall. She watched her mammy take a few steps down the front garden path before she withdrew her hand from the banister, walked down to the lobby and went into the bathroom.

Alone in the small room, the tears ran down Pauline's face. A mixture of joy, frustration and disappointment were fighting for space in her heart. She was delighted to see the children she had worried about so much when she left home were wonderful. She was getting to know them again and although they were the same, they were also different; they were better in every way.

Anger wasn't an emotion that Pauline nursed, and she seldom lost her temper, but she relieved her stress and disappointments with tears. She never fought anybody over anything. She had always felt emotional hurt, and learned to endure the pain.

When she had met Harry and he had praised her for doing things that she didn't even know she had done, every bone in her body fell in love with him. She went off to Canada with dreams of a future where she was loved and wanted. During the six years of her new life in Canada she never nursed anger, lost her temper or learned to fight, but she had cried.

Less than six feet square, the bathroom was always cold, but nobody complained; it had a bath. The door was in the middle of the wall off the lobby and the bath ran the length of the wall facing the door. That door didn't open all the way because a small washing machine lived in the corner behind it. The hand basin stood underneath the window that gave light from the back garden.

The yellow paint on the walls looked tired, and the room was cleaner than the rest of the house. But then it didn't have to absorb the grease from the cooking, the heat from the fire, or the smoke from cigarettes.

Alone in the small room with the door closed and bolted, memories of happy times when she would be getting ready to go to a dance overwhelmed Pauline. Unlike Josie, she had never denied that her mother didn't give a toss about her, but also like her older sister she always felt intimidated, nervous and scared when her mammy was storming around the house in one of her tempers.

On hearing Maura's shoes on the steps outside the back door, her thoughts went back to Canada and what she would tell Harry when she returned with the movie and told him that nobody had seen it. It was a dreadful movie that Harry has cut and spliced to show her family what he wanted them to see, but her mammy had asked for it.

With her hopes of coming home for good hanging on by a thread stretched to breaking while holding a button on an over-coat, Pauline recalled that Harry and her mammy had become such immediate good friends that she had believed her mammy had changed. Also Harry had been so pleasant to her mammy she had hoped he would change also. But after her mammy had left, Harry reverted to his old ways.

She closed her eyes tight and tried to picture her two blonde-haired little girls. Her eyes were shining and her cheeks were red but she still managed to smile when she threw her eyes up to the ceiling. She was remembering a letter from Una.

I do envy you getting two babies for the price of one, Una had written. But then Una hadn't been up nearly every night feeding them, or trying to stop them from crying so that Harry could get his sleep.

She closed her eyes to the memory of the bruises on Jenny's arms. 'They're all gone now,' she whispered. 'And they will never come back again. Never ever again.' While she was thinking, and talking to herself, Pauline folded towels and wiped over the windowsill and the sink. The smell of all sorts of soap and toothpaste soothed the bitterness in her heart.

Rubbing the hair over her ears after splashing water on her face, she whispered to her reflection in the mirror, 'After all this time, she is still a spoilt bitch.' She sat on the edge of the bath, worrying about why her babies didn't smile or talk much, when she heard the door rattle and saw the handle shake.

'I want to wash Sue's hair,' Josie shouted and continued to rattle the handle of the door.

Keeping her head down and setting her eyes on the bottom of the door facing her, because she didn't want Josie to see she had been crying Pauline crossed the lobby and went into the toilet.

Sanding with her back to the door of the very tiny room, Pauline closed her eyes to the green wall, that was just a little over two feet away from her face. Although she felt confined, isolated and lonely, she still needed to hide. She sat on the toilet, closed her eyes and focused her mind back to Friday afternoon.

The copper pipe that brought the hot water to the bathroom ran along the wall under the window of the toilet. Pauline bowed her head and listened to the water hissing into the bathroom taps. She stared at the black stains on the yellow-tiled floor along the skirting board and tried to remember what her mammy had said about showing the movie. After about thirty seconds, she decided that the toilet floor hadn't been washed properly for a year and that her mammy hadn't said anything. She had just walked out of the room.

When she raised her head she noticed that the window needed a couple of coats of paint. She thought of her own house with every room beautifully decorated and spotlessly clean, and wondered if she was doing right by her daughters in wanting to bring them home to Plunkett Road. But whatever she decided to do, she would still have to go back and face Harry. This brought her thoughts back to the movie. She recalled her mammy had been standing outside the hall door on the doorstep when Josie, Maura and herself had decided to show the movie either before or after tea, when most of the family would be home.

The clouds were still blowing across the window when Pauline recalled her mammy had come back into the room after they had decided when they would show the movie. She hadn't sat down; she stood at the front window. Just the same, her mammy would have heard them talking, and what they had decided on before she had walked out of the room again.

Running water, and the sink emptying told Pauline Josie was nearly finished shampooing Sue's hair so she hurried her thoughts and recalled a cold breeze had stung her legs after her mammy walked out into the front garden. She smiled as she thought back to the time, years ago, when Una had locked their mammy out of the house when she had walked out of the kitchen in a temper.

It was eight years ago and at the time Pauline didn't know what had happened because she was upstairs making the beds and Una had been cleaning the living room. It was the usual Saturday morning, and Josie and her daddy were working. It wasn't unusual to hear knocking on the hall door on a Saturday morning. There were always children calling for her brothers so Pauline ignored the banging sounds because she thought that Una would open it.

When the banging continued and became louder, Pauline glanced out the window into the back garden. When she saw Una was hanging out some washing she went downstairs opened the hall door, and found her mammy standing under the concrete shelf with her hands in the pockets of her apron scowling at a group of children that were standing at the gate.

Sheila Malone hadn't argued when Una had said that the door must have closed from the draught when she had opened the back one. It was a week later when Una had told Pauline that she had deliberately closed the door. Her mammy had walked out and just stood looking up and down the road after Una had asked her to wash the porridge pot.

Pauline hated spiders but she watched a little one with short legs slip and recover as it made its way along the top of the low slanting skirting board. She tried to remember other times when her mammy had walked out and stood at the door after the day that Una had locked her out. It took the spider a minute to reach the dirty corner and Pauline couldn't recall her mammy standing at the door again when Una was at home, until this morning.

What with meeting Una, and getting ready for the party, until now Pauline hadn't thought about the Friday afternoon, or the movie, or her cold feet. As her mind went back to all the times that her mammy had closed her eyes, or walked away from her before she had asked about the letter she had written, her hurt turned into rage. She started to feel cramped in the tiny room, so she stood and opened the top of the window as far as it would go.

'Pauline?' Josie called came from the lobby.

Pauline flushed the toilet so she wouldn't hear what her sister was going to say. She waited until she heard Josie's voice coming from the hall before she went back into the bathroom to wash her hands.

The mirror on the windowsill above the hand basin was fogged up with steam so Pauline couldn't see that her eyes were red. But they felt sticky, so she washed her face again before she sat down on the side of the bath. The sweet scent of shampoo in the bathroom reminded her of Saturday evenings when the family first moved into the house.

The room used to smell like a warm bar of soap for two days from all the baths. The happy memory of Saturday evening baths stopped Pauline from feeling she was a stranger in her family home. On hearing the voices of Una and Liam talking and laughing in the lobby, then the hall door closing, she wondered if it was important to come home often to keep her place in the family.

While pondering what she should do about her mammy and the movie, Pauline straightened the towels on the back of the door and thought how Una never showed any fear about having a fight with anyone.

The long bar screwed to the door came away when Pauline was drying her hands. A second towel slid down to the floor. She gazed in astonishment at the remaining old threadbare cloth that hung from one of the tiny screws in the door. Her eyes started to shine with more tears when she unhooked the very old towel from the rusty screw that remained on the door where the towel rack had been.

The faded yellow gloss paint on the door reminded Paul

ine of Una's wedding. She smiled at the memory of all the commotion when the house was being decorated. 'This is still my family home,' she said to the walls. 'I painted you lot and this door.' She washed her face again and left the bathroom.

Chapter Forty-four

Fred moved his hands towards his shoulders so he would see over the top of his newspaper when he heard the light sharp click of the living room door closing. The back of his chair touched the wall when he shifted his body. He saw Maura let one side of her newspaper slip from her hand as Pauline walked in. He sat up straighter in his chair and pulled in his legs when he saw Pauline walking over towards him. He didn't have long legs, but the power he saw behind Pauline's stride made him feel she wasn't going to stop walking.

Pauline imagined she could feel her heart throbbing over the ruffling sounds of the newspaper Maura was struggling with. She thought Maura looked like a little kitten striving to get in, or out of a paper tent. In between using her head and her knees to try and force the sheets of paper to fold in the middle, she kept glancing over her eyebrows at the fireplace. When Pauline turned round to see what her sister was looking so worried about, she saw Carl sitting in her mammy's easy chair, smiling at Josie's legs.

Pauline knew her sister would have seen what her husband was leering at, but she didn't care. She turned her back on Maura and moved so that she would block her sister's view to the fireplace. She felt a light thump in her back and took a step forward to stop from falling as Maura pushed past her and walked over to the door. She found Una standing in the doorway when she yanked it open.

'What on earth is your hurry?' Una shouted, stretching her arm out to try to catch the door Maura had yanked open.

Maura raised her arm as though she expected Una to hit her, then stormed out of the room.

Una didn't catch the door so it banged sharply against the back of the chair her mammy was sitting on.

Josie pushed Sue's head down and gave her attention to parting the back of her aunt's hair. She slid the tail of her comb under a slice of the hair, picked it up then held her hand out to her mammy.

Sheila Malone handed Josie a small rectangular tissue.

'The boys are gone off to play football,' Josie said, wrapping the slice of hair in the tissue as if Maura storming out of the room hadn't happened.

Una didn't really care why Maura had run out of the room. The spoilt little bitch was always showing off when she wanted something. Una often admired her, especially when her mammy or Josie were involved. She used to think that one of them should be spoilt. 'Is that why Maura stormed out of the room?' she asked, watching her mammy peel another tissue from the pack she was holding and start to smooth it between her thumb and her first finger like it was a delicate piece of satin cloth.

The soft sharp swish of newspaper brought Una's attention to her Uncle Fred. When she looked over to him he shook his newspaper again, shot glances at Pauline and Josie, then closed his eyes at Una and raised his newspaper to his face.

It was a long time since Fred had closed his eyes at Una, but then she had avoided giving him the opportunity to since she was thirteen years old. Her sharpest memory was the first time she had upset him. It was the day after Maurice was born. She was nine years old and the family lived in a small four-roomed two-storey house in Arbour Hill when she had told him she thought he was her mammy's brother. It was a

Sunday afternoon and she was spreading margarine and jam on the bread they would have for their tea after Josie, Pauline, and Sean came home from the pictures. By the time she was scraping the last of the jam out of the jar, her mammy and daddy had decided on a name for the new baby.

Una didn't know what the name for the new baby was because she hadn't been listening. She had been dreaming about what spiteful thing she could do to Fred because he hadn't given her the four pence to spend for herself, as she didn't go to the pictures with her sisters and brother. It had taken her ten minutes out in the scullery to wash the knife and the empty jam jar. When she came back into the living room, she found Fred sitting by the side of the fireplace. Her mammy was gone back to bed, and she could see through the front window that Sue and her daddy were standing out in the street. She could feel her uncle was watching her so she didn't take a slice of bread before she went out to wheel Maura around in her pram again.

'What made yeh think that I was yer mammy's brother?' Fred asked her when she was walking over towards the hall door.

'Because you're always sitting in one of those chairs like me mammy is,' Una replied, turning her face to the second easy chair on the other side of the fireplace. When she heard her uncle snort, and saw him close his eyes before he started to move forward in his chair, she ran out of the house. She thought that he was going to hit her.

While Una was thinking back, Josie continued to wind Sue's hair. Her mammy ironed each piece of tissue paper with her finger and thumb, then handed them to Josie, as her daughter needed them.

The boiler in the corner of the room belched out a light rumble when Pauline walked towards the table and said, 'I think Maura is upset because she won't see the movie.'

'What movie?' Una asked.

In response to the rumble from the boiler, and a rustle from a newspaper, Una looked over to the press in the corner in time to see her uncle raise his newspaper up to his face again. The paper brought her mind back to Arbour Hill again, and the second time she had upset him.

Like most of the families that lived in Arbour Hill in the late 1950s, the Malones didn't buy a newspaper every day. However, Fred bought two every day, and Sue used to bring the old papers over to her sister.

In addition to keeping the family supplied with paper to light the fire, Fred's extensive reading supplied the Malone family with enough toilet paper, and, when it was raining, floor mats. It was always on a Saturday afternoon when Fred came over with the old newspapers. Una used to lend the pile of newspapers to her neighbour Joe Furlong. Joe always brought the papers back the next day, and there would be bits cut out from the pages that were packed tight with long columns of small print.

At thirteen Una could read, but other than looking to see what was on at the local picture house, she never bothered to read the newspapers. When she saw the parts in the old newspapers beside the strips that Joe Furlong hadn't cut out Una imagined she knew why her uncle bought so many newspapers every week.

'Have yeh not found a job yet?' Una had asked her uncle one Saturday evening when he was minding them while her mammy, daddy, and Aunt Sue had gone to the pictures. She had wanted to cry when he ran his eyes over the old summer dress she had been wearing for a nightie, then close his eyes and raise his newspaper to his face.

The worst part for Una that time was listening to her uncle snorting through his nose while she finished warming the milk for Maurice's bottle.

While Una was recalling her misdemeanours with her Uncle Fred, Josie continued to wind the perm curlers on Sue's hair.

Pauline said, 'Maura's wedding.'

'Then why won't Maura be seeing it?' Una asked.

Carl stood, pulled his jumper down over his waist then placed his hands on Josie's waist, gently pushed her forward and walked behind her towards the door, opened it then turned back and said loudly, 'Harry made a movie of our wedding and Pauline has it in her case.' He raised his voice loud enough to be heard in the marquee and added, 'It will be sad if you don't see it because Maura looks beautiful.' He then walked out leaving the door open.

'Then why isn't she going to see it?' Una asked, kicking the door shut.

Pauline walked the few steps over to the table and waited for Josie to answer.

Josie placed her hands on the sides of Sue's face and raised her aunt's head as if she was presenting Una a prize. 'It's the time, Una.' she said, taking another tissue off her mammy and winding the last curler on the front of her aunt's head. 'It's the time,' she repeated.

'Josie, we arranged it at all on Friday,' Pauline said.

'I know what we arranged on Friday,' Josie said nervously 'but this is Sunday and things have changed since then.' She pushed Sue's head down and started fiddling with the curlers on the back of her aunt's head.

Surprised that Pauline was upset about the film not being shown, Una raised her head from watching Josie.

From where she was standing, Una couldn't see the face in the photograph on the wall beside the one of Eileen, but she knew it was a picture of Pauline's girls. She imagined that Pauline must be upset because there were pictures of her twins on the film, and that she wanted the rest of the family to see them. 'What's changed so much since Friday, Josie?' she demanded.

The seconds seemed like minutes while Josie stared at her mammy's bowed head as if she was expecting her mammy to tell Una to leave the room. But Sheila Malone continued to iron the tissue papers with her fingers. She wasn't going to tell Una anything because she never did. She always left that to Josie.

'What's the problem with the time?' Una persisted.

Josie didn't know because she hadn't asked why when her mammy had suggested they shouldn't see the film. She had just come back into the living room after she had been teaching the children to dance and Maura had been sullen so she didn't really care if the film was never shown. Right now all she could think of saying was, 'Maura won't be here for tea. She has decided to go down to her friend early.' She turned her head around to the clock.

Pauline moved back from the table. She was never able to fight Josie. She shoved her hands deep into the pockets of her trousers and worried about what she would tell her husband about why the family hadn't seen the movie. Whatever she decided to do she would be going back to get her children and she would have to tell him. She also knew he would blame her and not her mammy.

Believing that Pauline would forget about the movie when she moved away from the table, Josie bowed a weak smile of relief to her mammy.

Una wasn't worried about Maura seeing the film and she thought that Josie was right about the time. She expected that as well perming her mammy's and Sue's hair her mammy would also want her do cut Cathy's and Joan's hair as well. She stretched her hand into the table and picked up a tail comb. 'I'll finish winding Sue's hair and put the lotion on while you get Mammy washed and cut, and then I can wind mammy while you cut Maura's hair.'

'Una, if I need your help I'll ask for it,' Josie snapped, shooting out her elbow to prevent Una from getting near her aunt.

'I was only trying to help,' Una snapped and threw the comb back on the table.

This wasn't the first time Fred had watched Josie concentrate on doing something she had already done four times. It was what she always did when she was biding her time because she was afraid. He didn't know anything about the film that was upsetting the three girls, but he wondered what their mammy was up to as he watched her walk out of the room.

On many a Sunday afternoon, the light sounds of Josie's slippers on the worn carpet as she moved about behind Sue's chair had sent Fred to sleep. If today had been an ordinary Sunday afternoon he would be asleep because he was tired. His usual eight hours of sound sleep every night had been troubled during the past few months because Sue was fighting with her headaches again. Sleepy though he was, he recalled listening to Sheila's three oldest girls arguing since they could walk. He had also heard them shout and cry at each other many times. He had watched their mammy demand and receive more attention than any girl should be expected to give her parent.

On many occasions when they were still in their teens, Fred saw the girls worry and fret about pleasing their mammy when they wanted to go to the pictures or to a dance. And then watch them suffer pain and disappointment when, at the last minute, Sheila wouldn't allow them to go.

The boiler in the press beside Fred's chair gurgled again. Josie turned her head round to the fire. The silence was making her think and she never wanted to do that so she lifted her portable radio off the mantelpiece. The radio cackled and whined as she moved the dial to find a station with music then replaced it on the mantelpiece. As she walked back to the table Una walked over to the front window and joined Pauline.

Fred folded up his newspaper and rested it on his lap. He watched Josie read the labels on some bottles of liquid and tried to recall if Josie had ever disagreed with her mammy. Nobody had ever disagreed with Sheila, Fred concluded, and then quickly changed his mind. Una always said what she thought. He always felt something special for Sheila's third daughter. She was small and quiet. He was sure that Una bullied her as much as her mammy did, but he had never seen or heard Pauline complain.

Pauline was the first baby Fred held in his arms. At the time he had been courting Sue for three months, and Pauline was only two days old.

Ten children and eleven times pregnant, Fred counted as he waited for Una to say something to Josie. He never liked Sheila, and he never understood why Terry spoilt her so much. He remembered all the commotion when Sheila was pregnant before Maura was born. And he was bewildered when Sheila became pregnant again and again and again. But he knew it wasn't a coincidence when Sheila became pregnant so often just before a large bill was due to be paid.

Although it wasn't playing loudly, Fred wanted to stretch out his hand and turn off the radio: the Clancy Brothers singing 'The Holy Ground'. He liked the Clancy Brothers but he hated the song that was bursting from the radio.

It was the phrase 'Fine girl yeh are' that rankled Fred because he had heard women referred to as 'fine girls', just because they had given birth to six or more children. He picked his newspaper up from his lap and he was making his third attempt to read the same article when the Clancy Brothers bellowed out their last 'Fine girl yeh are'. With his eyes on the newspaper print, he told himself that there was nothing fine about a woman with ten children that sat on her arse all day.

'Are there towels in the bathroom?' Josie asked wrapping

Sue's head of curlers in a plastic bag. She wound her timer, then patted Sue's head and checked her clock again.

'I have no idea,' Una said, 'but there are plenty in the hot press.'

Josie didn't have the time to wait in the hall while her mammy completed her stroll up and down the garden path, so she walked quickly over to the hot press. Then as if her life depended on getting the towels, she yanked the door open and pulled the first towels she saw. Along with three towels, underpants belonging to her brothers, was the bag Pauline had kicked into the bottom of the press when she was getting Eileen's clothes. 'Who moved this bag?' she asked.

Fred turned to see the bag. 'Your mammy did when you were washing Sue's hair,' he said.

'They were on the windowsill when Joan cleared it for you,' Una said, walking over with her arm stretched out and, taking the bag, added, 'I'll sort it out.'

Light throbbing in the back of Sue's head started to spread down towards her neck. It was time to take her tablets. Dear God, she prayed, as she started to tidy up the table, make me do something. She wished she could swallow something to ease the heaviness in her heart. She didn't want to see a film of Maura any more than she wanted to go to the Glen. She had been looking forward to spending the evening with all her nieces together.

Half of Sue's mind was on Pauline as she gathered up pieces of tissue paper. The other half was wrestling with her feelings for her sister Sheila. She chastised herself for all the years she had watched her sister bully her children and hadn't tried hard enough to stop her.

When Sheila had walked out of the room, Sue knew that her sister was manipulating Josie. She didn't know anything about the movie or the plan to show it, but she suspected her sister had set Josie up to change the plan. Although the room was warm tiny streams of perm lotion running down the side of her face made her shiver. The liquid was cold and the sensation of anything touching her face aggravated the awful headaches that had returned since Christmas. The tightness along her nose and down the sides of her face would soon develop into a fierce pain in her head. She knew the headache she would have in half an hour wouldn't be the result of the perm curlers or the cold lotion.

Pauline was standing at the window watching her mammy walk down the path for the third time and raise her head to the sky as if she was worried about the weather. She had never wished poor luck on anyone, but right now she smiled at a vision of the clouds opening and her mammy running back up the path to find the hall door closed.

'Is Mammy out there?' Josie asked, pulling back the net curtains just as her mammy was walking back up the path again. She waved her arm to indicate to her mammy to come in. She had moved away from the window as her mammy turned round and walked back towards the gate.

Sue looked up as Josie walked out of the room. She felt sorry for Josie because she knew her sister succeeded with exploiting and controlling her more than she did her other children. She stood up straight and inhaled deeply like her doctor had told her to do whenever she felt the pain in the back of her head. Her stomach felt better when she exhaled but the headache was growing so she decided to take two of her pills. She waited until she heard her sister and Josie walking down the lobby to the bathroom.

'I just want to get a glass of water,' Sue said when she walked into the kitchen. She didn't care that neither Maura nor Carl answered her while she took a tumbler off the shelf above the table. She saw that Maura's eyes were red and suspected she had been crying, but she didn't care about that either.

The dish on the windowsill over the sink unit that held the remains of a bar of soap and a rusty Brillo pad didn't look silver any more. Sue wondered what had happened to the little silver spoon that come with the dish and recalled that when Maura was born the family were in need of more important things than a silver dish and spoon. Her memory rolled back twenty-one years and two months and she wondered if Maura would be as spoilt as she was now if Terry had agreed to Sheila giving the baby she was carrying to her friend Pam O'Hara in return for paying a very large bill. It's not the girl's fault she is spoilt and stupid, Sue thought as she tossed the two little white pills into her mouth, then chased them pills down her throat with the water.

Returning to the living room, Sue saw Fred folding his newspaper to a more manageable size. She wondered what he was making of the fuss about the movie. After all, it was his godchild's wedding, and because of her headache they never even came over to her party. She recalled he had never liked Maura, and although he had always given Pauline the most attention she believed that Una was his favourite.

A smile curled around Sue's mouth, recalling Fred laughing when he had told her about Una asking him if he was always looking for a job in the newspapers. 'She will be a match for any man she married,' he had said. Sue wasn't wishing Pauline's problem upon anyone else, but she believed that out of all Sheila's children Una would manage on her own no matter how far away from home she was. And Una would never write and ask her mother if she could come home. She would just come.

Fred always went shopping with Sue for the children's Christmas presents. He never complained when she also bought them socks, vests, and knickers, even after they bought the toys he insisted on getting.

Twice Una had been given a second present. Fred had

always been adamant that she should have something with a pair of scissors, a bottle of glue and some sticky paper. At Fred's insistence, they bought four different colours of paper to wrap the presents in. Even the boy's presents had to have ribbon around them.

'We could treat them to the pictures for the cost of the paper and ribbon,' Sue had protested the year they had only six presents to buy.

'That'll only last a few hours,' Fred had insisted. 'Una will make them all something nicer from the paper and the card that'll last a lot longer than that.'

Unable to stand the silence in the room any longer, Sue said, 'I take it Cathy and Joan are gone to the pictures?'

'I don't know,' Una said, turning round from the back window where she had returned the contents of the bag neatly to the windowsill. 'I told the pair of them to go off and do what they liked before Mammy came in from the marquee.' She picked up her mammy's handbag off the floor and put the two bills into it.

From the window where she was standing, Pauline saw Cathy walking down the road with two other girls. She didn't say anything in case Sue wanted her to go for cigarettes.

'There's only enough room in the kitchen for two,' Una continued, recalling Sue used to say the same thing to her when she was Cathy's age. The other one who used to do the washing up was her daddy. 'Cathy and Joan have enough to do when we aren't here.'

Sue wanted to hug Una, and she wanted to say that at least they have less to do than when Pauline and herself were living at home. It hadn't come as a shock, or even a surprise to Sue, when her sister's older children emigrated. She often wondered why they hadn't run away from home when they were younger. She used to think it was because they wouldn't have left their daddy. Now she wasn't so sure.

Recalling a promise she had made to Terry, Sue sat down on her sister's easy chair beside the fireplace and allowed her mind to wander back to the Saturday afternoon in the hospital before he died.

The ward had been as quiet as the living room was now, and Sue was sitting on her own at the side of Terry's bed, trying not to think about anything. Even now thinking back, it felt like both a long and a short three days. So much to be done in a short time, and every day had felt like a week. There were still times when she wondered how Terry could have played cards on a Tuesday and, by the following Tuesday, be lying in his grave.

Staring into the flames of the fire, Sue imagined she could see Terry's handsome face when he opened his eyes and said, 'Will you look after Sheila?' The memory made her feel cold. She picked up a towel and held it to the dribble of perm lotion running down the side of her nose. The coldness of the liquid and the smell of the perm lotion made her feel nauseous. Just like she had been in the yard of the hospital, when she had gone out for a cigarette after Fred and Sheila had come back into the ward.

It was unusual to see her aunt sitting down staring into the fire. Una asked, 'Are you all right, Sue?'

Sue stood. 'Just warming my head from the cold lotion,' she said, and went over to the table and started sorting through Josie's bottles, tubes and curlers.

On and on, the silent train of memories moved through Sue's mind, with more and more little memories jumping on each time she closed her eyes to block them out. She could hear every sound in the house; water running in the bathroom, and Josie talking. She could hear the legs of the old stools scraping on the tiles in the kitchen across the hall. But it was the whispering of Pauline and Una over at the window that bothered her.

The silence was broken when Josie came in. 'Should you not be going down for Shea, Una?' she demanded as she guided her mammy, who had her head wrapped in a towel, to a chair as though her mammy was blind. She cast her eyes up at the clock and said, 'Don't you think it's time you got a move on?' she ordered.

Pauline walked out.

'I'm not going,' Una said, turning round from the window in time to see Fred peep over the top of his paper at Josie. She watched Josie rub her mammy's hair with the towel until her sister lifted her mammy's head up and started to comb her hair back from her face and repeated, 'I'm not going down for Shea.'

'That's up to you,' Josie said. She combed her mammy's hair in the same place for twenty seconds. 'You know that Sue won't see him,' she said. She wasn't concerned about anyone seeing Shea; she wanted Una to go somewhere so that she wouldn't ask about the film of Maura's wedding.

'I never thought about that,' Una confessed, moving her eyes away from the top of her mammy's head to her aunt's face and added., 'Sue won't see Pauline's babies on the film either.'

The little clock Josie had wound buzzed.

Una sat down at the table and lit a cigarette.

'We still have three minutes,' Josie said, removing the plastic bag from Sue's head and nodding a weak smile at Una

Una didn't respond to Josie's nod, nor did she offer to rinse the perm lotion from her aunt's head. She smoked her cigarette and watched Sue sort out the perming curlers while she waited for Josie to ask her to do it. She followed Sue's hands as they moved across the stack of perming curlers. They were spread across the table and Sue was sorting them into groups of colours and sizes. 'Anyway,' she said, 'it leaves me free for the evening, so Pauline and myself are going to the pictures.'

A soft thud came from the fireplace. Una looked over to the grate in case a briquette had fallen out on the hearth but they had only burned down and collapsed. The fire needed more fuel. She though that Josie could worry about it so she watched Sue move the curlers about for another five minutes, then crushed out her cigarette and left the room.

Another thud from the fireplace and Josie turned round. She needed a good supply of hot water. 'I'll just get more briquettes for the fire,' she said, putting her scissors on the table.

'Tell Maura to get them,' Sheila said.

'Won't take a minute,' Josie said, nodding to her aunt. 'Come on, Sue, I can rinse your hair and bring the briquettes back in with me.'

The door to the kitchen was open enough for Josie to see Maura sitting on one of the stools. 'Give me fifteen minutes to wind Mammy's hair,' she said to her scowling sister, 'then wash your hair.' She followed her aunt down the lobby to the bathroom.

Fred was stunned that Josie had left her mammy to rinse Sue's hair. He was about to lower his newspaper to steal a glance at her when she walked over to her chair beside the fireplace and retrieved her handbag. Una hadn't closed it properly so as she picked it up it opened. 'Who was at my handbag?' she asked.

'Una put some letters into it,' Fred said. 'They were in a bag Josie pulled out of the hot press when she took out the towels.

Chapter Forty-five

For five minutes while Josie doused the cold, wet ammonia smelling liquid on her aunt's hair, she talked about the new long and short-life perms that were now very popular with her customers. Sue raised her eyebrows and nodded her head and wondered how the girl could ignore how upset Pauline was.

Josie unwound one of the curlers, 'It has taken a lovely curl,' she said, smiling at her mammy.

Sheila nodded her head in approval as if the roof wouldn't fall in if her sister's perm hadn't been successful.

'You're a great hairdresser, Josie,' Sue said and went back to sorting the curlers. She didn't want to hand the tissue papers to Josie so when her niece placed the little white bundle on the table in front of her, she slid them over to her sister's hands.

The curlers reminded Sue of people. There were long, short, thick, and thin curlers of all different colours. Sue thought that some of them looked happy because of their bright colour. While she was trying to find a group for a couple of old grey ones, she thought about her own parents and went on to think about when she and her sister were children.

As she twisted and caressed the two old grey curlers in her hand, Sue tried to recall some happy or warm memories of her own childhood. All she could remember was school and the maids that had looked after them when they had come home. She also remembered that she hadn't cried when her da had died. She remembered that Sheila hadn't cried either.

Most of the tension and hostility over the movie had evaporated after Una had left the room. But Sue still worried about Pauline. She doubted that Maura would become a friend, or even a companion to Pauline, like Una was.

Thinking about sisters as friends, Sue thanked God that she had never needed help or support from Sheila. Unlike Pauline, she had her ma. She had cried with her ma's arms around her every time she was disappointed when her doctor had told her she wasn't pregnant.

'Don't worry about the curlers, Sue,' Josie said, nodding her head at the small plastic bars that were spread on the table. 'I can use one or two of yours if I need them.' She moved the pack of tissue papers back towards her aunt's hand.

'I think you will have enough curlers,' Sue said and stood. She closed her eyes at the packet of white fine papers and moved away from the table. The easy chair was only four feet from the table, but she was sitting behind Josie so her niece's voice wasn't as loud while the stupid girl continued to prattle on about her business.

The two of them are in a world of their own, Sue thought and yet they are so different. Josie gives generously, and her mammy takes greedily. She closed her eyes and rested her head on the back of the chair. When she opened them she saw the blurred images of the photographs on the wall in front of her. She didn't need her glasses to see them because she knew every picture in the nine frames. Her favourite was a postcard portrait of her ma.

Sue closed her eyes again and recalled the day her ma had told her about when she had the photograph taken. It was the happiest day of my life, her ma had told her. Her brother had brought her to Dublin to buy her wedding dress. Sue imagined she could see her ma's kind gentle face as she went on to tell her about having tea in Jury's hotel. The teacups were so thin she could see the liquid through them, and the plate was lighter than the wafer-thin sandwiches.

Although her ma had seldom used the china tea set her brother had given her for a wedding present, Sue remembered her ma used to take it out of the cabinet every month and wash it. When she had given the tea set to Flo after her ma had died every flower and gold ring on every plate, saucer, and cup on the tea set were as bright as the first time Sue had seen her ma wash them when she was about four years old. She closed her eyes and thought back over her own life and what her ma had told her about da.

Sheila and Susan Duffy grew up on the south side of Dublin where their parents owned and worked a prosperous grocery shop in Clanbrassil Street. They never played out on the streets with other children. Da Duffy didn't think it proper for his children to mix with his customers.

Ma Duffy came from Cavan, a town outside Dublin. She married the serious and hard-working young man that had impressed her father, after the boy had come to work for them when he was sixteen years old. He had lived with a small farming family and in return for his bed and food, he helped with the animals. During the day he delivered groceries on his bike around Cavan for Ma's father.

It was after her da had died that her ma had told Sue that the cold and calculating manner her da displayed probably grew out of his childhood experiences in Cork. Her ma told her he was weaned on the worst stories about the famine and the ferocious way the British had treated the Irish before the country had won its independence. With help from a young priest, the sixteen-year-old Duffy boy boarded a train for Dublin the day after his grandmother was buried and never went back.

Sue already knew some of her Irish history but she listened attentively when her ma told her that at the time Ireland had numerous political and economic problems. And that her da never bothered who ran the country as long as neither himself nor his family had to spend their time sitting around, either inside or outside pubs, drinking stout and talking about the good or bad old days.

Sue's ma told her she would have liked more children especially a son to carry on the business her da had worked so hard to build. Sue didn't ask her ma if she didn't, or couldn't have any more babies.

The smell of turf oozing from the burning briquettes reminded Sue of the country. She had no idea if the people in Cork dug turf but her ma had told her that her da had cut the sods. She imagined it was hard and dirty work and she tried to feel sorry for him. She had never liked her da and she always thought her ma made too many excuses for him because he was so mean.

Money doesn't grow on trees, was one of Da Duffy's constant remarks. He paid for a live-in maid for the house rather than employ an assistant for the shop. Also, and more important, with his wife working as his assistant, he didn't have to worry about money going missing from the till

Although he never went back to his hometown in Cork, Da Duffy wrote regularly to the young priest who had helped him to leave. Her ma told Sue that every time he met the train from Cork, he prayed for his grandmother because the evening a few days before she had died she had told him that his mother hadn't been married. He prayed that the young girl he was meeting to work in his house would not be pregnant

Sue could remember six different maids, and she never missed any of them when they left. She never missed a maid at all until three months after Sheila's eighteenth birthday when her da died suddenly of galloping consumption and all three of them moved into a rented house. Ma Duffy's brother helped her to sell the shop and invest the money so that she would be able to live the rest of her life without having to work again.

Sue finished two more years at secondary school after her da died, and she never earned as much money as Josie, or Una, and both of them left school at fourteen with a primary school certificate. Sheila never earned much either when she worked for one of the best shops in Grafton Street, where she served many of the most affluent Dublin ladies.

Closing her ears to Josie droning on about her customers, Sue thought: no wonder the girl has nothing else to talk about with the meagre education her mother had allowed her. The poor girl barely finished primary school before she started work.

Sue went on to recall Sheila had spent her money on herself. Most evenings after work she would have her tea her in Bewleys, and the best seats at the cinema in town with her friends from school or work. Her memory began to get angry recalling the only times they had together were Sunday afternoons in the summer when they would cycle out to Portmarnock and meet other groups and go for a swim in the sea. Some of the groups were made up of boys. They would all cycle home together late in the evening, singing Irish ballad and rebel songs.

By the end of the summer when Sue was twenty she was attracted to a shy young ginger-haired man with a slight stammer. She didn't care that his family reared pigs. Sheila laughed, but when she learned that his family also owned a row of terraced houses in the city she started talking to him. Terence Malone was more impressed and flattered by Sheila's attention than by Sue's, and it was Sheila he married eighteen months later.

With anger in her heart for her sister and her husband,

Sue moved back to the table while she thought what a cheek Terry had to ask her to look after her sister. How dare he!

After allowing her thoughts to go back over her own teenage years, Sue was ashamed of seeing her niece as boring and stupid. When she leaned into the table to get the curlers for Josie, she heard her sister breathing through her nose. Sue wondered if the lotion on Sheila's head had turned to ice by the severity of the expression on her face as she stared at the wall in front of her.

When the little timer went off again Sue stood. 'I'll manage, Josie,' she said resting her hand on her niece's shoulder. 'I'll take my time and I'll call you if I need you.' She needed to be on her own to think about what she would do to stand up to her sister over Pauline.

Without her glasses Sue couldn't see the extra lines on her forehead when she looked in the mirror on the windowsill in the bathroom. But four basins of hot water had rinsed away the neutralizer and her head was warm. After a bout of sneezing she blew her nose, wrapped her head in a dry towel and sat on the edge of the bath. She didn't need her glasses to search through her memory for what Sheila's friend Ena had told her about Harry Harper. She still found it hard to believe what she had been told, but she had no trouble with seeing the motives behind Sheila's reason for preventing Pauline from leaving him.

Sue knew that Pauline would have to decide for herself about leaving her husband, but she would find a way to get the movie shown and give Pauline proof that her mammy had received her letter. She left the bathroom with a warmer head and phoned Sheila's friend Ena.

Chapter Forty-six

When Pauline heard the bedroom door open she pulled her knees up tighter towards her chin. She was lying with her face towards the wall on the double bed inside the door.

Welcoming the silence, Una lay down on the bed beside her sister and tried to make some sense of what was going on downstairs since Pauline had walked out of the kitchen when they were washing up. She turned her head towards the wall and listened to Pauline sobbing for a couple of minutes. 'There's nothing wrong in crying, you know,' she said. 'It's good for the eyes. Gives them a good wash out.' She waited a few seconds and said, 'Anyway, you and I are going to the pictures tonight.'

Pauline stretched her legs down the bed, turned onto her back and asked, 'What pictures?'

'Whatever is on at the Star', Una said, lifting her leg and wriggling her toes.

The springs on the old bed squeaked when the sisters shifted their bums and elbows until they were both lying on their back and gazing at the ceiling.

Fifteen minutes earlier, when she had walked out of the living room, Pauline hated Josie. She could still see her sister's long slender arms curled round her mammy's head and shoulders as if her mammy was blind and needed to be guided to the table.

Una continued to raise her legs and wriggle her toes.

'Do you do exercises?' Pauline asked.

'No, I don't,' Una retorted, 'do you?'

'Every day since the twins were born,' Pauline said. She stretched her legs down the bed and tucked her hands under the small of her back.

'You must have looked like a little elephant.' Una said raising her head off the pillow and looking down at her sister's stomach.

'How can you talk like that to anyone and then complain about Josie?' Pauline said raising the top part of her body sharply off the bed into a sitting position then touched her toes.

The springs on the old bed squeaked like angry birds when Una moved her body around so she could straighten the candlewick bedspread with her feet.

Pauline put her hands under the small of her back then raised the bottom half of her body towards the ceiling.

'You really do take it seriously, don't you?' Una said rolling over towards the middle of the bed so she could try and throw her legs up towards the ceiling. When she tried to lift her shoulders onto her elbows she dropped her head back down on to the pillow. 'This bloody bed, she moaned, 'I'll bet you a pound to a penny that the mattress hasn't been turned for over a year.'

'I'll give you the penny,' Pauline said, shooting her feet up to the ceiling again. She couldn't hold her legs up because of the dip in the bed so she lowered them. 'It never made any difference to the dip when the mattress was turned. I always thought the lumps were worse.'

'We made the lumps when we used to jump up and down on it when we were children,' Una giggled. She shifted her body so that her arm would move away from the cold iron bar. 'I can't remember ever hearing this bed creak when mammy and daddy used to sleep in it.'

'They probably had sex during the day when we were playing out in the street.' Pauline said recalling how much she used to enjoy sex with Harry when she was first married.

Jesus, Una thought lifting her head off the pillow, 'That's probably why we were sent off to the pictures on a Sunday afternoon,' she said recalling some of the things that the girls in the factory used to say about men and sex. She had been horrified at some of the stories they had told but she laughed with everyone else, though not as loudly as Jack did when she told him some of the stories she was able to remember.

'Can you remember what baby mammy was going to have when you first found out that she was pregnant?' Pauline asked.

Una laughed loudly. 'It was Joan. I was fourteen, and Josie told me.'

Pauline also enjoyed a hearty laugh. 'I was only thirteen when you told me. And it was another two years before I found out that the baby didn't get born through the belly button.'

'Josie told me about Joan when we were waiting for a bus to go to work. I often wonder if she would have told me at all if I hadn't been complaining about mammy keeping you home from school so often that she could stay in bed.'

'What did Josie say to you?' Pauline asked.

'I can't remember what she actually said to me,' Una said, 'but I remember asking her if daddy knew.'

Pauline lifted her shoulders off her pillow quickly and turned to look at her sister's face and asked, 'what did Josie say?'

'I really don't know,' Una said smiling at the memory of Josie's face when she had asked her. Then when she saw the smile fade on Pauline's face she raised her voice. 'That's what Josie said. She said, "I don't really know."'

The smile returned to Pauline's face and she flopped back on her pillow. 'Do you think she did at the time?'

'If I didn't know how a baby was conceived at that time, I doubt if Josie knew.'

If laughing could be seen the room would have been littered with whatever form it would take. The two girls laughed so hard they could scarcely draw breath. Even the squeaks from the springs on the bed softened, as if they were also enjoying the joyous mood in the room.

'It's hard to believe that there are empty bed spaces in the house now,' Una said, there is enough room for me to stay here now when I come home.'

'Would you come home for good?' Pauline asked.

'To Ireland, or to Plunkett Road?' Una asked.

'Ireland,'

'Not at the moment,' Una said, 'but one never knows what is down the line.'

'And Plunkett Road?'

Una thought a moment then said, 'I would have to be on my own because Jack wouldn't live on the same road as mammy let alone the same house. I wouldn't want to but with daddy gone now and Josie only coming for holidays mammy would be as easy to control as we were when we were children. What about you, would you come home to Plunkett road?'

And the children are all grown up now, Pauline thought. 'I never thought about it,' she lied, 'but mammy will never change.'

'She doesn't have to,' Una said swinging her legs off the bed. 'We all have to change and not put up with her tantrums.' She searched the floor with her feet for her shoes and when she found them she said, 'let's take Eileen into the village for a walk.'

For an awful moment when she saw the door to the small

back bedroom open Una thought that Eileen had got out of bed and made her way downstairs. When she went into the room Eileen was sitting up on the bed watching Maura search through the case that Josie had put on the end of the bed to stop her daughter from falling out.

Maura looked like a half drowned poodle with her thin wet hair clinging to her neck. She was half naked dressed only in her bra and pants. 'This is my room,' she said taking the garment she had in her hand and holding it to her chest. But she didn't hide the bruises on her arms and shoulders.

'I have come in for Eileen,' Una said stretching over to take the young girl. Her hand rested on the dress Maura had been wearing. The top half was all wet like Maura had been wearing it buttoned up to neck when she was washing her hair. She picked Eileen up off the bed and left the room.

Chapter Forty-seven

The smell of ammonia from the perm lotions floated out through the top window when Una and Pauline were walking up the garden path as they came back from their walk.

Una welcomed the sweet smell of shampoo that blew up the lobby when she opened the hall door just as Josie came striding from the bathroom behind Joan.

'Nearly done,' Josie called over her young sister's head as she piloted her into the living room.

'Take your time, Josie,' Una said.

'Just the two cuts to do,' Josie smiled at Pauline as though she was pleased to see her.

Pauline returned Josie's smile then un-strapped Eileen from the pushchair.

'Okay Sue.' Josie threw the words over to the back window whipping the towel away from Joan's head. The scent of the shampoo from Joan's hair helped to mask some of the remaining smells from the perms that lingered in the room.

Sue handed the hairdryer she had been holding to her sister. At the same time Cathy jumped up from the easy chair and ran out to the bathroom in front of her aunt.

Una winked at Fred as she walked over towards him and opened the top window over her mammy's head. Walking back towards Josie, she wondered if Fred was stuck to his chair. He looked as if he hadn't even moved his elbows since she had left the room and joined Pauline upstairs nearly two hours earlier.

'Una, will you hold the dryer?'

'No Josie, I won't,' Una interrupted expecting Josie was going to ask her to hold the hair dryer for her mammy. 'You know mammy's well able to hold it herself, and to tell you the truth, Josie, if I so much as hold a newspaper near her head right now, I would hit her with it,' she said, pulling the old circular skirt that Josie was using for a gown off the back of the chair and draping it around Joan's shoulders. 'You hold the dryer and I'll cut Joan's hair'.

'That's ridiculous,' Josie snapped, picking up her comb and scissors off the table and shoving out her elbows to form a shield over Joan's head.

Una was wrong about Josie not caring when her siblings were upset. Josie never forgot anything; she just chose not to remember because it was easier than fighting a battle with her mammy that she knew she would never win.

From the minute the hall door had closed, after her two sisters had tucked Eileen into her pushchair and left, Josie decided the problem over the movie had gone with them and she felt she was alone in the living room. When she was cutting her spoilt sister's hair, Maura hadn't spoken to anyone and nobody had said anything to her.

As usual, the music from the radio had soothed Josie's anxieties and helped her not to think about why her mammy didn't want the movie to be shown. She heard Fred rustle his newspaper, thanked Sue for sorting her curlers, and she was gentle with her mammy while she was winding the rollers in her hair.

Welcoming the distraction from the silent heaviness that had lingered in the room when Una and Pauline had gone, Josie greeted Joan and Cathy with a bright smile when they came in to have their haircut. Now while she was cutting

Joan's hair she started to feel uneasy again. There were times when she was as much afraid of Una as she was of her mammy.

'The boys are at the gate,' Pauline called from the door walking in with Eileen in her arms.

'Would you hang on a little while?' Josie said happily, shoving Joan's head forward. 'The cuts won't take long and we only have to hoover up. Sue has packed away all the curlers.' She wanted to help with getting the tea ready.

The Gallowglass Cheili band were playing a medley of waltzes on the radio as Una stood in front of Joan and watched Josie cutting her sister's hair. She swayed with the music and smiled at the wide grin on Joan's face.

Joan's grin was contagious and Josie smiled all the time she was cutting. Most young girls in England were wearing their hair short with a fringe, in imitation of the Beatles and Twiggy. It took Josie less than ten minutes to remove nearly all of Joan's hair. 'There,' she said, patting the sides of her sister's head. She snipped some more hair off Joan's fringe then raised her face to the back window and called out, 'It'll be dry in five minutes, Mammy.'

'You look lovely, really lovely,' Una declared. She touched Joan on the side of her face and added, 'Just like Maura.'

Joan knew that she didn't look at all like Maura, but she smiled back at Una. From when she could remember people had told her that she didn't look a bit like any of her older sisters. But just the same, she was delighted to have latest haircut. She turned round to her eldest sister and said, 'Thank you, Josie.'

'Not quite,' Josie said, 'Maura's hair is thicker.' She didn't notice Joan's smile fade. But then she wasn't thinking about how plain or pretty her young sister was when she raised her head over towards the back window again and smiled at her mammy.

God Almighty, thought Una, you can be a real bitch at times, Josie.

Out in the hall Sue and Pauline were teaching Eileen to climb the stairs when Cathy came out of the toilet. The door to the living room was open so they heard Josie say, 'I've cut it a bit shorter than Maura because young hair grows quicker.' She knew that her mammy wanted her young sisters' hair cut short so that they wouldn't have to go to the hairdresser's for a few more weeks.

Eileen was halfway up the stairs when the hall door opened and Donal and Liam came in.

'You mind Eileen,' Sue said to Pauline. I want to talk to Liam and Donal.' She then brought the two boys into the kitchen and closed the door.

'Where's Sue?' Josie demanded of Cathy when her young sister came in.

'I think she's tellin' Liam off fer somethin',' Cathy said.

Josie pulled in her chin and looked over to the door as if she expected to see Liam walk out with tears in his eyes.

Thinking that Josie didn't believe her, Cathy said, 'I saw her call him into teh kitchen.'

'Really?' Josie said, bowing her head, as if she was satisfied that Sue was telling Liam off for anything.

'Don't cut my hair any shorter than Joan's,' Cathy pleaded. 'It takes ages and ages te grow.'

Josie fixed her mouth in a tight grin, looked at Una, then started to comb Cathy's hair.

'No it doesn't, Cathy,' Una said. 'It just looks like it does because the ends curl back like mine and Pauline's.'

Josie smiled gratefully at Una.

'Besides,' Una continued, 'you will never have to have all those smelly chemicals on your hair like Mammy and Sue if you want it curly.' Watching Josie fighting with the tangles in Cathy's hair she added, 'It will also be easier and quicker to comb.'

Josie gave Una a nod of approval.

'Take your time Josie,' Una said, 'Pauline, Sue and myself will get everything ready for the tea.' She left the room.

When Josie had finished cutting Cathy's hair, Sheila got out of her chair and walked over to the hot press.

'I don't need any more towels, Mammy,' Josie said.

Sheila stretched her arm up to the top shelf and pulled at some old sheets. Everything that was on top of the sheets, including the bag that Una had stuffed up there came tumbling off the shelf onto the floor.

'I would have got that down for you,' Josie snapped. She could hear her sisters and her aunt's voices out in the kitchen and she wanted to join them. 'What do you want the sheet for now anyhow? We won't be showing the film,' she said as she went over to pick the mess up off the floor.

Ignoring her daughter, Sheila bent down and picked up the bottom of the bag. All the things spilled out on to the floor. She withdrew the letters Una had put into her bag from the sleeve of her cardigan and dropped them in the mess then walked back to her chair and left Josie to pick them up.

Frantic to get out to the kitchen, Josie scooped everything into the bag. She recognised the envelopes: 'You have some bills here you will be looking for, Mammy,' she said. 'I'll leave them on the bottom for you so you don't have to stretch up again.' She then pushed the bag into the press and closed the door. 'Come over to the chair now, Mammy,' she ordered, 'and I'll comb out your hair.

Chapter Forty-eight

While Josie was frantically combing out her mammy's hair, Sue, Pauline and Una were laughing and bumping into each other in the small kitchen as they prepared the food for the tea.

'Una! Where's Una?' Josie asked Maurice when he came out of the kitchen with a plate of bread.

'I'm in here,' Una called out from behind the kitchen door.

'Out here,' Josie demanded.

Una wiped her hands on a tea towel and reluctantly left the kitchen. She was curious to know what Sue had told her brothers off about even though she suspected it could not have been that bad, because they were also laughing. Liam came in three times and asked if they needed any help. She was looking forward to them all having their tea together. There were feet stamping up and down the stairs, doors opening and closing, and voices calling out everywhere.

'In the bathroom,' Josie ordered, ignoring the enquiring glances from Sue and Pauline.

Una obeyed, walked out to the hall and followed Josie down the lobby and into the bathroom.

The bath was full of mucky clothes that were just about covered with water. She knew what the clothes were and why they were there. 'I'm not washing them,' she said.

'I'll do them,' Cathy said, ducking her head under Una's arm.

'You?' Josie said loudly, her voice bouncing off the walls of the small room.

'Yes, me,' Cathy retorted sharply, placing her hands on the back of her head behind her ears as if she was holding her head on her neck. Her head felt cold with her hair cut away. Her expression softened when she looked at Una. It wasn't Una that had cut all her lovely hair away.

'Do you always do them, Cathy?' Una asked, nodding her head at the bath and the dirty football kits.

Cathy lowered her head and spoke into the bath. 'They give me a pound every time,' she said, leaning into the bath and shoving the mucky clothes under the water. 'All I have te do is teh put them in and out of teh machine fer a couple ev minutes, then hang them out on teh line.'

'A couple of minutes won't wash those,' Josie said.

'Or in teh shed if it's rainin,' Cathy continued as if she hadn't heard Josie. She stepped on Josie's toe when she moved so that she could turn on the tap. 'And if they're not dirty,' she continued, 'I just hang them in teh shed.' She felt Josie pull her foot away.

'That's fair enough,' Una said nodding her head in approval.

Encouraged with Una's support, Cathy said, 'I always take teh muck off them first.' She squeezed past Josie and leaned into the bath so she could pull the mucky clothes back and check that the plug was still in the outlet.

'What do you do with the money?' Josie asked, scowling at her little sister's bum.

'I spend it,' Cathy said, standing on Josie's toe again.

'Good for you,' Una said, delighted with her young sister for standing up to Josie.

'If yeh will get out of teh way, Josie, I'll put some powder in teh help them soak fer a while,' Cathy said quickly before Josie had time to shout at her for stepping on her toe again

'With so many of us here we'll need the bath so I'll have te do them this evenin'.' She sloshed the football kits around the water.

That's three pounds a week Una calculated, and thought how smart her little sister was for her age.

Cathy turned off the tap and raised her head defiantly to Josie and said, 'Sometimes I get more when they forget it's not their turn te pay me, or they have forgotten that they have paid me on teh Friday.'

Josie stared at the disgusting pile in the bath and although she wouldn't wash such stinking smelly clothes for three pounds a minute she said, 'How often does that happen?'

'Not often enough,' Cathy said, pulling Josie's hand off the hand basin. She then bent her knees so she could shrink her body down to the floor to get the packet of soap powder from underneath the sink.

'Well, at least you don't have to iron them,' Una said, watching the blue grains in the soap powder pouring into one of Cathy's hands. Recalling when she used to wash nappies by hand when she was Cathy's age, and with only a bar of soap she thought that maybe Cathy wasn't doing too badly. Also from talking to Angie when she was having her breakfast, she had a good idea of what her young sister spent her money on. She thought that Cathy went to the pictures too often, but she was pleased that Cathy was spending some of her money on food even if it were bags of chips and cream cakes.

'I'd give it back if they asked,' Cathy said, holding her cupped hand full of soap powder steady while she bent her knees again to put the packet of soap powder back under the sink. She tilted her hand and watched some of the soap powder slide off and run into one of Josie's slippers. 'Sorry, Josie,' she said when her sister pulled back her foot. She stood up quickly and threw the remains of the soap powder into the bath.

While Josie was standing on one foot and shaking the soap powder from her slipper into the hand basin, Una watched Cathy move the clothes about in the bath. 'I wouldn't give them back their money,' she said. 'If they don't want to pay you they can always wash the kits themselves.' She leaned over her sister's back and helped her to move the dirty clothes around in the soapy water.

The fine soapy grains had blown into Cathy's face when she threw the powder into the bath, and now they made her sneeze a couple of times. She rubbed the back of her hand along her nose and turned round to the hand basin again. Her nerves were tight and the sneezing made her eyes water. She could hear Liam shouting from the hall and she remembered him telling her that neither Josie nor Una had any right to tell her what to do. Her brother's voice gave her some cour-age. She sniffed twice and turned on the tap. 'Then I won't either,' she said.

The water was cold but Cathy's hands were sticky from the soap powder. She wondered if Josie would be able to get all the soap powder out of her lovely slippers, but she didn't care.

Josie dropped her slipper on the floor and tried to ease her foot back into it.

'That stuff's sticky, Josie, isn't it?' Cathy said. She didn't care if Josie knew she had spilled the washing powder into her slipper on purpose. She thought her snobbish sister had plenty of money to buy herself new slippers – and anyway it served her right for cutting her hair so short. 'I'll do them when I've had me tea,' she said and left the bathroom, drying her hands on the sleeve of her jumper as she rolled them back down again.

'I wonder how often she gets three pounds a week,' Josie said when Cathy left the bathroom.

'She won't be overpaid, and they can afford it,' Una re torted and moved to go back into the kitchen.

The unpaid bills Josie had picked up off the floor fluttered before her eyes, 'If the boys can afford to give Cathy a pound a week then they can afford to give Mammy more money,' she said.

Una closed her eyes and thought: will she ever give up? She wanted to get away from her sister as much as she wanted to leave the reek that came from the muck and the detergent in the bath.

Josie removed her slipper again.

'Mammy will never have enough money, no matter how much any of us give her.' Una said. 'I admire your generosity Josie, and always have,' she continued, 'but has it ever occurred to you that you have always made things difficult for the rest of us?'

Josie pulled her head back as if Una had smacked her.

'If you're worried about Cathy getting money from the boys then you do the washing while you're here and give the money to Mammy,' Una snapped.

The stink from the bath bothered Josie as much as the thought of washing the clothes. She increased the intensity of her stare into the dirty water, but the football kits still wouldn't vanish.

'At twelve years of age Cathy is too young to be doing any washing. But at least she is getting paid for it. I never was and I was washing when I was ten,' Una reminded her sister.

Josie continued to stare into the bath.

The last of the bubbles from the soap bursting reminded Una of the popping sounds that came from the potato guns her brothers used to play with. She hated the smell of the dirty bits of potato when she used to clean them up and this brought her thoughts to when they were talking about the different jobs that women and men do. 'The boys could do their own washing and some housework as well,' she said.

'Even so,' Josie said closing her eyes at the wet floor. 'Even so,' she repeated, tossing her head back as if she was shaking some unwanted snow off her hair, and as if she could blow away the bag with her mammy's unpaid bills that she returned to the hot press.

Even so was a common enough expression that meant, 'just the same' and whenever Josie said 'even so' Una knew that her sister wasn't able to think of anything else to say. After a few seconds of watching her sister struggle with her slipper and the corner of a towel, Una echoed, 'Even so, Josie what do you think about Cathy doing washing at all at her age?' She snatched the slipper and the towel off her sister and removed the soap powder. 'Try that,' she said, dropping the slipper on the floor.

'That's much better.' Josie smiled gratefully, sliding her foot into the slipper.

'What about Cathy doing the washing? And the boys doing some of the housework?' Una persisted. 'Do you think you should have a chat with Mammy about Cathy being so young and doing so much? And the boys '

Josie didn't have to concentrate long to understand that what Una had said was correct. Her mammy would never be satisfied, no matter how much money she was given. Cathy was too young to be doing washing, and her brothers could so some cooking and housework like her daddy had. Mike did all the ironing since Una had taught him how to do his shirts. He even enjoyed doing it. However the thought of suggesting any of this to her mammy, coupled with the stench from the bath made her feel sick.

'Well Josie,' Una encouraged. 'I think if Mammy will listen to anyone it will be you,' she lied because she knew that Josie wouldn't say boo to their mammy. She didn't really care; she would be satisfied if Josie would stop expecting the rest of them to be like her.

The football kits hadn't moved, and the walls hadn'

changed colour but Josie ran her eyes over them twice. She bowed her head and said, 'I think you are absolutely right. It's up to Cathy and the boys.' She glanced into the bath again and added, 'I just hope she gets them out of there after tea in case Mammy wants to have a bath before we go out.'

Una wanted to close the door to the room and not open it until Josie told her why she was so afraid of their mammy. If she had, and Josie had unblocked her memory and told her Una would have started a different relationship with her sister. But Una didn't know this so she said, 'Mammy will never change, Josie, but we can, and for Mammy's sake we will have to.'

Josie continued to stare into the bath.

Una continued, 'It's unlikely that Pauline, Maura, yourself, or myself will come to live here for good. And I think that it is also likely that within the next six years Joan and Cathy will also be living away from home. We can't un-spoil her but we can stop.'

Josie raised her face to the window.

'Let's get on with the tea, Josie,' Una said and walked out of the bathroom wondering if her mammy would meet her match one day when Cathy was a little older.

Chapter Forty-nine

The temperature had dropped below the middle fifties but the marquee retained some of the warmth that had come from the afternoon sun. The big tent seemed brighter than when the family were having dinner.

Maurice walked in with two plates of cut bread. He smiled at his mammy, who was sitting at the top of the table hopeful that she would be in better temper now that she had her hair all curly

Sheila clenched her teeth, closed her eyes, then bowed her head to her joined hands.

Not for the first time Maurice felt as if his mammy had slapped him across his face and as usual when his mammy displayed anger he blamed his older sisters. His negative attitudes towards his older sisters stemmed from the summer after Cathy was a born. It was also the year they had moved from Ballymore, and ever since that time he blamed his older sisters when his mammy had a cold, a headache, a toothache or a pain in her belly. He even blamed Josie when his mammy had a corn, because he believed Josie had bought her the wrong shoes. 'Your hair is very nice, Mammy,' he said.

Sheila raised her head and stared in front of her as if her son had asked her to get up and sweep the floor.

Maurice put the plates of bread on the table and turned to leave.

'Stay where you are, Maurice,' Josie ordered, walking in with the plate of meat.

Maurice continued to make his way down the side of the marquee and he was halfway down when Una walked in carrying two bowls of lettuce. 'You may as well move up, Maurice,' she said, 'because everyone else is on the way out and we can manage to bring out the rest of the food.' She held one of the bowls out to him. 'Put that one in front of Mammy so she won't have to stretch for it.'

Ignoring Josie was easy for Maurice but he knew that although Una seldom told him what to do she always expected him to do as she asked. He took the bowl and put it on the table in front of his mammy and was about to make his way out again when Donal, Joan, Liam, Pauline, Cathy, and Sue marched into the marquee like soldiers on parade carrying trays with food. Fred followed with the big teapot and walked up the side blocking Maurice's exit. Maurice had no option but to sit down beside his mammy. By way of excusing his mammy for the angry mood she was in, he allowed his thoughts to dwell on his older sisters again.

Saturdays were the worst days for Maurice when all the family were living at home. Una didn't work on Saturdays and it was nearly half nine when she would get up. She always made porridge for the breakfast. She never made toast for his mammy, but she always had enough time to wash and polish the kitchen floor, change the sheets on all the beds, and hoover all the other floors.

Nearly every Saturday morning was the same, and Maurice was sure that his mammy didn't like Una because she used to stay in bed until just before half past one when their daddy would come in from work. Una never made his mammy toast to go with the stew. It was always his daddy that made his mammy's toast. Maurice also hated the three hours in the afternoons when Una was doing the ironing because she used to send him upstairs with different bundles of clothes to put into the wardrobes. He knew that his mammy hated that time, as well, because she used to walk around the different rooms and she never closed any of the doors after her.

Sometimes Sundays were even worse for Maurice when Josie was home as well, but Josie always made toast for the breakfast, and she often made Yorkshire puddings for the dinner even if they had sausages.

Maurice never knew or wanted to know what his three sisters used to fight about on Sundays. They always closed the door of the room they were in, but he knew that they were fighting because he could hear Una and Josie shouting. Then one Sunday his sisters had been fighting more than usual, and three months later the family moved to Ballyglass. Ever since that time Maurice believed the move had something to do with his sisters fighting. He recalled this time now because since shortly after Christmas his mammy was behaving the same way as she had then.

It was eleven years ago now, but whenever his older sisters were upsetting his mammy Maurice's mind would go back to their last summer in Ballymore. He was only nine at the time but he remembered the fighting between his three older sisters for weeks, and that afterwards his mammy was sick.

The scorn his mammy had shown him when he came in with the bread encouraged Maurice to feel little hammers trying to pound nails into the back of his throat. It was the same Sunday afternoon when he had come home from the pictures and found his daddy sitting on his own in the kitchen crying. At the time he thought his mammy was dead or that she was going to die. His sisters had been very quiet all morning after the doctor and the nurse had left, and Josie had given Sean money to bring all the younger children to the pictures.

The only times Maurice would remember that Sunday

were if he was early for mass and he would shove it quickly to the back of his mind. Una had sent them off to mass so early that Sunday they were in the church before the altar boys lit the candles. They also had their dinner early, and he had been so hungry he ran home from the picture house looking forward to Pauline's apple pie for his tea.

Two months later they moved to Ballyglass. His mammy hadn't died, he never saw his daddy cry again, and his sisters continued to argue and fight with each other. As these memories condensed and sped across Maurice's thoughts like a flash of lightening, he stole a glance at his mammy. She continued to stare at her hands as if she was measuring how long her nails had grown since she had last looked at them.

The smell of tea dragged Maurice's attention away from his mammy's hands. Fred filled the cups and Una passed them up and down the table.

'Come on everyone,' Pauline called out, 'let's eat before the tea gets cold, and butter melts.' She handed Maurice three large plates and said, 'Pass one to Mammy and one to Josie.' After he had handed his mammy a plate and placed one on the empty place in front of him for Josie he filled his own plate with lettuce, cold pork, and tomatoes. The smell of the meat brought his thoughts to Josie again.

When he had heard that Josie was going away to England, Maurice was delighted, and he had believed that his mammy was pleased. Although she had been very quiet and she had walked around the house, she didn't slam the doors. Then when Una was getting married and going to England, Maurice became hopeful that his mammy would be home more often when he came in from school. Because Una did so much housework on Saturdays and Sundays, he believed that his mammy went into town or to Arbour Hill to see her friends on Mondays because there was nothing for her to do.

Two things changed for Maurice when Josie and Una

went away. He didn't have his hair cut so often, and he had a little more room to move his arms when the family sat down to dinner together on a Sunday. His mammy was always at home for dinner on a Sunday, so they never had turnips.

Whenever Maurice saw turnips, he thought about his sister Una. She used to cook turnips at least four times a week. She would peel and chop them in the evenings and leave them steeping in a pot of water until she came in from work the next day. He could smell the yellow vegetables all over the house. Although she cooked turnips sometimes, he missed Pauline when she went to Canada. She had to work on Saturdays in the shop so she had two afternoons off every week. She always made rissoles for dinner on Tuesdays and Thursdays and she never cooked turnips.

'There's no doubt about it, Josie, but yer a great girl fer pickin' out a joint ev meat,' Liam said, stretching his hand into the table for a slice of bread.

'Yeh know yer fat from yer lean parts,' Donal cut in. He loved roast meat.

'Yeh should join her on the football club fer a while and have her pick out teh best players,' Liam said, glancing down the table at Maurice.

'I don't know the first thing about football,' Josie said, smiling in appreciation at her brothers for praising her cooking.

Returning Josie's smile, Liam said, 'Yeh don't have know about any sport to pick out a good team. All yeh need te do is look at how fit they are.'

Una had no interest in sports, but she was afraid that Liam would tease Josie again, so to stop him she said, 'Josie's talent is in cooking.' She looked at Maurice and added, 'You could get her to teach you while she is here during the week.'

Pauline was still uneasy about standing up to her mammy but she had no qualms with embarrassing Maurice. She raised her voice and said firmly, 'Don't say it is a woman's job because all the famous chefs are men.'

Fred was used to Una firing off at all her siblings but this was the first time he had heard Pauline speak up so strongly. He was also concerned over the movie that was to be shown and the tension that was in the living room before she had walked out. 'Women's sports have never been popular in Ireland,' he said, hoping to take the conversation away from men cooking. 'Schools have never even encouraged girls to do the cheaper sports, like running,' he added.

Una's memory shot back to when the family had lived in Arbour Hill and she had borrowed a hurling stick from a friend. She hadn't minded that it had taken her more than an hour to walk up to the Phoenix Park. She loved the cheers from the side of the field when she ran after the ball, but to be on the team properly meant she had to turn up two evenings a week and Saturday mornings.

'Convent schools do sports,' Pauline said, stretching her arm into the table to get a slice of bread.

On the rare occasions when Josie thought back over her early years they were always about her days at school. The mention of the word convent triggered her memory now and she recalled when she was twelve and she used to come home from the shop with the bread. Every Thursday at half past four, the same three girls from the local convent school passed her on the way to their tennis lesson. How she had loved those short white pleated skirts, and the way the girls used to swing their racquets as they stepped into the road so they could continue to walk three abreast.

Pauline knew her mammy and Sue went to a convent school so she raised her voice like she had heard Cathy do and asked, 'Did you do sports in school, Mammy?'

Eileen banged the spoon she was playing with on the tray

of her chair like she was demanding everyone's attention to hear her granny's answer.

Sheila stood, then stretched her hand into the table and picked up the plate with the coffee cake and tilted it away from her. The cake started to slide off the plate and would have ended up on the table if Una hadn't picked up the plate with a couple of slices of bread and caught it. 'That was a stupid thing to do,' she snapped. 'All you had to do was ask me to pass it to you.'

Sheila sat down, smiled at Sue and said, 'Only when I had to.'

No Sheila, Sue thought, smiling back at Sheila, you won't threaten me any more. The memory of her thoughts in the quiet living room after Pauline and Una had gone out for their walk were still so fresh she could fill a book with them. The memory of when Sheila had broken a girl's ankle out of spite slipped easily into her thoughts as if it had happened that afternoon. She stared coldly at her sister and said, 'We played hockey in school.'

Fred always thought that some day Sheila's children would have enough of her manipulating them and fight back. He was pleased to hear Pauline speak to her as though the selfish woman was a stranger, but he worried about Sue because of her headaches. He knew about Sheila not being allowed to play games in school after she had used the hockey stick on a girl's ankles. He was also unhappy with the way Sue had stared at Sheila, so to change the conversation he raised his cup of tea as if he was making a toast and said, 'I hope we will have many more parties, perms and blue rinses before Cathy gets married.'

'I'm never gettin' married, or havin any children either,' Cathy bellowed.

'Good,' Una said, 'I think we can all contribute and send you to a good convent school then.'

'I'm fine where I am,' Cathy retorted. 'I don't want any nuns beatin' me.'

'How do you know the nuns beat the children?' Maurice asked.

'Doreen's ma told us,' Cathy said. 'She went to a convent school.'

Maurice wondered if the nuns had beaten his mammy when she was at school but he was afraid to ask her because he didn't want to know. He made another effort to eat his cake but no matter how many pieces he divided it into he still didn't want to put it in his mouth. As he brought his finger up to his mouth to lick the cream the smell of coffee made him remember when he was sick, and he had been very sick when he was five years old.

Whenever he smelt coffee Maurice would imagine he was sitting on a stool by the fireplace in the living room in Arbour Hill. He was too sick to go to school that day. He didn't know he had fainted, and he didn't remember banging his head on the fender, but he remembered the strong smell of coffee that had come from the black syrup in the long square bottle his mammy's friend Ena was pouring into a hot cup of milk. He didn't remember going into the hospital, but he remembered feeling dizzy all the time he was in there. He also remembered that for weeks after he came home from the hospital, Pauline and Una used to put a plenty of marmalade on his bread.

'I go ice skating in the winter,' Pauline said.

'Do thee mean like waltzin' around with music and everythin'?' Cathy asked.

'Sometimes,' Pauline said. 'It depends on where you go. I'll take you if you come out but it will have to be winter and it is very cold. The only thing I don't like about Canada is the cold in the winter.' She looked at Joan and said, 'You could both come out for Christmas.'

'It would take years te save enough money,' Cathy bellowed.

'You won't need any money,' Pauline said. 'I will buy your tickets, and give you all the money you need when you are there.'

Doubting that her mammy would allow them to go Una said, 'And I'll make you both some warm clothes.'

'We will need passports to go to Canada,' Joan said meekly, recalling the day she had picked up her mammy's photograph.

'I'll treat you to passports,' Sue said.

Sheila Malone shoved her chair back from the table and Josie closed her eyes.

'If yeh don't like it over there,' Maurice said, 'then why don't yeh come home?'

'I'm thinking about it, Maurice,' Pauline said as her mammy walked past her.

Younger than Maurice by ten months, Donal had shared beds, bottles, and nappies with his brother when they were babies. He was an assemblage from all the Malone children He had an oval face and straight hair like Josie, thin like Liam's. He was as quiet as Joan, and like Pauline he never argued with anyone. Like Sean he was always happy to see his older sisters when they came home. He was always smiling, and like Cathy he never seemed to worry about either pleasing or upsetting his mammy. He thought it would be great for Joan and Cathy to have a holiday in Canada. 'Will yeh come home before Christmas?' he asked.

'Certainly not if Cathy and Joan come out,' Pauline said ,warming to the idea even though she also doubted her mammy would allow them to come.

Una glanced at her watch and said, 'Let's get cleared up or we will be late for the pictures.'

'Leave them,' Sue said and looked from Una to Pauline a couple of times then nodded her head at Donal. 'I hope you won't be annoyed with me,' Sue said, resting her hand on the table in front of Pauline. 'I asked Donal to set up the projector while we were getting the tea.' She paused when Pauline glanced over at Josie then continued quickly, 'So we could see the movie that you brought with you.'

'Now?' Josie gasped.

'Yes now,' Sue said firmly, moving her eyes to Una, 'but if you'd prefer to go to the pictures, it's all right, I won't mind in the least'.

The spindly legs on the table squealed as if in pain from the pressure it was bearing. It hadn't stopped wobbling after Donal and Liam had pressed down on it so they could get up off their seats. Joan and Cathy were also holding the table while they threw their legs over the bench.

Una didn't want to go to the pictures any more than she wanted to see the film of Maura's wedding, but she was delighted that Sue had stood up against her mammy so she felt the least she could do was to support her. It might even put an end to all the misery of the afternoon. 'Great,' she said and swung her leg over the bench.

'Maura's not here,' Josie moaned as her mammy was walking back into the marquee.

'That won't make any difference,' Una said, watching her mammy sit down again. She wasn't going to allow her sister, or her mammy to stop the family from seeing the movie now. 'Maura doesn't have to be here, Josie,' she said gently, 'Pauline brought the film for us to see.'

Soft sharp tingles creeping up the back of Sue's head told her it was nearly time for her to take her tablets again. But her head felt warm, just like when she was in the bathroom and she had decided what she would do to get the film shown. From what was said, and not said in the living room when Pauline first asked about the film, Sue was sure that Sheila had managed Josie and she felt sorry for her niece. 'Maura chose to go out this evening before anyone even tried to see if we could show her movie,' she said.

Like all bullies when they are faced with more than one person that was fighting back, Sheila sat quietly as if she was on trial.

Una moved her eyes from her mammy's grey face to Pauline and said, 'And Maura also knew that Mammy had written to Harry to tell him not to forget to send the movie with you.'

Although Josie had agreed with her mammy earlier in the day she had no idea why her mammy changed the plan they had made to show the film. 'I didn't know that,' she said apologetically to her mammy as though it was someone else who didn't want the movie to be shown.

Sheila stared angrily at her sister, then lowered her face to her hands.

Chapter Fifty

Dull green was a weak substitute for black but the new curtains blocked out enough light in the room for the family to see the movie.

Liam pinned a white sheet to the curtain on the back window, and Donal mounted the projector on a chair.

'Where's Mammy? Josie asked when she walked into the room after putting Eileen down for the night.

'She's on her way in,' Liam lied. He had no intention of waiting for his mammy to start showing the film.

Josie sat down on a chair at the table.

Donal had already started to roll the film when his mammy came in from the front garden. She made her way over to her easy chair beside the fireplace and sat down.

Carl was right. Maura was beautiful, but Pauline's house and garden were stunning.

No wonder she needed a gardener Una thought as the camera completed four tours of the large house with three dormer windows in the roof and a double garage.

The film started with pictures of Maura leaving the house for the church, then Carl and Maura walking out of the church. The remainder was taken back at Pauline's house.

'Who is that?' Cathy called out when the camera zoomed in on a large woman dressed in pink sitting at a table eating.'

'That's Carl's mother,' Pauline said.

'She seems to be enjoying her dinner, 'Liam said as the camera zoomed in on the table laden with food.

'Did you do all that cooking, Pauline?' Josie asked.

'Harry had caterers in,' Pauline said, leaning her body towards the screen in an effort to see something in the distance on the film.

The quality of the twenty-minute film was poor compared to the cinema, and even though there was no sound the family watched in silence. The Toronto spring sun beamed on everyone and everything. The bright colours of the clothes, the shiny cars and the fresh green of Pauline's garden made the film look like the introduction to a Hollywood movie.

During the first showing, Pauline explained where each shot was taken and who was in the film.

Josie was bored, Sue was sad, and Una was angry.

If a picture paints a thousand words, like many art collectors never seemed to tire of saying, then the film that Donal was trying hard to keep steady on the chair painted a thousand different words to every one that was watching it.

Josie didn't have her own garden, so Pauline's was of no interest to her. All the women wore hats so she couldn't see their hairstyles and apart from Harry, Pauline and Maura she didn't know any of the other people.

Though she was still nursing feelings of resentment against her dead brother-in-law, Sue was glad that Terry wasn't there to see there was so few of the family in any of the pictures. Whatever doubts she had about why her sister didn't want Pauline to come home faded before the film was finished.

Una was angry because the family had been upset all day over the stupid showing of a piece of rubbish. As it turned out, there were only a few clips of Pauline's twins, and most of those were taken at a distance.

Only Cathy and Joan seemed to be enjoying it. They were enthralled with the glamour of the big cars, the flowers, the satin ribbons, all the dresses, and the hats. Donal rewound the film a few times so they could see parts of it again.

Sheila sat in silence and worried. She had worried before, but this was the first time she didn't know what to worry about the most.

Chapter Fifty-one

Una glanced at the clock while she shuffled the cards. 'Two more rounds, she said, 'and you two are off to bed.'

Joan shrugged her shoulders, smiled, and moved her tiny pile of money coins about on the table.

'Three more,' wheedled Cathy. With her mass of hair cut away, her head seemed smaller. 'And if yeh don't stop tellin me what te do all teh time then I won't swap yeh back yer Irish money fer me English.'

'Then I'll just have to throw my Irish money in the Liffey when I'm on the boat, like I usually do,' Una returned. She winked at Pauline and dealt out the cards.

'Why do you do that?' Pauline asked when the fifth card flicked on the table.

'Don't mind her,' Joan said as she picked up her hand of cards. 'Una always gives us her Irish money before she goes back to England.'

'She never gives us her pound notes, though, does she? Cathy cut in.

'Why do you give your Irish money away at all?' Pauline asked picking up her cards.

'Because I can't use the Irish money in England,' Una said throwing a coin into the middle of the table. The penny chimed out a dead tune until it stopped rolling. 'Okay Cathy three more rounds after this one, then off to bed,' she said smiling at Joan. 'You have school tomorrow.'

'I'll open fer an Irish shillin,' Cathy called out. Before she had sat down to play cards she knew that Una was going to talk about school. For one thing she always did, and for another when her sister was helping her to wash the football kits earlier, she kept talking about what she could and couldn't do when she got in from school.'

Pauline moved the coins about in her bank searching for a small silver coin with a harp on it. 'I don't have an Irish shilling,' she said.

Except for the three-penny bit and the sixpence, all the Irish coins were the same size and colour as the English ones. The English coins were accepted in Ireland but apart from occasional use in vending machines, the Irish coins were not used in England. Nevertheless, Irish people had no problems using a mixture of both currencies in Ireland.

Una searched through her pile of coins: 'If you want to play,' she said, 'then give me your English shilling and I'll put a florin in for the two of us.'

Pauline slid her English shilling over to her sister.

'I hope you have a good set of openers, Cathy,' Una said holding her youngest sister's worried stare for a few seconds.

'Teh only thing yeh need te worry about is that I have me openers,' Cathy returned, bringing her elbows up onto the table. She hid her face behind her little fan of cards and added, 'I know teh rules and I don't cheat.'

'Proper rules, or Granny Duffy's rules?' Pauline asked.

'Are you good at bluffing?' Una asked, moving her cards about, then placing two of them near the centre of the table in front of her. 'I'll play,' she said. She watched her sisters pull their cards in and out of their fans and glance at the two cards she had put down. She suspected they were trying to decide if she was bluffing because she held three cards in her hand.

It was a long time since Pauline had played cards, and she had never enjoyed playing poker. Like all her brothers and sisters, she sat down with her Granny Duffy and learned the rules of the game. But she could never keep up with the rules that her granny kept changing, and adding to. She never lost any money when she played with her Granny Duffy because Sue used to give them all the money to play with in the first place.

Fred told Pauline that bluffing was about making other players think that you held cards that you didn't have. But just the same, she always thought that it was cheating. Her Granny Malone had never cheated, and she never had to be minded or allowed to win anything. Pauline never played cards with her Granny Malone, but she liked her the best. She studied her hand of cards as though bluffing was excluded from the game.

Pauline won the kitty. She held two tens and got another one when she asked for three cards. Cathy showed her openers of two Jacks. Una didn't have to show her three sevens but Cathy said, 'Well played, Una,' when she saw them.

Does she really need me to moan at her, Una wondered smiling back at the sad and defiant shine in her young sister's eyes? She also thought she could save herself a great deal of worry if she allowed everyone to take care of themselves in their own way. But she knew that saving herself worry wouldn't help Cathy, and she also knew that Josie, Pauline and herself would have been smarter if they had been allowed to go to school and she couldn't allow that to happen to Cathy. She sat up straight and said, 'I don't suppose it's a lot better than when we were going.'

'What is?' Pauline asked dealing out the cards.

Eighteen, nineteen, twenty, Una counted the cards Pauline was dealing, then picked up her own five cards. 'School,' she said. She made a little fan with her cards and continued, 'Just the same, I liked school, but I bunked off one day.'

Joan laughed heartily.

'It's the truth,' Una insisted, 'I really did like school, and I did bunk once, and I managed to get my primary certificate.'

'That's right, and I remember it well,' Pauline said, placing three cards near the centre of the table. She moved her coins about and added, 'You were lucky that you didn't get pneumonia instead of your primary.'

'I'm not sure it was as bad as all that,' Una returned. 'But just the same I should think that you would remember because it was you who really paid the price.'

'Is anyone openin'?' Cathy called out.

'I will,' Pauline said sliding a coin into the table. 'I'll open for one of these.' She threw an English sixpence into the centre of the table. 'I'll have two cards.'

Joan also played and took two cards.

Cathy stared at her hand of cards as if she could will one of them to change. She didn't have two matching cards in her hand so she leaned back in her chair and said, 'I'll pass. I'll just listen te yer conversation.'

Una saw Joan's bet of a shilling with two sixes. 'I though you were bluffing,' she lied when she saw Joan's three fives. She wanted her sister to win the money.

Cathy smiled triumphantly at Una.

Along with losing her mop of hair Cathy also lost a couple of years. Instead of looking a couple of years older she looked a couple of years younger.

Dear God, Una prayed, while she shuffled the cards, for Cathy's sake help me to get this right. She knew from Angie that her sister was close to getting into very serious trouble because she was skipping school so much. And she knew that Cathy was worried about it.

Cathy already knew about how awful schools were years ago because Angie had told her. She wanted to know why Una had played truant. 'How did yeh nearly get pneumonia?' she asked.

'Because when I came home from school I was soaking wet,' Una said smiling, because Cathy wanted to know. 'It was raining all the afternoon and I didn't have anywhere to go, so I walked around the streets and got soaked to the skin.'

Some of the stories that Angie had told Cathy about about schools were so dreadful that she didn't believe half of them. She knew her older sisters went to old schools like Angie, because they used to live in the city at the time. However, she thought that it would be true about getting pneumonia from being out in the rain all day. 'Why did yeh mitch?' she asked.

Una recalled she had been frightened when she had decided not to go in through the hard iron gates all those years ago. She now felt ashamed because she had never given any thought to Pauline, and she knew that her sister had suffered afterwards.

'Did yeh get an awful hidin' or somethin'?' Cathy persisted. The defiant attitude she had adopted as a defence against her sister's sermon about going to school melted when she saw Una raise one of her hands to her mouth and bend her head. She thought her sister was going to cry.

But Una wasn't going to cry, she was trying to prevent herself from laughing. 'No, Cathy,' she said, 'I didn't get a hiding. I liked school because I liked learning but I hated most of the teachers. I managed with my Irish and my English because I was good at writing stories, and I was great with my sums.'

'It's easy te go te school when yeh know everythin', Cathy,' said. 'I don't mind me sums,' she continued, 'but its teh angle things that I can't get teh hang of at all.'

Angles? Una had no idea what Cathy was talking about because she had never been taught any geometry. But her sister's softer attitude prompted her to say, 'I suppose I was a vain little bitch because I used to love holding my hand up when I knew the right answers. I think it made up for being kept back in the same class so often.'

'Why were yeh kept back?' Cathy asked.

Pauline didn't know that Cathy was skipping school. 'For poor attendance,' she explained. 'We were all kept back because we were absent so much.'

'They're both too young to remember,' Una said, 'we were both working when Cathy was born.'

'Yez must have done a lot ev mitchin',' Cathy gasped.

Most of the children that mitched in those days were also suspected of shoplifting and Una didn't want Cathy to think that any of her older siblings brought shame on her family so she said quickly and firmly, 'I was the only one that ever did any mitching.'

'Did yez get hit in school?' Cathy asked.

'We were all hit in school,' Pauline said, closing her right hand into a fist like she used to so the sting from the cane wouldn't go up her arm.'

'Was Josie hit?' Joan asked.

'What were yez hit fer?' Cathy asked.

'Being late, not having jotters, or pencils, broken nibs, not learning our tables, or catechism,' Una said.

'For whispering answers to your friend,' Pauline cut in, 'then both of us got the cane.'

'The reason why I mitched that day,' Una said, 'was because I had been away for two weeks and I didn't think that I would be able to answer all the questions the teacher would ask us.'

Pauline didn't know that but remembered the water running down Una's face when her Granny Malone brought her home.

'Where did you go?' Cathy asked.

'I left home as if I was going to school. I went to mass and stayed in the church praying until everyone else had left. I then walked up and down Manor Street as if I was shopping I was home in time for dinner. It was raining when I left the house again and when I was in the Phoenix Park the heaven opened.' The memory of the heavy rain that day made her imagine the water was running down her back again. She unwound her fingers and entwined them again leaving her two index fingers straight, like the steeple on a chapel and said, 'I was a long time ago now.'

'And that's how you got soaking wet,' Joan said, sounding like she was going to cry.

Una felt she had relived the day all those years ago. She wanted to tell Pauline she was sorry for the year that followed but her memory was so sharp now that she wanted to tell her young sisters how Pauline had suffered as well so she said, 'When I turned into Oxmantown Road, Granny Malone was standing on the pavement.'

'That awl cow,' Cathy roared. She lowered her shoulders and laid her fist on the table. 'Did yeh tell her everythin'?'

The vision of her Granny Malone standing under her wide black umbrella in the middle of the pavement brought tears to Una's eyes. She sat back in her chair and locked her eyes with her youngest sister and said, 'Cathy, I was soaking wet I was so wet that the cardboard in my shoes was all squashed between my toes.' She calculated she had been a year older than Cathy at the time. 'I was tired, and I was terrified.'

'That woman'ed frighten anythin',' Cathy said. 'Mammy used te go green in teh face when she saw her walkin' up te garden path.'

'I didn't have to tell her anything because she knew,' Una said. 'She was on the bus and she saw me walking along the North Circular Road. She brought me home and put me to bed.'

Pauline wanted to tell Cathy that their Granny Malone was the nicest woman she had ever known but right now she thought it was more important to continue with when Una had come home drenched. She rolled a penny coin on the table and said, 'No, she didn't. I put you to bed. I remember that very clearly because I woke Liam up when I was looking for the hot water bottle.' She raised her head to Cathy and said sternly, 'Granny Malone was not an old cow.'

'That's right,' Una said, 'Liam was only a few months old.'

'Was it winter time?' Cathy cut in, concerned that Pauline had spoken so firmly.

'No. It was the end of April,' Una said, turning her head to Joan. 'You were born just after Christmas that year.' Una didn't want to talk about the last few years when the family had lived in Arbour Hill. She was afraid she would tell them things they didn't need to know until they were a lot older. She pointed to the deck of cards that Joan was still holding and said, 'Deal the cards for one more game.'

But Cathy's curiosity was roused now and she wanted to know more. 'Did Granny Malone not say anythin' te yeh at all?' she asked. 'And how did Pauline pay teh price fer yer mitchin'?'

School had never given Pauline any pleasure. She couldn't do her sums and she couldn't write stories. She had never minded when she was kept back because for a while at least, she wasn't the worst pupil in her class. She was small, so she didn't look two years older than most of the other forty-five girls that had been crammed into the stuffy room. And because she was small, she was allowed to sit in one of the middle desks. She used to feel sorry for Josie and Una when they were kept back because they were much taller, and were made to stand or sit at the back of the class. She continued to play with the penny. 'I didn't pay the price,' she said. The coin made a sharp click when she put it down on the table. Her emotions had settled down since she had seen the movie. The fear of not pleasing Harry was now faded from her mind like a toothache recedes when a bad tooth has been pulled. 'What Una is saying is that she wasn't kept away from school any more,' she said, 'but that I was.'

Cathy stared at the coin in front of Pauline and counted the children that were in the family at the time that Una had mitched but she was more interested now in why Una hadn't got a hiding than why Pauline had been kept away from school. She wanted to know but was afraid to ask if one of them had been in one of the terrible big grey buildings with the high wall around it that Angie had told her about when children were taken away and put into because they didn't go to school.

Every time Cathy remembered the attendance officers Angie had described she expected to see one walking up the garden path.

Even if the man Angie had told her about had wiped his nose, or wasn't wearing his red knitted gloves with the fingers cut out, or wasn't carrying his big thick exercise book with the navy cover and the red stripe down the back, Cathy knew that she would know him. He probably wouldn't be still wearing a grey rubber cloak and matching hat with stitching around the edge to keep him dry when it was raining, because the women would never let him into their house.

But Cathy would know, if a small man with a limp came walking up the garden path, that he was coming to take her away. She ran her hand down the back of her head and wondered about Josie. For the first time since before tea, Cathy didn't miss her hair. 'Did Granny Malone not do anythin' at all?' she asked.

'I'll tell her,' Pauline said firmly to Una, 'you were in bed.'

Una lowered her head to her hands and worried. Even before now, she regretted she hadn't spent much time with her younger sisters since she had left her family home. There were no children in the house now for Cathy and Joan to look after so they were bound to have an easier time with their mammy and she wondered if they needed to know how hard she had been on Pauline, Josie and herself.

'I remember that I was disappointed with Granny because she didn't take her coat off,' Pauline began. 'The first thing she did was put a penny into the gas meter and boiled some water. She then made two cups of cocoa. She brought a packet of biscuits out of her bag and gave me three of them to take up to Una with one of the cups of cocoa. When I came back downstairs she gave me two biscuits and told me to drink the other cup of cocoa. When Maurice, Maura, and Sean came in from school, and Donal from playing out, she gave them the rest of the biscuits. She then sat at the table and waited until five o'clock before she sent Sean around to Ena's to tell Mammy she was waiting to see her.'

Una remembered the biscuits, and how cold she had been.

'We can finish with playin cards,' Cathy said. She was afraid Una would insist herself and Joan go to bed soon and she wanted to hear about the granny she could only remember seeing twice. 'Go on and tell us what Granny Malone did.'

'Cathy,' Pauline said with tears in her eyes, 'I don't know what she did.' She wiped her mouth with her hand in an effort to stop her tears from falling then said, 'When Mammy came in, Granny Malone walked out to the scullery. Then when Mammy walked out after her, she closed the door. I went upstairs to see if Una was all right and when I came back down, Granny Malone was walking out of the hall door.'

Una didn't want her young sisters to go to bed with sad memories of the family. 'We still have time for another round,' she said.

'Do yeh want te swap fer me English coins before I go te bed?' Cathy asked.

Una smiled and said, 'It can wait until before I go tomorrow.'

'That's right. Yeh'll still be here when I get in from school,' Cathy said, winking at Pauline.

Chapter Fifty-two

Sparks flew up the chimney and fell into the hearth when Pauline jammed the poker into the fire to break up a couple of half-burnt briquettes. She could hear her two younger sisters talking while they were walking up the stairs. She wanted to beat the briquettes because she felt like beating something. She would never have hit Cathy, but she had wanted to slap her when she had said that her Granny Malone was an old cow.

There were fewer sparks when Pauline rammed the poker into the fire a second time. She felt some relief as though she had defended her Granny Malone. She used to feel the same way when she was a child and had been to confession. She always used to imagine she left her sins behind her when she slapped the bushes while walking down the church steps.

The bright light and the heat from the soft embers of the turf in the grate encouraged Pauline to feel as if she was coming out of a dark room. Her Granny Malone had had a very hard life, and she had lived to be ninety. If the embers hadn't looked so soft, she would have beaten them again. She settled for putting more briquettes on the fire while Una was making them tea.

The fire seemed dead when Una pulled the two easy chairs over to the hearth. She nodded at the foggy smoke that was twirling up the chimney and said, 'Put the blowers on for a minute or two.'

'Do the neighbours still borrow this thing?' Pauline asked as she kicked the bottom of the square sheet of tin she had put over the front of the fire to make sure it was steady.

'Not if Cathy answers the door and they don't have a shilling in their hand,' Una chuckled.

'She's smart,' Pauline said.

It was just gone ten. The two sisters ate slices of coffee cake, sipped their tea and listened to the purring, and soft sharp thumping of the hand on their daddy's clock as it jumped around the seconds.

Pauline tried to gather all her family together into one patchwork quilt like they used to be before she had left her family home. One second she would see them as they had been before she had gone away, and another she was seeing them as they are now – grown up and talking like adults. Still she nourished the memories of when they were children. In some ways her young siblings were easier to look after than her own two girls were now.

One of the briquettes in the grate slipped and spouted a blue flame. Pauline shoved her chair back. 'I want to turn the light off,' she said, getting to her feet. 'It's like old times in the dark,' she said when she sat back down again. With talking about when she was a child living in Arbour Hill, her memory was on a roll and she wanted to bring back as many memories as she could to Canada with her because she had decided she would not come again while her mammy was alive.

Soft rapid flashes of lights coming from the fire roamed around the ceiling as though they were looking for a place to rest. They reminded Pauline of birds. 'I love the smell of turf,' she said, smiling at the fire that was now starting to flare up the chimney. She saw many visions in the flames as they changed colour and danced around the briquettes. 'Children in Canada don't play out on the street like we used to,' she said, recalling winter evenings when she would come in from playing out and the only light in the living room came from the fire. 'It's a wonder none of us were killed from the swings that we used to make on the lampposts,' she said recalling more memories she had long forgotten.

'At least we weren't in a war zone,' Una said, raising her foot and wagging it at the fire. She usually enjoyed talking about her childhood, but now after talking about when they had been deprived of their schooling she didn't want to go there again, so, to change the subject, she said, 'The people in London were much worse off than we were when we lived in Arbour Hill. Our turf was wet, but we could leave it in the hearth to dry. Some people in London couldn't even get poor-quality dirty coal.'

Not now, please Una, not now. Pauline thought closing her eyes. She didn't want to hear about other people's troubles. Right now she had enough of her own. But her sister's reference to the war brought her thoughts back to her Granny Malone and Cathy again. She could see her tall, proud, white-haired grandmother wearing her tiny wire-frame glasses as she hugged a brown paper bag of white flour, and thanking God for the end to the war. She sighed, thinking that she would gladly give all the money in her bank account right now if she could just talk once more to her Granny Malone. A slight curl grew around her mouth.

'What are you smiling at?' Una asked.

'The wireless,' Pauline said her thoughts still on her Granny Malone. She had lent the family a wireless one Christmas. When her daddy had carried the huge box into the house she thought it was a wooden gas meter because it was so big. The living room used to feel warm on a Saturday after her daddy had washed the floor. 'Daddy used to get a good fire going all the time,' she said, still thinking about the wireless, and how the fire used to blaze up the chimney.

Like all men who worked on a building site, Terry Malone would bring blocks of wood home from work. Every Saturday he used them to get a good fire going before he placed the tub in front of it and filled it with hot water. After he had bathed his children he washed the floor.

'Thanks to Granny Malone,' Una agreed.

'I don't remember Granny Malone ever lighting the fire in our house,' Pauline said frowning.

'She never lit the fire,' Una said wondering why Pauline was smiling. 'But she sent us down a fairly regular supply of dry turf and logs.'

'I never knew that.'

'Oh yes, our Granny Malone was a shrewd and smart woman,' Una said, raising her voice. 'She filled her garage with turf and logs a year before Germany invaded Poland.'

Pauline didn't know the significance of Germany invading Poland, and she didn't want to know and to prevent Una from telling her said, 'We learned all the latest songs from the wireless.' The first sounds she had heard from the wireless was the voice of a man who sounded very posh. The only light in the room had come from the fire because her daddy had to take the plug out of the light socket so that he could plug in the wireless.

'Do you know that I have never heard Mammy sing?' Una said.

'Neither have I,' Pauline said, recalling the atmosphere of those winter evenings when they had lived in Arbour Hill She didn't know that the family sat in the dark because it saved money on the electricity bill. Now, with her mind on times that she seldom tried to remember, she could almost hear her daddy whistling softly as she, Una and Josie sang the songs they heard on their Granny Malone's radio.

'They used to sing in England during the war,' Una said trying again to move the conversation away from Arbour Hill

'They probably had more radios over there,' Pauline said recalling the radio her mammy had bought on hire purchase a few years later.

Una's memory of when they used to listen to the radio was also alive now. 'The very first mystery I ever heard was when I listened to the Perry Mason serial,' she said. 'It was *The Case of the Martyred Mother*. I can't remember if it was on every night or every week but I actually used to pray that we would be able to tune the wireless in.'

'That wasn't real,' Pauline asserted and laughed.

'It was to me at the time,' Una insisted. 'I actually lit a candle so that Perry would find the mother, or the child, I forget which now.'

'Was that on Radio Luxembourg?'

'I think so.' Una laughed too. 'God, I don't think I will ever forget all the radios blaring out the latest songs on a Sunday night when we used to listen to the top twenty on Radio Luxembourg.'

'Harry loves his records,'Pauline said,'and he's always playing them. Whenever I sing he puts on a record.' She paused and glanced over at her sister with a guilty smile. 'Maura sings to his records.'

'But Maura can't sing,' said Una.

'I know, I know.' Pauline glowed with suppressed laughter at the memory of her daddy encouraging Maura to sing and repeated, 'I know, but I'll never tell her.'

Laughing at the memory of scenes of her daddy trying to get Maura to sing, Una thought, God knows, the girl had tried. She recalled how their daddy had insisted they all listen as Maura murdered another new song. 'I thought Maura knew she couldn't sing. What does Harry do when Maura sings?'

'He sings with her but he can't sing either and I'll never tell him either.'

'Are you kidding me?' Una had never known Pauline to be unkind.

'I'd only have to listen to the pair of them practising,' Pauline said, laughing at the memory of Maura and her husband singing.

The long blue flame twisting like a corkscrew in the centre of the fire held Pauline's attention. She watched it spinning slowly for a while before she asked, 'Did you hate Jim Byrne before you were married?'

Una looked down at her outstretched feet, 'I didn't marry Jim. I married Jack.' She had never met Harry's father. 'Is Harry like his father?' she asked.

No, but he's getting there, Pauline wanted to say, but she knew she would have to tell her why so she said, 'His father is very fat.'

Una held her mug in her lap and gazed at the flames while her thoughts crawled over the scene of Maura in the bedroom when she had gone in to get Eileen. 'Tell me about Maura,' she said, 'because I don't know her any more?'

'Maura is just like you have seen her this weekend. Spoilt and selfish,' Pauline said into the flames, waving up into the chimney like blue and yellow flags, and tried to recall what she had written in her letters to Una since Maura had come out to Canada. It was like trying to do a jigsaw puzzle without a picture to help her.

Una raised her head to the soft sharp thumps of the clock and saw it was gone eleven. She wanted to be gone from the house when Josie and her mammy came back from the Glen. Until now she hadn't said anything to anyone about the dark colours she had seen on her spoilt sister's arms. 'I saw some bruises on her arms when I was in the room getting Eileen,' she said.

Pauline nodded her head as if she knew and said, 'He probably shook her when she was screaming to get her way over something. There were times when I felt like shaking her myself.'

'It's not her fault, Una said, thinking back to the day she had heard her mammy telling her friend Ena how she had tricked her daddy into believing she was going to give the baby she was pregnant with the her friend Pam O'Mara.

'It is her fault,' Pauline said, 'but that is no reason why he should shake her.'

'I meant it is not her fault that she is spoilt and she has always gotten her own way when she screams,' Una said. 'We have all spoilt her.'

Pauline nodded her head knowingly again and said softly, 'I didn't know how spoilt and selfish she was until she came out to Canada.'

'When we were all living at home she was one of ten and although she always got what she wanted there wasn't much to give her then,' Una said as though she was talking to herself. She wondered if Pauline would be lonely on her own now so she asked, 'How often is Harry away?'

'Sometimes five days, it depends on how far away he has to go.'

'What does he sell now?'

'Beer,' Pauline said. She was tempted to tell her sister that he wasn't making the money he put into her bank account from what he earned as a rep for liquor. She looked down at the mug in her hand as though it would tell her what to say next. The aroma from the turf reminded her of the awful smell in the small room Harry used for an office. 'He also sells some things for his father,' she added and closed her eyes against the vision of the short fat man that came for dinner every time Harry came home.

'Will you miss Maura?'

Pauline sighed. She was tired of telling lies. 'No,' she said firmly, then continued quickly, 'I was pleased when she asked

263

to come out because at the time I thought she would help me with the twins. But instead I had another child to look after.'

Una nodded her head in agreement as though she had also had Maura living with her. 'We are all to blame,' she said again.

'We were too young to know any different,' Pauline said staring into the fire.

'We weren't supposed to know why she was so special to Daddy,' Una said and told Pauline what she had heard her mammy telling Ena when she was in the kitchen and her mammy and Ena were sitting by the fire.

Pauline raised her head from the fire. 'Do you think she really would have given Maura to her friend?' she asked.

'I have never thought about it, but I think she would give her away now,' Una replied, then added quickly, 'You are the only one I have told.'

Pauline smiled: 'I wonder what Josie would say if you told her now?'

Una wondered what her mammy would say if she told her she had heard her telling her friend Ena. 'I must admit I have been tempted to tell Josie many times, but much as I fight with her I don't want to hurt her.' She retrieved her packet of cigarettes from the mantelpiece. 'There is no need for any of the family to know. It won't un-spoil Maura now,' she said taking a cigarette out of the packet.

'Do you like Ena?' Pauline asked.

Una lit her cigarette. 'Yes,' she replied, 'and I like Pam.' She smiled as she added, 'I have often wondered what the pair of them see in Mammy to remain friends for so long.

Images of her mammy's two friends appeared in the flame Pauline was staring at. Ena, tall and horsy looking with long grey hair that she wore in a thick plait down her back. She had one child a boy called Dominick who was a couple of years older then Josie. Pam was small and dainty with curl hair, a small nose, and a rich husband. She had no children. The three women made an odd trio. Her mammy had a houseful of children and no money. 'I was always terrified of Ena,' she said, 'because her voice was so loud.' She pulled her eyes away from the flames and looked at Una and asked, 'was Ena married?'

Every neighbour in Arbour Hill would like to know if Ena Dwyer's son was legitimate. 'I don't know, Pauline,' Una said, 'but she had enough money to bring up Dominick and send him to secondary school, and he used to stay with his father's family in the country during the summer holidays.'

Pauline smiled with her eyes. 'Dominick,' she whispered.

'And Josie,' Una added, joining her sister in a conspiratorial smile.

Neither Pauline nor Una had ever seen a man go in or out of Ena's house. Her only child Dominick was a year older than Josie. He never played out on the street but sometimes he would stand and watch them play 'rounders', or 'hit the can' when he was coming home from the shop with bread or milk. Una asked him a couple of time if he wanted to play but he always said no, and walked away.

'I never knew if Dominick was looking at me or over my head,' Pauline said, recalling the thick glasses he used to wear.

'I used to think he was smelling me,' Una said, 'by the way her used to screw his nose up as though he was trying to stop his heavy glasses from falling down over his mouth.'

'Josie was the only one he talked to,' she said, 'he used to carry the shopping for her. Was Josie fond of Dominick?' she asked.

Una pulled on her cigarette. 'I think she was, she said, 'and I think that Dominick was fond of Josie, but I think Ena wasn't too pleased.'

Pauline didn't need to ask why because she knew a bricklayer's daughter would not be good enough for Ena's son. She recalled her own fondness for Jimmy and how she had missed him when they had moved away from Ballyglass. But she had known enough about his mother that she didn't want him going out with a girl that lived in a corporation house so it was no surprise when he had gone to England for his summer holiday when his school had closed.

'There's no turning the clock back,' Una said, nodding over to the wall where underneath the clock four wedding photographs made a square on the wall. They were Josie's, Pauline's, her own, and her mammy's. She had bought the frames and put them on the wall the year she came home when Shea was a baby. She was wondering if anyone would add a photograph of Maura's wedding.

Pauline turned her face towards the wall and although she couldn't see the pictures in the dark she knew what they were. The photograph of her mammy's wedding used to hang on the wall beside the front window when they lived in Arbour Hill. She must have spent hours staring at it when she was on her own in the house and the baby she was minding was asleep.

In the remaining glow from the fire, the two sisters chatted and laughed about the news and gossip that Cathy and Joan had told them when they were playing cards until Una said 'It's time I was going. I don't want to be here when they get back from the Glen.'

'Neither do I,' Pauline said, picking her empty mug off the floor.

'We'll have a great day in town tomorrow with Liam and Shea,' Una said. 'We'll pick him up on the way into town. I'll be over here for nine.'

Chapter Fifty-three

A cold breeze hit Una in the face when she opened the hall door. She was about to go back and borrow a coat when her Uncle Fred's car turned the corner so she changed her mind. She was at the gate when the car pulled up so she waited to say goodbye to Sue and Fred. The street lamp was on the other side of the road so all she could see were four bodies in the car.

Expecting her mammy to be in the front seat beside Fred she opened the car door, and was surprised to find Josie.

'I can manage,' Josie shouted, pushing the door out so sharply that Una had to step away. She turned her head round to the back and said, 'Open the door for Mammy.'

When Una opened the back door her mammy continued to sit clasping her handbag to her chest as if she was expecting her daughter to snatch it off her. Una left the door open and walked around the back of the car to say goodbye to Sue and Fred.

Sue held Una in a long hug. 'Will you be able to get Pauline into Bewley's tomorrow by three o'clock?' she asked.

'Of course,' Una said as Fred came up and took her in his arms. When Fred released her from a hug Sue was walking in the gate behind Josie. Sheila was still sitting in the back seat of the car because Josie had assumed that Una would help her mammy out, and Sue didn't care if her sister never got out of the car. While Fred was holding the car open for Sheila to decide if she would get out or stay there, Una was walking up the path of Angie's house and Josie was walking into the hall of her family home.

'Are they all gone to bed?' Josie whined when she pushed in the hall door and saw the light wasn't on in the living room.

'It is nearly twelve,' Sue said, closing the hall door after Fred had followed Sheila into the hall. She walked into the living room behind her sister and started to unbutton her coat. 'They have left a lovely fire going,' she said, nodding to the fireplace.

'Even so,' Josie moaned, scanning the room for something else to complain about. Her evening had been very gloomy and disappointing: neither Sue nor Mammy had asked her any questions at all when she was telling them about her customers, and about how well her business was doing. Most of the time they talked about card games.

Fred stayed standing at the door of the living room and watched Sheila walk over to the fire and sit down in her favourite chair. He tried to feel sorry for her because he wondered from the events of the afternoon if her older children would soon not bother coming home. He hoped he was wrong because he would miss them, and he knew that Sue would too. He rattled his car keys and nodded his head over to Sue and said, 'We aren't stopping. It's late and we're all tired after the weekend.'

'I'll see you on Tuesday then,' Sheila said, assuming Sue would do as Fred had said.

Sue turned back from walking towards her husband and said, 'I will ring you tomorrow.' She had no intention of waiting for half an hour outside the hospital for Sheila not to turn up. She hadn't asked her to come and like the last time she was sure all her sister wanted was a free lunch.

Sheila lowered her head to her feet and fumbled around her legs for her handbag.

'I'll see you during the week, Josie,' Sue said, smiling weakly as she walked behind Fred out into the hall. She prayed she would have enough time left to make up for all the damage she had allowed to happen. She also knew her sister was very angry, and for the first time in her life she didn't care.

Both Liam and Fred opened the hall door at the same time, with Liam coming in and Fred going out. Liam walked down the front pathway to wave Sue and Fred off.

Sue caught Liam's arm while Fred was unlocking the car and said, 'Can you arrange for Pauline to be in Bewley's tomorrow for three o'clock.' She thought she would tell both Una and Liam in case one of them forgot.

'Which one?' Liam asked frowning

'Grafton Street,' Sue said. Putting her arm around Liam's neck, she pulled his head down and kissed him on the side of the face. He hugged her back and stayed at the gate until the car had turned the corner at the top of the road. When he pushed in the living room door and saw the sad face of his eldest sister Liam suspected that she hadn't enjoyed her evening. But the fire was smiling at him, so he walked over and sat in the low chair facing his mammy.

Sheila returned the notebooks, tubes of pills, keys and envelopes to her handbag then stood. She glanced briefly at her eldest daughter as she walked towards the door and said, 'You can bring my milk up to me,' and walked out of the room.

Although the fire was every bit as bright as it had been an hour earlier, Josie didn't feel as warm and cosy as her sisters had been when they were sitting beside it. But Josie had never sat around the fire and chatted with her siblings.

As usual Sheila left the door open. To avoid looking at the tired wallpaper or the dreadful curtains Josie gazed into the fire. The bang of the toilet door closing made her jump and bring her hand up to her shoulder, and Liam looked up from undoing the laces on his shoes.

On seeing the look of pain on his sister's face, Liam asked, 'Are you all right, Josie?'

This wasn't the first time Josie imagined she felt pain in her shoulder when she heard a bang. But like now she would shut her memory down. 'What's happening on Tuesday?' she asked.

'Don't ask me, I can just about manage temarra,' Liam lied, removing his shoes. They made a soft thud when he dropped them on the floor in front of the fire. 'If no one else wants teh hot water, then I'll have a bath,' he said.

The memory of the imagined pain in Josie's shoulder returned when she saw the shine on her brother's black shoes. She imagined she was sitting on one of the stools her daddy had made for Pauline, Una and herself, showing her sisters how to write numbers on a slate with chalk. Her mammy was shouting at her daddy and when she looked up she saw her daddy lower his body as a black shiny object whizzed past him and hit her on her shoulder.

The pain in Josie's shoulder had gone when she had left the hospital with her Aunt Sue but she couldn't sleep for weeks because of the hard white board the doctor had put on her arm and shoulder. Thinking about it now, she felt she could cry with relief because she didn't feel the pain any more.

'Have yeh a pain in yer shoulder, Josie?' Liam asked.

'Not any more,' Josie said as a tear rolled slowly down the side of her nose. She stood. 'I'll get Mammy's milk, then get off to bed myself.'

'I'll get Mammy her milk,' Liam said. 'You go up to bed.'

'No need,' Josie protested, smiling gratefully.

'I get it for her when you aren't here,' Liam lied, taking her by the elbow and walking her over to the door. 'Up you go now,' he said, 'and get asleep before Mammy goes up.'

When Liam ran the water for his bath he wanted to pee. He estimated his mammy had been in the toilet for ten min utes. He stared at the closed door for a few seconds, then turned off the light. He waited a few more seconds for her to call out, then went out the back door and peed on the old rose bush. When he came back in the toilet door was open and his mammy was walking up the lobby.

After he had checked the water running into the bath was still hot, Liam went into the kitchen and poured his mammy a glass of milk. As he hadn't heard her climbing the stairs he assumed she was in the living room, so he went in and put her milk on the table. 'I sent Josie to bed,' he said.

Sheila's face looked like a squashed prune because she had closed her mouth so tight when she delivered her son a glare she usually reserved for Josie.

Liam smiled at his mammy, thinking if she looked at her glass of milk it would turn sour, then left the room.

When Sheila heard the bathroom door close she got out of her chair and went over to the hot press and retrieved a small bottle of whiskey from behind an old pair of shoes. She then went into the kitchen and poured the milk down the sink, rinsed the glass under cold water, filled it with whiskey and returned to the living room.

Chapter Fifty-four

The lace curtains that Una and Angie stood behind were old, but, like the rest of Angie's house, they were spotlessly clean. They were looking over at Una's family home where Carl and Maura were standing at the hall door.

'The pair of them look like they are going to Siberia,' Una said.

'They might need them thick coats and fur hats in Galway at this time ev teh year,' Angie said as a light green car pulled up at the gate.

The windows were closed so they didn't hear what Maura said when she turned and shouted into the house. She was walking down the path behind her husband when Liam came out of the house with a large suitcase. He plonked it down on the path, then went back into the house. When he came out with the second suitcase Maura and Carl were sitting in the back of the car. He placed it beside the other one and shoved his hands into the pockets of his trousers.

Angie shoved her glasses up on her nose, then moved the curtain back as if to make sure she was seeing all right. 'Is tha big bloke sittin' in teh back ev teh car expectin' Liam…'

'Yes, Angie, the conceited git is expecting Liam to put the suitcases in the back of the car,' Una said.

From Angie's window they saw Maura gesticulating with her arm. Liam waved back and the car drove away. Liam wen back into the house leaving the two cases standing like deserted children where he had left them.

'They will miss their train if they have to come back for them,' Una said.

'If they don't miss teh train, they will miss their cases when they get to Galway,' Angie said, dropping the end of the curtain as a neighbour came out of the house directly facing her.

By the time the neighbour had crossed the road to the house next door to Angie, another woman was making her way over from two doors up from Una's family home. This made five of them staring at the two deserted cases as if they were waiting for them to sprout wings and fly after the mini cab.

'How often does the train to Galway run? Una asked.

'Regular as clockwork every Monday and Thursday,' Angie replied, shoving her glasses up on her nose.

'You are kidding,' Una gasped, swinging her head between Angie and the two-orphaned cases as though she was afraid one of them would disappear if she weren't watching them.

'It was the last time I needed te know,' Angie said sniffing to stop from smiling at the horrified face of Una.

'When was that?'

Angie sniffed again. 'I can't remember exactly,' she said smiling, 'but it was after the war.'

Una laughed as she said, 'Angie Dolan, you are getting as bad as Liam.

'Anyway,' Angie said, 'it won't make any difference te you f Maura and her husband come back to stay till Thursday because yer off this evenin."

Una wasn't thinking about herself: 'I'm concerned for Josie,' she said.

Angie was about to walk away when the light green car returned. Along with the three neighbours Una and Angie watched Carl get out of the car and lift the orphaned suitcases into the boot. He was getting back into the car when the three neighbours cheered and clapped.

Angie moved away from the window.

'She is some flower,' Una said as she followed Angie.

The only flowers Angie had in her garden were roses. She knew the phrase Una used was a saying but she never knew what it meant, but Maura wasn't a rose. 'She is indeed,' she said as she walked over to the small back room that was her kitchen.

A widow with two daughters, Angie Dolan had moved into Plunkett Road a year before Una's family. She made it her business to know as many of the neighbours as she could, because she relied on them to tell her what her two young daughters got up to when she was out at work doing all sorts of cleaning jobs. She didn't like all her neighbours but the only ones she disliked were Sheila, Josie and Maura Malone.

Returning from the kitchen, Angie poured coal black tea into two cups and moved one of them over to Una. 'Drink that,' she said. 'It'll set yeh up fer yer day in town.'

The two spoonfuls of sugar Una put into her cup felt heavy on her spoon, and she was still stirring them when Angie had taken her first sip of tea. The smell of the tea was so strong she wondered if she had used enough sugar to enable her to drink it.

Angie studied her lodger for a few seconds, then picked her cup of tea off the table and said, 'What's botherin' yeh, Una?'

Una gazed at the four flying swans on the chimneybreast behind Angie's head for a few seconds, then picked her cigarette packet up off the table. She placed a cigarette in front of her friend and put another one in her own mouth.

'Now what's botherin' yeh, Una?' Angie asked again, taking a small gleaming brass container from the mantelpiece and placing it on the table.

Una lit her cigarette. 'I think the conceited git Maura is married to is hitting her,' she said, raising her face from her cup of tea.

'What makes yeh think that?' Angie asked, frowning.

'I saw bruises on her shoulders and arms when I went into the bedroom yesterday to get Eileen.'

'Sorry Una, I can't help yeh there,' Angie said, drawing her chin into her neck and lowering her head to the table. She knew about physical and sexual abuse after her mother had died and her father came into her bedroom every evening. At fourteen she was too young and innocent at the time to know what was going on.

'I know, Angie. I know, but that's what's bothering me,' Una replied. She passed her lighter over to Angie, raised her eyebrows, smiled and said, 'You did ask.'

'Did yeh say anythin' to her?'

'No. She covered herself up quickly as though she didn't want me to see.'

'Did yeh tell anyone?'

'Pauline.'

'What did she say?'

'Pauline said he probably shook her to stop her screaming when she was in one of her tantrums. She also said that there were times when she felt like shaking her.'

Angie would never have shaken the girl but there were times when she used to hear the little bitch screaming out on the road and she was tempted to go out and bang a potato into her mouth. 'It's up te Maura te get help with that,' she said, patting Una on the back of her hand. 'It's time yeh stopped worryin' about yer family. Yeh can't live their lives fer them.'

Una turned her hand and held Angie's. 'Thanks for having me for the two nights. I really do hope you will come over to me for a holiday. We could have a great time taking the girls round London.'

'Any time, Una, and yer always welcome.' Angie had no desire to go to London.

Una was about to tap her cigarette into the brass ornament Angie had put on the table for them to use as an ashtray. She picked it up and took a closer look. 'Is this what I think it is?' she asked.

'And what do yeh think it is?' Angie said, sitting up straight and sniffing.

Una turned the little object upside down then put one of her fingers into the hollow centre. She waved her head and tried to look offended. 'Angie Dolan, you ought to be ashamed of yourself for using church candle holders for ash trays.'

'Finish yer tea and get off with yeh,' Angie said.

Una closed her eyes and swallowed as much of her tea as she could. 'Jesus, Angie,' she said, 'if you don't put more water into that teapot you will have ulcers on your arse by the summer.'

Chapter Fifty-five

Birds swooped up from the pavement into the air as if they were clearing a space for a queen when Una was crossing the road from Angie's house to her family home. There were only about five or six of them but they seemed like a dozen and they swooped around so fast as they glided over the tops of the houses and along the road.

A familiar sound coming from the top of the road made her turn her head. A nearly empty bus was making its way into town. She smiled remembering she used to see the birds when she was running to catch the earlier bus into town to go to work before she was married. She inhaled the chilly air, thinking how different it was when she was going into London. The tubes were crowded and noisy. Her eyes followed the creatures up into the blue sky, her thoughts still on the rattling, cramped trains, and the boredom because none of the people talked to each other.

As she was turning the key in the door, the birds dropped down again as if they were closing a gate behind her. She inhaled the smell of hot toast and butter when she opened the door. She sniffed again and smelt eggs. When she walked into the living room she was surprised to see that the fire wasn't lit because the room was warm. Angie didn't light her fire as often as her mammy did. She couldn't afford the coal or the turf, so her house was never as warm as her mammy's.

The table was set for four. Josie and Pauline were sitting at the table, and Eileen was in the high chair Joan had borrowed. Liam was standing at the window as if he was waiting for her. Una noticed a clean cup and saucer, and side plate on the table. 'Ready when you are,' she said. She wanted to be gone before her mammy came down.

'I'll get my coat,' Pauline said. She kissed Eileen on the side of her face and left the room.

'While you are up there, see if Mammy is awake yet,' Josie called after Pauline.

'Yeh needn't bother with anythin fer teh rain,' Liam sang. He picked a crust of bread up off the floor beside Eileen's chair and threw it into the fireplace. 'Because we aren't goin' teh have any.'

'And what makes you so sure about that?' Josie asked, smiling at her young brother. She was still grateful to him for getting their mammy's milk.

'Cos I've ordered it.' Liam smiled back like a puppy that had been given a treat. 'I always do after I've heard teh weather on the radio.'

'If it's not going to rain we will be as quick walking down to Ballymore for Shea,' Una said, walking out into the hall as Pauline came down the stairs. She also wanted to be gone when her mammy came down.

'That's fine by me,' Liam said, following her and opening the hall door.

'As long as we get our cream cakes,' Pauline said, zipping up the front of her fleecy coat, 'because that's all I'm going for.'

'Did you check to see if Mammy is awake yet?' Josie asked

'No, Josie, I didn't,' Pauline said, then walked out of the house.

'We'll bring back a couple of Bewley's bracks, Josie,' Una said.

Chapter Fifty-six

At half past ten in the morning they had their choice of seats on the bus into town, so they sat on the four front ones upstairs. For the first ten minutes of their journey into town, Liam told Shea all the history of Ballyglass and Ballymore he had learned from his friend Brian. He knew how old most of the buildings were, and what they were used for when they were first built. Pauline and Una soon became more interested in Liam's lectures than Shea was.

Monday mornings were usually quiet in the city so they were able to walk four abreast along O'Connell Street.

'Have yez made a plan fer where yez want te go?' Liam asked when they were passing the Gresham Hotel.

'Eason's, Cleary's and Hickeys will be enough for me,' Una said.

Pauline was just glad to be out of the house and away from her mammy so she said, 'That will do me.'

Liam had no interest in dress fabrics so he waited outside the shop when his sisters went into Hickey's.

Ten years rolled back for the sisters when they walked into the small fabric shop. Rolls of dress fabrics of all colours and patterns were fighting for space on the shelves. A small grey-haired woman was tidying up after the usual busy Saturday.

'Sorry about the mess,' the woman said, picking up a roll of fabric off the counter.

Pauline recognised the woman. She had sold her the white organdie for her wedding dress. 'If I could get you to go back to Canada with me,' she said to Una, 'I would buy some of every fabric that's here.'

'I could make you some dresses for the summer and post them out,' Una said. 'You could hem them yourself.'

'I was thinking about the twins,' Pauline said, running her hand down a pastel-coloured cotton print and recalling the dresses Una used to make for her when they were teenagers. She estimated that Una used to make a dress every week.

'I could do some for them as well,' Una said. 'I love making for Joan and Cathy. All the dresses are in one piece now so if you like that fabric I will get some and make some dresses for the twins and post them out to you.'

Still not sure if she would come home for good and not ready to tell Una why, Pauline bought fabric for two dresses for herself and two each for her daughters.

Liam and Shea were waiting for them under the clock at the front of Cleary's department store.

'What do yeh want in here?' Liam asked when they walked into the store. He hated the shop because it reminded him of his mammy and the suit she had bought him for his confirmation as though it was yesterday instead of four years ago. He imagined he could feel the softness of the grey suit he had wanted on the back of his neck and his legs. He had known at the time that his mammy was going to buy him one of the dark grey suits that was made from a coarse hard-wearing cloth, but he had hated having to try on four expensive ones before she bought the one she knew she was going to buy before they even walked into the store'

'Plain old-fashioned flat shoes,' Una said smiling at the lovely wide wooden staircase.'

As it was early on a Monday morning the customers were only starting to come into the store. Pauline and Una probably looked like they were staking the place out for a robbery because they were wandering around reminiscing and talking about when they used to love the January sales. They were leaning over the balcony looking for Liam and Shea when a woman came over to them.

'Can I help you?' the woman asked the back of the sisters' heads.

'The shoe department,' Una said, turning round.

'Pauline Malone?' the woman said, smiling when Pauline turned round.

Pauline thought she recognised the woman but couldn't remember how she knew her.

'Ann Kennedy,' the woman said, holding out her hand.

When Pauline saw the bracelet on Ann Kennedy's wrist she knew who she was, but she had known her as Mrs Kennedy, and as the owner of the shoe shop where she used to work before she married Harry and went to Canada. She was a small pretty woman, and she had two young children. She lived in the flat over the shop, and there were days when Pauline used to be in the shop on her own because Mrs Kennedy had bruises on her face.

After a short awkward silence Ann said, 'Are you home on holiday or for good?'

The black dress and neat appearance of Ann Kennedy suggested to Pauline that she was working as an assistant in the shop. 'On holiday,' she said, then turned to Una and said, 'This is my sister Una.'

Una had never met Ann Kennedy before but she remembered that Pauline was happy working for her. She sensed a friendly feeling between Pauline and Ann so she said, 'I am looking for some old-fashioned flat shoes, but I don't need Pauline with me so I will leave you to talk on your own.' She walked away and looked at the shoes that were on display.

Anticipating what Pauline was wondering and knowing that Pauline wouldn't ask, Ann said, 'Yes Pauline, I left him.'

Still seeing Ann as her employer Pauline bowed her head knowingly.

Ann looked down at her charm bracelet. 'I had twenty-two when you left,' she said.

Pauline looked at the bracelet.

Ann smiled. 'I now have twenty-four, and I would probably have another twenty-four if he hadn't started hitting the children.'

Pauline nodded her head, recalling the bruises on Ann's face. 'How are the children?' she asked, really wanting to know if she had left them with her husband. 'They must be teenagers now.'

'Twelve and thirteen,' Ann said, 'and they are doing great in school.' She looked around the store to see if there were any customers needing help. 'It was more difficult to make up my mind to go than it was to actually leave him. His parents supported me until we sold the shop. They didn't want me going to the police.'

Pauline nodded her head as though she knew what Ann was talking about. She wanted to know more about how Ann had managed so she said, 'Show me a couple of pairs of shoes.'

For ten minutes Ann sat on the footstool and helped Pauline to try on three pairs of shoes while she told Pauline how her husband's family had supported her and the children until the shop was sold.

'They were prepared to do anything to prevent me going to a solicitor or the police,' Ann said, slipping the third shoe on Pauline's foot as Una came over to join them. 'If you have time you might come and see the children,' she said to Pauline as she stood and started to pick up the shoes.

Pauline felt mean because her first thought about going to visit Ann and see the children was that it would give her somewhere to go to get away from her mammy. 'I'll have the second pair I tried on,' she said and followed Ann over to the till. She needed to get Ann's phone number and address. With her purse and her heart a little lighter, Pauline joined Una and they both went off to find Liam and Shea.

Chapter Fifty-seven

True to his promise, the sun Liam ordered was shining on the pavements and tall buildings when they came out of Cleary's. 'It's great to be home,' Una said as they waited to cross O'Connell Street to go into Eason's.

Yes, Pauline thought, looking around the wide familiar street and recalling how she used to stand in the queue at the Meteropole cinema with Harry. Her whole body felt warm with memories that encouraged her to wonder if Harry would come home to Ireland. Unlike Ann Kennedy's husband, Harry had never hit her, and she knew he shook the children to stop them from crying. She also knew her father-in-law wouldn't support her if she left Harry. She thought about all the money Harry had put into the bank in her name and wondered how many charms she could buy with it.

Liam wasn't interested in looking at books, but he liked to wander around the music and children's department 'You two do yer own buyin',' he said, holding the heavy door open for his sisters as they walked up the few steps into Eason's. 'I'll take Shea to the children's part and see yez back here in half an hour.'

After ten minutes of watching her sister sorting through the large variety of exercise books, Pauline said, 'Why don't you ask Liam?'

'I'll just get a selection,' Una replied. 'If Cathy doesn't use them, then Joan will.' She inhaled the scent of the fresh paper from one of the jotters as she rolled the pages over. 'I wish I was getting them for myself. I used to love writing in new books.'

'Are you saying that new exercise books helped you to learn?' Pauline giggled, stooping to pick a jotter off the floor.

'No, I'm not,' Una replied smiling, 'and new exercise books won't help Cathy learn either, but they might get her into school more often. Even if it's just to show them off.'

'I used to hate the paper in our jotters,' Pauline said, recalling all the holes she used to make in the dull grey paper from rubbing out her mistakes. 'This paper is lovely. It's thicker and shinier than what we used to have.'

'I'm more concerned with getting Cathy into school,' Una said, handing Pauline her shopping bag so she could use two hands to search through the exercise books and jotters. 'I don't care what she does when she is there, as long as she walks through the doors every day.'

'There's no reason why Cathy shouldn't be in school every day.'

'I know,' Una said, cradling a bundle of exercise books to her chest. 'But just the same, she isn't going.'

'And Joan?' Pauline gasped, glancing over her shoulder to see if anyone was listening.

'Only Cathy,' Una replied, picking out another bundle of jotters. 'The pair of them are very close to a day in court.'

'What pair?'

'Cathy and Mammy,' Una said, looking up from the jotters in her hand. 'You know, Pauline, when I think back on it now, we wouldn't have missed Mammy all that much if she had been put into a home.'

Used to hearing her hot-tempered sister utter wild accusations about people, Pauline lowered her head to her feet and moved her toes and recalled the morning when her daddy wheeled his bicycle beside her to make sure she went into the school. At the time she had been absent for so many days that she didn't want to go. She was in the confirmation class, and she hadn't learned her catechism. 'I don't remember any mother being taken away,' she said.

'They weren't. It was always the children that were taken away,' Una said, handing her sister some jotters to hold. 'What we have to do with our smart little sister is to get her to see some reasons why she should go to school.' Una giggled: 'It's Cathy that is going to land Mammy in court. I'm not saying that Mammy doesn't keep Cathy away when she wants her to do something, but I don't think she knows that our smart little sister is able to write her own notes.'

The exercise books and jotters were in packs of three. Una put two of the packs back on the shelves and picked up three different ones. 'Anyway,' she said, 'I don't want Josie to know. She will blame Cathy for all the absences.' She selected four packs of exercise books and handed them to Pauline. 'Don't let on that you know because I don't want Cathy to know that Angie told me.'

Chapter Fifty-eight

Liam continued to give Shea a history lesson on every building they passed. When they were outside the General Post Office, he pointed to some jagged holes in the huge columns and said, 'Put yer finger inte these, Shea.'

While the young blond haired boy was trying to scrape some gravel from the hole with his fingernail, Liam sang the praises of the Easter Rising and told Shea how proud he should be to be Irish.

Shea smiled at his mammy, and said that he was.

Liam continued to narrate the history of Dublin as they sauntered towards the Liffey.

'Does he really know what he's talking about?' Pauline asked Una as they gazed into the dirty green waters of the River Liffey; waiting for a Guinness barge to pass under O'Connell Bridge.

Una cast her eyes over the back of her brother's short den-im jacket. She smiled at his thin curly hair blowing around his face. 'The pity is that Shea is too young to take it all in,' she said.

Pauline followed her sister's gaze. 'Does it matter?' she said. 'Just look at him, he's absolutely spellbound.'

'Aren't we all when Liam starts going on?' Una said. She then remembered that Pauline wouldn't really know. 'Anyway,' she said quickly, 'I think we have had enough of this smell for now and I don't like the way Shea is sticking his head through those concrete posts.' She was terrified that Shea would slip into the water between the posts on the bridge. She called over to her brother and they moved on after Liam promised Shea that they would see a barge on the way back.

Originally the home of the Irish Parliament the massive grand building they were admiring was now the Bank of Ireland.

'I didn't know that my daddy had any money,' Shea confessed after Liam had told him that the Bank of Ireland was so big because it minded all of their money.

'The cream in the cakes will be sour if we don't get a move on,' Pauline said when she saw her brother squinting his eyes from the sun while he looked over at Trinity College. She knew the building was important, but she didn't want to hear about it now. Her talk with Ann Kennedy was still in her thoughts. It was a tonic for her worries and she knew that she had options, but she needed time to think about what to do.

They took their time, just the same. It was a lovely sunny day and although there was a fair number of cars and buses they didn't seem to be in a hurry. Una thought how much calmer her home city was, compared to London.

They could smell the coffee two shops down from Bewley's when they were in Grafton Street.

'Upstairs, upstairs,' Liam shouted after his sisters, when they walked into the most famous coffee house in Dublin.

Liam didn't like coffee but he loved to sit in this famous Bewley's café. He didn't really know for sure if all the great Irish writers and political thinkers had developed their best ideas in the place, but he believed that they had because Brian had told him and his friend never told lies.

The lunch hour customers had already left to get back to work so they were able to take a table over by the window so that Shea could look down at the traffic in the street.

'That's handy,' Pauline said when Liam showed Shea where to put his bag on the shelf under the seat of his chair.

'That is what teh little shelf is fer, my dear girl,' Liam said. 'These chairs were made fer ladies who wore long dresses and corsets, hence teh high round back.' He ran his hand over the curved smooth thick wooden tube on the top of Shea's chair and continued, 'Such ladies of distinction came to Bewley's fer coffee and cream cakes when they were doin' their shoppin in Grafton Street.'

'It's very small for shopping,' Pauline said.

'The ladies Liam is referring to had most of their shopping delivered,' Una cut in.

Liam had no idea how ladies of distinction managed their shopping but he wasn't going to allow Una to upstage him so he said, 'Such ladies of high birth always carried a string bag to hold teh smellin salts, and a small white cloth.'

'Why the white cloth?' Pauline asked, raising her eyebrows.

'To cover their bad teeth as a result of them eatin' so many of teh cream cakes,' Liam said.

'The shelf was for their hats,' Una finished. She knew her brother better than Pauline, and she thought he was making more than his usual effort to entertain them. She smiled with her eyes, but her heart was uneasy because she sensed he was unhappy about something.

'What were the smelling salts for?' Pauline asked. She didn't care what they were for. She wanted to gather as many memories of her young brother as she could before she went back to Canada even if she would be only staying for a year or two until they sold the house and came home. The idea of getting Harry to come home was maturing into a plan in her mind.

'They used te pass out from the tight corsets,' Liam said before Una stole his story again.

'It's true, and it served them right,' Una said, 'and I'm not talking about the ones we used to wear with a couple of bones down the front to pull in our tummies.'

'The whole world has changed since yez women got out ev yer corsets,' Liam said, winking at Pauline.

They could only manage two cakes each, with Liam helping Shea with both of his so that he could taste two different ones.

'Are you sure about paying for all this, Liam? We could easily go one third each,' Pauline offered.

Liam tapped the table in front of Pauline. 'This is my treat, and I've been lookin' forward to it fer a few months with just teh three ev us.'

Una was certain now that her brother had something on his mind. She expected it would have something to do with Cathy. She moved the ashtray to her side of the table. 'Now give us the bad news first, Liam,' she said.

'I don't really know which ev teh two things that's on me mind is teh bad news.' Liam said, stirring his half-full cup of coffee. He sat back in his chair so that, if necessary, he could avoid a scream or a slap from either of his sisters and said, 'I'm goin te join teh airforce.'

'Jesus' Una whispered into her cup of coffee.

'What airforce?' Pauline asked.

'Teh English,' Liam said, strumming his fingers on the table.

'What about all the history you were talking about to Shea up to half an hour ago?' Pauline asked, recalling how he had blamed the English for all Ireland's misfortunes.

'Very good point, very good point,' Liam agreed. He rested his arms on the table. 'If yeh read more about yer Irish history yeh'll see that it's no more than the English owe me.'

'Why?' Una asked, sitting up to better scrutinize a tall woman wearing a black and red poncho, who had just walked into the cafe. She recognized her at once.

'Because I want an education,' Liam lied, turning round to see what his sister was looking at.

'You could go back to school for that. We could all chip in a little, you know we would,' Una said as she watched Ena remove her poncho and sit at a table near the door.

'You could, Una,' Liam said. He knew his older sisters had missed out on school and he was sorry for them.

Una could only see the top of Shea's head because he was bent over the colouring book that her brother had bought him. She knew her son would have his lips puckered up, just like his daddy always did when he was writing. She wanted to tell Liam that her son could write his name and read some words, but she was afraid that he would ask Shea what he could read and she knew that he would say: 'The Labour Party.'

'We can't go to school fer each other, Una,' Liam said breaking into his sister's thoughts. He was often weary, listening to her talking about the value of education. Seeing the sadness in her face, he decided not to tell her now that he also wanted to leave home. 'The school is rubbish and the teachers are worse,' he said. Expecting her to tell him the schools were better than when she was going, he added quickly, 'Ask Maurice and Donal.'

Seizing the opportunity to talk about schools, Una said, 'Do you know that Cathy is not going to school?'

'It's the journey,' Liam said. 'You two never had te do teh journey down te Arbour Hill, fer te go te school.'

'She could go to a nearer school,' Pauline suggested.

Liam sighed. 'The biggest excuse that Mammy has always used fer keepin' us away from school since you girls went was, and still is, is teh journey. She blames teh buses fer bein' full, and all teh colds we didn't have because we had te stand in rain waitin' fer teh next bus.'

'But I still don't see why Mammy wants to keep Cathy at home at all,' Pauline insisted.

'She probably doesn't,' Una cut in. 'She just doesn't care that Cathy doesn't go to school once the fire is lighting.' She moved her cigarette around the ashtray and said, 'If Cathy doesn't go to school she'll be put into a borstal, or whatever they are called these days.'

Liam softened his tone and said, 'She won't be.' He wasn't sorry he told his sister off. He thought it was time that someone told her that she wasn't the only one who cared about the family, even if her heart was always in the right place. 'I have already bought her a little calendar.'

'A calendar?' Pauline said frowning.

'Yes, a calendar,' Liam said, lifting his cup of coffee to his mouth to stop from smiling. 'Cathy knows that she has to turn up fer school so many days a month, even if she is late. So she is going to tick off all teh days she doesn't go te school, and add them up, so that she'll know when she is getting to her limit.'

'Will that work?' Pauline asked.

'It did fer me,' Liam said, taking a sip of his coffee.

Una smiled with relief. At least he knew and he was trying to help her. 'I still think it's an awful shame, because Cathy is a bright girl,' she said. 'Anyway, when do you leave?'

'I don't know yet we have only got the application papers.'

'We?' Una asked.

'Brian Farley and meself.'

'Is that the same Brian you used to play with; the one that was always getting into fights?' Pauline asked. She sat back and stared at the wall behind Liam for a few seconds. 'I remember seeing him one day and the side of his face was nearly as dark as his hair.'

'Yes and no,' Liam said, pressing his elbows down on the table. 'Yes it's the same fella that's been me pal since I started school. But no, he wasn't always gettin' inte fights.' He paused 'However he has always got beat up a lot.'

'That's what happens when you get into fights,' Pauline said, recalling the day she had tried to find shoes to fit his big feet.

Liam counted three vertical lines across Pauline's forehead. 'It usually does,' he said, 'but not always. Brian has been gettin beat up by his da since he was six. He always let everyone think that he had been in a fight because he was ashamed.'

'Are you saying that he's been getting beaten up like that for more than ten years?' Una asked.

'If that's as long as I've known him, then yes he has,' Liam said, feeling his chest tighten. He worried for a second that his fiery sister would march them all off to the police station.

'What did he do to get beaten like that so often?' asked Pauline.

'He stood in front of his mother,' Liam said, lowering his face to his coffee. He felt ashamed for telling his sisters about his friend getting beaten by his father. After all, a secret is a secret. He was tempted to drink the full cup of coffee in one go as punishment for betraying his friend.

Una didn't remember seeing bruises on Brian's face. 'I used to see him going into eight o'clock mass nearly every morning,' she said. 'I used to measure if the bus was late by how near Brian was to the church.'

'How did you know he was going to mass?' Pauline asked, wondering if Brian went to mass to pray that his daddy would stop hitting him. When she went to mass she prayed all the time for Harry to have more patience with their babies.

'I would see him walking into the church if the bus was late. And when we were on short time and I didn't have to be in work until nine, I often saw him coming out of the church.'

'Why did he get beaten for standing in front of his mother?' Pauline asked, recalling that every time she was smacked when she was a child she would stop picking the centre out of the loaf of bread for a few days, and stop swinging the can of milk. But she had never suffered any blue or purple marks

She used to smack Maurice whenever he threw cups o water out of the bedroom window. And she also smacked Donal when he used to dip his bread into the bowl of sugar but she had never marked either of them.

'So that his da wouldn't keep hittin' his ma,' Liam replied

Smacking, hitting and beating were for Una entirely differ ent things. Smacking was done with hands. Hitting was don with an instrument of some sort, and beating was repeated hitting. With Cathy and school still on her mind, she though that if teachers at school had had to use their hands instead c canes or sticks, very few children would have gotten beaten because the teacher would feel as much pain as the children

The beatings Una hated most were given out to other girl in school because they couldn't answer the teacher's ques tions, or for some trivial offence, such as not bringing pencil or exercise books with them.

Listening now to Liam telling them about Brian, a pang c shame pierced Una's conscience. She wondered if she would have stood in front of her mammy if her daddy had given he a clout. 'Did you know about the beatings all that time?' sh asked.

The last person Liam wanted to talk about was Brian. ' guessed,' he said. 'Brian didn't tell me himself until last weel And I don't know what I could have done anyway.'

From where she was sitting, Pauline could see her mammy friend sitting on her own, stirring her coffee. She wondered she was waiting for her friend Pam, or even for her mamm She turned to Liam and said, 'You're under age. You will nee Mammy to sigh some papers, and she won't let you go away

'That's what I want te talk te yez about,' Liam said.

Una doubted the airforce would take him. He was to small, thin and scrawny-looking. 'Pauline's right,' she sai stubbing out her cigarette, 'because if you go away she won't be getting any money from you.'

'Don't let that stop you,' Pauline cut in. She thought of all the teas and cream cakes her mammy had enjoyed over the years and probably sitting in the chair she was now. 'Mammy will never have enough money, no matter how much we give her.'

'But Liam is under age and he will have to get Mammy to sign his papers,' Una cut in.

'What if you don't like it, and you can't get out?' asked Pauline.

'I'll make teh best of it as long as I'm getting an education, or good training fer somethin'.'

Una now thought her brother could do worse, and he was just bumming around anyhow. 'How are you going to get around Mammy to sign your papers?' she asked?

All the answers that Liam had rehearsed for when Una would ask him about how he would handle his mammy were either stuck to the ceiling over his bed in Plunkett Road, or floating around the gardens in Ballyglass. 'That's what I want te talk te yez about,' he said, interlacing and undoing his fingers as if he was demonstrating how to crochet. 'I'll run away,' he said, slipping one of his hands into the inside pocket of his jacket. He pulled out a brown paper packet and placed it on the table in front of Una.

Visions of her younger brother sitting in a trench shooting at wretched souls like himself, or even getting shot, receded as Una dwelled on the disappointment that awaited her young brother. She was sure the airforce would reject him. 'What is it?' she asked, picking up the packet.

'Open it,' Liam said, trying to look more confident than he felt. He looked at his watch, then around the room. He wanted to tell his sisters about his plan before his Aunt Sue came in.

Tips, Una thought, removing a post office book from the dirty bag. She ran her eyes over the pages that were nearly full with entries of five and ten pounds that now had a total of nearly three hundred pounds. She smiled with her eyes, but her heart was sad because she still thought that the air-force wouldn't accept him. She wondered what her mammy would spend the money on as she handed the book to Pauline.

'Enough fer me te get te you, Una, and back home again,' Liam said. 'I don't want any police, because I will join teh air-force and they won't take anyone with a criminal record. Will it be all right if I turn up on yer doorstep?' he asked.

Although Una was disturbed that her young brother would run away from home, she wondered if anyone in the family would get in touch with the police to bring Liam back to Ireland if he did. 'If you can, let me know you are coming,' she said, and laughed. She had thought he was going to give the money to their mammy. She wondered what Josie would say and do, and decided she didn't care.

Liam moved his hand across the table and took hold of his sister's fingers and said, 'What about Jack?'

Una pulled her fingers away, patted her brother on the back of his hand and said, 'As I understand, the law says that I own half of the house and if Jack has any objection, you can stay in my half all the time.'

'Mrs Byrne, yer a hard woman,' Liam laughed, 'but I'm glad that yer on me side.'

The electric light didn't help Pauline's eyesight. She squinted as she turned the pages of her brother's savings book. Then she raised her head and spoke like a schoolteacher. 'You started saving in '63,' she said.

'I can't remember the year.'

'Up until six months ago, you didn't leave any of you money in for more than two weeks.'

'That's about right,' Liam nodded.

Pauline closed the little book, and ran her thumb and first finger along the folded edge of it. 'You must have started it when you made your confirmation,' she said, feeling ashamed for wanting to come home because she was running away from a problem she shouldn't have allowed to happen in the first place. She was so proud of him, and the way he had worked everything out that she wanted to cry. 'Was that the bad news?' she asked.

Not now, Liam thought, pleased that neither of them tried to convince him not to send in his application. Pleased though he was with support of his sisters, he couldn't bring a smile to his face. 'The bad news is that Sue is not well.'

After about ten seconds silence Una said, 'Her headaches?'

'Sue has always had headaches,' Pauline said.

'She has been getting them too often for the last few months,' Liam said looking around the room again but there was still no sign of his aunt. 'I wasn't told but I know she has a hospital appointment on Tuesday.'

'Then how do you know?' Una asked, feeling guilty because she had always thought that Sue had pretended to have a headache to get away from her mammy.

'I heard Mammy telling Ena on the phone,' Liam said, bringing his hand up to his face where his aunt had kissed him before she got into the car.

Una nodded her head, thinking that Sue wanted to meet them to tell them about going to the hospital. She looked at her watch. It was getting on for four and there was no sign of her aunt so she thought that her aunt wasn't able to get the time from work. It then dawned on her that they were in the wrong Bewley's. They should have gone to the one in Westmoreland Street because it was nearer to where Sue worked. There was nothing she could do about it now, but they had to pass Bewley's in Westmoreland Street on the way to get the bus so if they hurried they might be able to see her for a few minutes. 'It's time we were going,' she said.

While Una and Pauline were gathering their shopping Ena was folding her newspaper, Liam walked over to the door. He stopped in front of his mammy's friend. 'Hello Ena,' he said. 'If Sue comes in will yeh tell her we were here but we couldn't wait any longer because Una has a boat to catch this evenin'.'

'I am the reason why your Aunt Sue asked you to bring Pauline in here,' Ena said, glancing over at her friend's two daughters. 'I didn't want to interrupt you earlier.'

Liam turned round to where his sisters were leaving the table where they had been sitting. 'They are on the way,' he said. 'Tell them I will see them downstairs.'

Una held Shea's hand and guided him in front of her as she walked towards her mammy's friend. 'Hello Ena,' she said, smiling.

Ena was often angry with her friend Sheila. There were also times she was jealous of her, now as she saw Una's young boy, jealousy swept over her like a heat wave. 'This is your son,' she said to Una, bending down to shake the young boy's hand.

'And the heir to my millions if I ever get them,' Una said laughing.

Ena knew the expression 'heir to millions' was used when people talked about their eldest child. She also knew they meant money. She laughed with Una and said, 'There are more important things to leave him than money.'

'How is Dominick?' Una asked. 'I haven't seen him since we left Arbour Hill.'

'He often asks about you all,' Ena said, pretending a cough to give her time to swallow back the tears that were gushing to her eyes, and suppressing the memory of last night when he had told her he had envied her friend Sheila's children. 'I would like to talk to Pauline for a few minutes,' she said.

Una nodded her head as if she expected Ena would want to talk to Pauline more than herself because this was the first time that Pauline had come home since she went to Canada. She also remembered she had promised Josie she would bring back a couple of bracks with her. 'I'll see you downstairs,' she said to Pauline.

'I'm the reason Sue asked Liam to bring you in here,' Ena said to Pauline. She opened her handbag and pulled out a blue airmail envelope, shoved her wire-framed glasses up on her nose and handed it to Pauline.

Pauline read her mammy's name and address on the front of the envelope, then turned it over and read the titles of some movies and the cinemas on the back. She raised her eyes to Ena and asked, 'Where did you get this?'

'I stole it,' Ena replied in the softest tone Pauline had ever heard from her mammy's friend's lips. 'I didn't see the letter because your mammy burnt it, but she told me what was in it.'

'Why are you showing it to me?' Pauline asked, raising her tear-filled eyes from the envelope.

Ena took the envelope out of Pauline's hand and said, 'No tears now, Pauline, they can wait until tomorrow. I take it you still remember where I live and you can find your way?'

Too stunned to speak, Pauline nodded her head.

'Can I expect you to come tomorrow at about three o'clock?'

Pauline nodded her head again and repeated, 'Why?'

'Many reasons,' Ena replied, 'but we don't have time for to go into them now.' She picked up her newspaper and opened it like she was going to read it. 'It might be better not to tell your mother you are coming,' she said.

Pauline nodded her head again and stood, 'I'll see you tomorrow,' she said and left.

Ena ordered another cup of coffee she didn't want, but

she needed to be sure her friend's children had left before she went home.

The waitress that brought Ena's coffee was tall with straight brown hair. She reminded Ena of Josie Malone who was now Josie Cullen with a young daughter. Ena imagined the little girl was like her mother although she had no idea what the child looked like because Sheila never talked about her grandchildren. It took her ten minutes to drink half of her cup of coffee and during that time she cried in her heart for her son Dominick because she now knew he had been so fond of Josie that he would have married her if Josie would have had him. She also cried for herself because she would now have had a granddaughter.

While Una was buying the bracks and Pauline was talking to Ena, Liam waited outside on the pavement with Shea and recalled the last time he had seen Ena. It was the day he had walked up and down Cleary's, modelling the suits he knew his mammy wasn't going to buy him for his confirmation. He had seen the price tickets, and they were all over ten pounds.

Four of the suits were so soft and light that Liam felt he was only wearing a shirt. His disappointment at knowing that his mammy would end up buying him the cheapest, heaviest and roughest suit was lessened because she had promised him they would be going for cakes in Bewley's.

After his mammy had bought his suit he had waited patiently while she admired a beautiful display of scarves, and sampled a selection of perfumes.

Eventually they were making their way over O'Connell Bridge when they met Ena and Pam. He would never know if his mammy would have kept her promise and taken him into Bewley's, but ever since that day he always blamed her friends because she didn't.

The sun was still shining but it was cooler as they walked back down Grafton Street.

With her face turned up to the clouds rolling over Trinity College, Una said, 'Did you order the rain to stay away for the evening, or just the day?'

'Fer the week,' Liam said, pretending to shiver. 'I was freezin' when Pauline was tellin' us about teh cold in Canada, so I ordered teh best spring weather until she went back.'

Chapter Fifty-nine

When Pauline stepped down off the bus at the top of Plunkett Road her mind went back seven years. She felt she was coming home from work because she could smell the fumes from the bus before the breeze from the fields behind the houses blew them away. She didn't know any of the children playing out on the road but she said hello to them all. She let go of Shea's hand and watched him run to Cathy. She had enjoyed her day, and she was looking forward to seeing Ena tomorrow, and Ann Kennedy during the week. She had somewhere to go to get away from her mammy for two days at least.

Liam waved to a neighbour as he walked up the path towards the door in front of Una and Pauline. Liam and Una were at the door when Pauline saw Josie at the kitchen window, and by the time she raised her hand to wave, her sister had dropped the curtain.

'Is Liam not with you?' Josie panted, walking out of the kitchen.

'I'm here,' Liam called out from the living room.

'Have you got a penknife?' Josie demanded, and as if she expected Liam to have one, she returned to the kitchen. Her face flushed with relief when she came back with a handful of pencils and saw her brother opening the blade on a small metal bar. She handed him the pencils and said, 'Sharpen these for Joan.'

Liam would have sharpened Joan's pencils with his teeth if she had asked him, but he hesitated before taking the pencils out of Josie's quivering hand.

'I've made your sandwiches,' Josie told Una as she waited for Liam to take the pencils.

'Thanks Josie,' Una said.

'I have the dinner all ready,' Josie said when Liam took the pencils out of her hand.

'What's the panic over them?' Una asked pointing to the coloured pencils Liam was holding.

'They're Joan's,' Josie snapped, moving towards the kitchen.

'I gathered that, but what's the panic?' Una repeated.

'She can't take them to school like that,' Josie said.

'It's only six o'clock,' Una said, 'she doesn't go to school until tomorrow.'

'Even so,' Josie said, bowing her head to her brother's hands. 'It's better to get them done now so that she doesn't forget. It won't take Liam five minutes, and Joan won't get into trouble tomorrow. I'll dish up the dinner while you're doing them.'

'And I bet yeh have done them lamb chops,' Liam said, sniffing and raising his face.

'How did you know that?' Josie demanded.

'Because I could smell them when I was at the top of the road,' Liam lied and smiled before he put his knife to the red pencil. All the stories Angie had told him about what schools were like in her day had stopped sounding funny to him when he saw fear in Josie's eyes when she had seen the penknife.

'I have everything ready,' Josie said, 'I was going to show Joan how to make a steak and kidney pie, but when she came in from school, she had homework to do.' She bowed her head to the kitchen. 'Luckily I already had the lamb chops in for tomorrow, so I have cooked them instead.'

I'll give you a hand,' Una said. She draped her coat over the banisters as she asked, 'Is Mammy here?'

'Una, you know that Mammy always goes into Arbour Hill to see Ena on a Monday,' Josie snapped, then went into the kitchen.

'That's right,' Una replied, 'I forgot.' She brought her finger up to her mouth to indicate to Liam not to say anything about seeing Ena in Bewley's.

The Malones often ran out of sugar, they seldom had butter, but there was always plenty of milk. As part of the household furniture, the family kept two milk crates. One held bottles of milk and was kept in the hall. The other one held the empty bottles and lived outside on the step underneath the concrete slab that was over the hall door. Every morning at six o'clock, the milkman would take away the crate full of empty bottles and replace it with a crate full of fresh pint bottles of milk. One of the boys would then swap the two crates around.

While his sisters were setting the table and serving up the dinner, Liam sat on the milk crate outside the door and sharpened twenty-one pencils. His knife was sharp so he pared away at the little coloured sticks as fast as Shea brought them out to him. Not all the pencils were blunt, but he sharpened them anyway. He smiled when he saw Shea rub his fingers along the tops of them, as if the young boy was making sure that his uncle had done a good job. He was starting on the last pencil when he noticed the tops of his fingers were stained mauve blue from the flakes and powder that came off the pencils. He rubbed his hand on the side of his trousers but the colour of his fingers still reminded him of the bruises on Brian Farley's face.

'Poor Josie,' Liam whispered to the little pink pencil he was putting his penknife into. He stole a glance over to Angie Dolan's house because he was sorry he had laughed at her when she had told him about the children in school that used to be beaten because they broke the nib of their pen or the point off their pencil. He wondered how old Josie was when she had been beaten in school because she had broken the top of her pencil.

'I'm sorry, Liam.' Joan's gentle voice brought Liam's thoughts away from his snobbish sister being in such a state over blunt pencils.

'I'll get yeh a sharpener temarra,' Liam said, handing the last pencil to Shea.

'I have one,' Joan replied, grinning at her brother's raised eyebrows. 'The pencils Josie gave you were the first ones that I took out of my box. She just whipped them up and ran out to the kitchen with them. When I followed her out, I found her trying to sharpen them with the carving knife. She was so frantic that I told her that I had more pencils and that Donal always sharpens them for me with his chisels. I thought she would forget about them then.'

Convinced that no teacher would ever hit any of Una's children, Liam watched her son examine the freshly pared ends of his own five new coloured pencils. He brushed the wooden flakes off his trousers. 'Did yeh get all yer homework done?' he asked Joan.

'Even some I don't need until Wednesday,' Joan said grinning guiltily. 'With Josie cooking the dinner I had more time.'

'I'll miss her too,' Liam said, returning Joan's grin with a broad smile handing her the last pencil. 'And that's the way it should be, and doin' the pencils got me out of mashin' teh potatoes.' He put his hand around Joan's shoulders and hugged her to him. 'I enjoyed doin' them, and at least Cathy won't have an excuse fer not goin' teh school temerra.'

Chapter Sixty

Concerned that someone would trip over her small bag, Pauline lifted it up on the crate of milk. She was determined to be ready to walk out of the door the minute Fred and Sue came to take her to the airport. She prayed in her heart that her mammy wouldn't get home until after she was gone.

She had cried so much during the day she was with Ena she was sure she wouldn't pee for a week, but she knew she would cry again when she said goodbye to her young sisters and Liam. But she wasn't going to tell them that she was never going to come home again while her mother was alive.

'Were yeh able te get everythin' in, Pauline?' Cathy asked.

Pauline smiled and said, 'I think so.'

Maurice poked his head out of the kitchen but Pauline ignored him, and continued, 'I'm going to check my handbag now.' She could hear Joan and Eileen in the bathroom. She smiled, recalling Cathy and Joan fighting over bathing Eileen. She thought back over the last twenty years, but she couldn't remember a single time when Una and herself had fought over bathing Liam, Maurice, Maura, Cathy or Donal.

Footsteps walking around the room above her head brought a more recent memory to Pauline's mind, and she wondered if Josie was moving the beds around again. She checked the inside pocket in her small bag to be sure she had the little book with Ena's and Ann Kennedy's address an recalled the evening she had come back from Ena's and her mammy had insisted the beds were moved so that she would not be sleeping in the same room as herself.

It was the last time Pauline had slept in the same house as her mammy. She had stayed with Ann Kennedy every night and came home every day to spend as much time as she could with Joan, and Cathy. She was securing Ena's and Ann's address in a small pocket in her handbag when the hall door opened and Liam came in.

The cases in the hall reminded Liam that Pauline would be gone soon and he felt mean because he intended to use her troubled situation to get his mammy to sign his papers for the airforce.

'The pair ev yez,' Liam said nervously, 'are like two school girls discussin' yer homework.'

'I never discuss me homework with anyone,' Cathy shouted.

'And quite right too,' Liam returned, raising his hand like he was stopping traffic as if he could prevent the next shower of words that Cathy was likely to fire at him. 'I wasn't meanin no offence at all,' he said, 'I just thought that yez looked like a pair of somethin' and I said teh first thing that came inte me head.' He ran his eyes over Pauline's very short hair. 'Teh pair ev yez look like two very strong women with yer hair cut shorter than a fellah's.'

God, he has an answer for everything, Pauline thought, winking at Cathy and patting her hair. She liked her hair short like Cathy's. Josie had cut it on the afternoon after she had come home for staying the night with Ena and her mammy went out on her own. She knew her brother meant well with calling them two strong women, but she wondered if she would ever be as strong as Cathy. However, she was determined to try.

Although no words had been exchanged between Pauline

and her mammy on the Wednesday morning after she had come home she knew her mammy sent Josie into the village to buy an English newspaper get her out of the house. At the time, Pauline was pleased to get a respite from her sister fussing about, and trying to find things to do to please their mammy.

Twenty minutes after Josie had left the house, her mammy walked into the living room wearing her coat. Pauline continued with writing her letters, and an hour later when Josie asked her where her mammy had gone, Pauline told the truth when she had said she didn't know.

When Eileen was down for her afternoon sleep and Josie was still rambling on about where her mammy might have gone, Pauline asked her sister to cut her hair like Cathy's. She decided she would find it less annoying to listen to Josie telling her about her business again than to hear about what they should all be doing to help their mammy.

Curly hair is very easy to cut. It doesn't matter if the hairdresser doesn't cut straight, because the ends curl up anyway So instead of droning on about her business, Josie began remembering when she had started cutting hair. Her first customers had been children with curly hair. She cut Pauline's hair slowly, like she was eating a bar of chocolate and she wanted it to last.

More pleased with the twenty minutes of silence than she was with her haircut, Pauline embraced her sister when she was finished. Every time Josie snipped away a clump of her hair, Pauline told herself that her sister was cutting away her misery.

The four-day-old English newspaper that her mammy had sent Josie down to the village to buy on the Thursday morning was still on the long shelf beside the boiler when Pauline sat down at the table in the warm living room.

The newspaper was smooth and flat because it hadn't been

opened. Pauline picked it up so she could put it under her page of notepaper while she checked her list of things to do.

'Have yeh done everythin' now?' Cathy asked from the other side of the table. She couldn't see what Pauline had written on her list because the paper was upside down, but she saw all the ticks down the side of the page.

'Not quite,' Pauline said, struggling to hold back her tears. She pretended to cough and blew her nose so she would stop the tears from coming. 'Just one more thing to do.'

'Yer havin' a grand time with stayin' in two countries on yer holidays,' Cathy said, leaning into the table but she still couldn't see the last two items that were on her sister's list. 'Yer goin' te have four days in London with Una before yeh go back to Canada.'

'You will have many grand times when you join the navy,' Pauline said. She raised her head when she heard the door open. She closed her eyes at Maurice who had came in. She removed her purse from her handbag and emptied the coins onto the newspaper.

Hearing the coins rattle, Maurice looked over at his sisters and asked, 'Are yez goin' te play cards now?'

Pauline glared at him and asked, 'Why?'

Maurice looked at the clock and said, 'I expect that Mammy will be here in a minute.'

'Why should Mammy coming in have anything to do with us playing cards?' Pauline asked, raising her head. During the five seconds while she ran her eyes over Maurice's face, he reminded her of Josie. She knew by the way he was closing his lips tightly that he was stopping himself from saying anything. Josie always closed her lips like that. The gesture reminded her of a little puppy that was afraid to bark.

'I just thought yeh were, with yer money out on teh table,' he whined.

'No, Maurice, we aren't going to play cards,' Pauline said,

'and no, Maurice, Mammy won't be in until after I am gone.' The frustration she felt towards him faded slightly when she saw a young lonely boy in his face. Recalling when he was a child and he had to take second place to Maura, she thought, it's not his fault. But she also thought it was time he woke up and saw that their mammy was no different to him than she was to the rest of them. 'Until well after I am gone,' she said and lowered her eyes to the table.

'Mammy's never in before teh last bus,' Cathy shouted.

Pauline spread her coins around the newspaper. 'I don't remember her being in much at all before I left for Canada,' she said. She ran her hand over her coins so that they would spread out on the table. 'Okay, Cathy, pull out all the Irish coins and you can divide them between yourself and Joan.'

Maurice welcomed the sounds of Josie's feet on the stairs because he knew she would do all the talking when she came into the room and she never said anything bad about their mammy. He made sure that his feet were not in the hearth.

Josie didn't come into the room. Maurice heard her talking to Joan in the hall before she went back upstairs again.

As his two younger sisters were dividing out Pauline's Irish coins, Maurice remembered that when Pauline was living at home, she was always very quiet, and she had always done what she was told. He wondered briefly why his mammy was so angry with her.

It would be over ten years before Maurice learned why Pauline was angrier with their mammy than their mammy was with Pauline.

Chapter Sixty-one

If silence had volume, then the air in 34 Plunkett Road would have been so thick that nobody would have been able to move for an hour after Pauline had left.

With Pauline now gone back to Canada, and Maura and Carl not expected home until the weekend, there were enough beds for all the family. Josie had already moved, with Eileen into the bedroom that Maura and Carl had slept in.

'I suppose Mammy will want to sleep in the small front room?' Maurice said hopefully.

'She might not,' Cathy said. She had slept in the small front room with Pauline the night after Pauline had come home from Ena's and the beds were moved around. 'Joan can sleep with me now.'

Josie didn't care where any of the family slept, but she knew her mammy would, so she said, 'I expect Mammy will want to get back into her own bed.' She looked coldly at Maurice and said, 'Anyway it won't make any difference to you.'

It would make a difference to Maurice, but he didn't say that to Josie, because he would have to tell her that he was uncomfortable with his mammy sleeping in the same room.

Everyone was in bed when Liam came in. He knew his mammy wasn't home yet because for the last two hours he had been standing at Angie's front window watching for the mini cab he was sure she would come in. He also knew she would be home because Pauline had told him that Ena wasn't going to allow her to stay.

It was just gone twelve, and Liam was sitting at the table playing patience when the mini cab stopped in front of the house. He had his application papers opened on the table with small neat-pencilled crosses on all the parts where his mammy was to sign. 'Had a good evening?' he asked his mammy when she walked into the room.

Sheila delivered her son one of her ice-cold stares, then walked out again.

Liam scooped up the cards and followed his mammy out to the kitchen. 'Pauline asked me to give you this before she left,' he said, handing her a small envelope. 'When you have read it, come into the living room I have a paper I want you to sign.' He turned back at the door and said, 'The spellin' in that—' he pointed to the letter '—is not too good, but we done er best.' He watched his mammy feel the letter as if she was trying to see how thick it was. 'If yeh can't understand the writin' call Maurice because he's good at readin' all sort ev things.'

Five minutes after Liam had left his mammy in the kitchen she signed his papers.

Chapter Sixty-two

Brian and Liam sat on the church wall watching a tall Garda in the middle of the road waving his arms across his chest and up into the air.

'What time de yeh make it?' Brian asked.

'It's seven minutes past twelve,' Liam replied.

Brian rolled his body so he could shift his legs on the hard wall and glanced down at his friend's wrist. 'How do yeh know that, when yeh didn't look at yer watch?'

'I didn't need te look at teh watch,' Liam said, continuing to keep his eyes on the small woman that was walking across the field towards the traffic lights. When Angie was standing on the kerb he said, 'And when teh Garda holds his hands up fer teh cars te come down teh road, it'll be nine minutes past.'

'How can yeh say that if yeh haven't looked at yer watch?' Brian said, impatiently lowering his head to his knees when three girls on the far side of the road waved over to him. 'How did yeh know what time it was, when yeh didn't look at yer watch?'

Liam nodded his head at the church and said, 'When the angelus was bangin' in me ear I knew it was twelve. Then I saw Angie in the distance comin' across the field and I knew it takes her eight minutes teh make teh journey on a bright sunny mornin' so I added it up.'

'Yer so good at yer sums and workin' things out I think teh airforce'll put yeh in engineerin',' Brian said. He nodded his head over to the Garda that was holding up the traffic. 'And when yeh come out, yeh'll be young enough teh join the boys in blue and do detectin'.'

Five seconds after the Garda turned his back to the building site and waved his hand at the road to Belfast, the cars started to glide or cough their way along the road into the city. There were no lorries tractors, or high winds so there was no grit blowing about. A small horse pulling a cart trotted up to the traffic lights. When the Garda held his hand up and stopped the traffic, so that the horse and cart could cross the road, Liam thought of Peter Carey and Brian's da. 'Did yeh pray fer yer da at all when he was bein' hauled off to teh hospital?' he asked his friend as he continued to watch the tired horse and scruffy cart.

To stop himself from smiling, Brian rubbed his nose. 'I was so busy prayin like teh devil fer all teh neighbours that I can't remember.'

Numerous different accounts still circulated Ballyglass about what had caused Brian's da to be taken into hospital at seven o'clock on the morning after Pauline returned to Canada. Liam was still working in the pub, and Cathy related all the gossip she had collected to him, so he heard them all After he had pieced together the facts from all the stories he had heard, he believed he knew what had happened, so he didn't embarrass his friend with asking him. 'Somebody prayed hard fer yer da, because he was lucky he didn't break his neck,' he said.

'Yer right there,' Brian said, 'and not only fer me da either Mary Madden could have been up fer murder fer chasin' him out of teh room.'

Brian was at mass the morning his da had been taken into hospital. There was no reason why he should have noticed that his da hadn't come home the night before. His da was always late when he was on the evening shift, and sometime he didn't get in until one o'clock in the morning and the whole family would be asleep.

On seeing a bright white van waiting for the Garda to wave it on, Brian started to feel ashamed again. He turned his back to the white van after he dropped down off the wall, and nodded his head over the railing at the side of the church. 'I was lockin' yer bike over there when teh ambulance was speedin' up teh road.' He looked from the road into the city towards the railing, and continued: 'Me mind was so filled up with wonderin' about how yer friend Paul Carey's talk with me da went that I didn't say a little prayer fer teh person that teh ambulance was goin' fer.'

'Did yeh not even hold yer collar?' Liam asked, hoping that a little humour would ease the guilt Brian had over not caring that his da was in hospital.

'What would I want to do that fer?'

'I suppose it wouldn't have been easy seein' as yeh were goin inte mass,' Liam said, lowering his head to the ground so that he wouldn't laugh. 'It's probably only superstition, but er Una told me that when she was a girl, and they saw an ambulance, they used to hold their collar until they saw a dog.' He jumped down off the wall and he was tucking his shirt into his trousers when he said, 'They didn't have te do it very often because there weren't that many ambulances about in them times.'

The laugh that burst from Brian's lungs was loud and hearty. 'I was lucky that I was goin' inte mass then, wasn't I?' he said and started walking into the village.

'Did yer da tell yeh why he went inte teh wrong house teh night before his accident?' Liam asked, falling into step beside his Brian.

'Goin inte teh wrong house was teh least of his troubles. It was getting inte teh bed and goin' asleep that nearly got him killed.'

'With all teh houses lookin' teh same sure I've nearly gone inte teh wrong one meself a couple of times,' Liam said. 'When it's late in teh evenin's, and it's dark, and it's rainin' all yeh want te do is get inte any house.'

'It was dark all right, but it wasn't rainin', and thank God he wasn't drunk,' Brian said, stepping down into the kerb.

'That's luck fer yeh again,' Liam said. 'It's not always generous.'

Brian saw a faint golden light along the top of his friend's mouth so he said, 'I see yer growin' a moustache.'

'About time too,' Liam said.

'Yer not seventeen yet,' Brian slapped back, smiling.

'This,' Liam said, pointing to his upper lip, 'has been there fer three days. I was beginin' te think that nobody was lookin 'at me any more.'

'Yer a man now, Liam, Brian said. 'I'll introduce yeh te Mary Madden any time yeh like.'

An old lady walking in front of them heard what Brian had said. She turned round and looked down at the smaller boy's feet.

'Mornin', Mrs Doyle,' Liam said to the woman as they walked past her. They were still laughing when they passed the Beggars Lodge. 'How's yer ma doin' now?' Liam asked.

'Not as well as Mary Madden's doin', if yeh measure teh attention that teh pair ev them are gettin',' Brian replied. 'But then me ma's man has two legs and an arm still in plaster. And that means he can't follow her around everywhere, like Mary Madden's man is still doin'.'

Still, Liam thought Brian's da wouldn't be able to beat his ma for a long time. 'Anyway,' he said, 'yeh got yer papers signed and we didn't have te bother Paul Cleary after all.'

'Except that I told me da that yeh had,' Brian confessed 'I wasn't lyin because at teh time I though that yeh did,' he added quickly. 'It was when I told him that Mary Madden' man wanted to come inte teh hospital te see him that he took teh Biro out of me hand. I think he would have signed anythin right then.'

'So yeh think he was afraid of that miserable little runt?' Liam laughed.

'And yerself?' Brian asked. 'How much did yer ma cost yeh?'

'Nothin,' Liam retorted, 'luckily a bit of blackmail came along. I'm not proud of it, but it got teh job done.'

Luck has a funny way of granting her favours, Brian thought as he stepped up on the pavement again. 'Me da's bit ev bad luck landed him in hospital, and that has led te Mary Madden struttin' up and down te road every hour, like she is a queen and all teh men fancy her. And that has led te all teh other women on teh road standin' at their gates waitin' fer their men te come home.'

'And you got yer papers signed,' Liam said. He thought that Brian's da deserved his bad luck, what with going into the wrong house and falling down the stairs.

A young woman came towards them with a child in a pushchair so Brian stepped down into the kerb. 'Are all yer sisters all gone back?' he asked.

'Just one more te go this evenin',' Liam said, raising his head from the ground. He kicked a stone off the pavement as though he was swiping at his shame and said, 'I told her that I had helped Pauline te write the letter she had left her.' He then told Brian about Pauline's husband Harry selling drugs.

'That's a dreadful bit ev bad luck fer yer sister,' Brian said.

Liam sniffed. 'We all get er share,' he said, 'and we have two choices when we get a poor dose. We can sit on er arse and wait fer it to change, or we can stand up and fight teh bad luck away.'

Brian stopped walking but he remained standing in the

kerb as they waited at the bus stop. 'Me da won't be standin'' up fer a few weeks.'

'How many is a few?' Liam asked while he wondered if it would be a long time before his mammy ran up more bills for the rest of them to pay.

'Anythin' between three and five,' Brian said, stepping up on to the pavement because a bus was coming.

More like three or five months, Liam thought, before Brian's da would be able to take a swing at a paper bag. He boarded the bus and followed Brian up the stairs, recalling the sad face of Brian's da when he saw him sitting in the chair 'Will yeh move over a bit?' he said when he went to sit down

Brian shifted in his seat. 'The space is too small,' he said 'That's why I always sit on the outside.'

'Then let me in first,' Liam said, handing Brian the money for the fares. 'Yeh paid the last two times.' His small body only took up one third of the double seat. 'Yer lucky though,' he said.

'About what?'

'Yeh don't have te sleep with yer brothers.'

'I don't have any brothers,' Brian said, 'and I don't think that is lucky.'

'I was meanin that yeh don't have anyone tellin' yeh te move over all the time,' Liam said.

THE END

Lightning Source UK Ltd.
Milton Keynes UK
UKOW03f0723060714

234623UK00008B/106/P